DELUSIONS OF THE PAST

ALSO BY THIS AUTHOR

High-Tech Crime Solvers
Virtually Harmless (Coming Soon)

Cowritten with D. D. VanDyke
California Corwin P. I. Mystery Series
The Girl in the Morgue

Stand Alone Suspense Novels
Looking Over Your Shoulder
Lion Within
Pursued by the Past
In the Tick of Time
Loose the Dogs

YOUNG ADULT FICTION:

Between the Cracks:
Ruby
June and Justin
Michelle
Chloe
Ronnie
June, Into the Light

Tamara's Teardrops:
Tattooed Teardrops
Two Teardrops
Tortured Teardrops
Vanishing Teardrops

AND MORE AT PDWORKMAN.COM

DELUSIONS OF THE PAST

REG RAWLINS, PSYCHIC INVESTIGATOR #6

P.D. WORKMAN

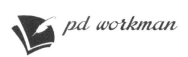

ISBN: 9781989415436

To those in search of their heritage

⋆ CHAPTER ONE ⋆

R EG DIDN'T RECOGNIZE HER RIGHT away. She looked at the woman who stood on the doorstep of the cottage and raised her eyebrows questioningly, wondering who she was and what she was there for. She didn't have a lanyard with ID to identify her as a canvasser for any charity or a utility repair person. She wasn't someone that Reg recognized from the area. She might be a client that Sarah, Reg's landlord, had lined up or someone who had seen Reg's advertising and decided to drop by instead of making an appointment as requested in all of her posters.

Reg cocked her head and was about to ask the woman who she was when she suddenly realized. The woman looked a lot different now. Clean and tidy, her shoulder-length brunette hair smooth and silky, her face enhanced by a little makeup and not covered with sores and pockmarks. She'd had her teeth done. Maybe a full set of dentures or implants. She bore little resemblance to the mother that Reg remembered.

"Norma Jean," Reg said, heart sinking.

Norma Jean smiled brilliantly, showing off the perfect teeth. "Oh, my baby. It's been so long since I saw you!"

She fell upon Reg, embracing her, trying to pull her in close for one of those warm Hallmark moments. Reg pulled back, pushing her away, trying to get her personal space back. "Don't do that! Don't touch me."

Norma Jean's eyebrows went up, and the corners of her mouth went down. She gave Reg a kicked-puppy-dog look, all hurt and offended.

Reg held her hands up in front of her in a 'stop' signal. "You can't just go around hugging people. You're not my mother. Not anymore."

"I am your mother and will never stop being your mother, no matter what you say or do." The slight southern cadence and accent were the same as Reg remembered. That woman had lived in her head for decades, from the time she had died when Reg was four, until… Reg shook her head to try to rid it of the feeling of vertigo she felt whenever considering the timeline and the changes that Weston had caused when he went back to see her mother.

Norma Jean had died when Reg was four. But not in the timeline Reg now inhabited. Whatever Weston had done had changed essential parts of Reg's past. Norma Jean had not died. Her spirit had not attached itself to Reg, her guilt making her a constant companion, always telling Reg what to do and attempting to undo the harm she had done while she had been alive.

Reg just stared at Norma Jean, trying to comprehend it all.

"Well, aren't you going to invite me in?" Norma Jean queried, giving a flirty little pout, acting the role she had made up. Why had she suddenly shown up in Black Sands, Florida? Reg had made it clear that she didn't want to see Norma Jean. Either Norma Jean was thicker than Reg believed, or she had wholly disregarded what her daughter had said, deciding to fly in from Maine regardless.

"Fine, come in," Reg said finally, glancing around the yard to make sure Norma Jean was the only one there. She wasn't sure who else she was looking for. Weston or a more current boyfriend? There was no way for her to prevent the powerful immortal from entering even if she tried.

She opened the door wide enough for Norma Jean and stepped back.

Norma Jean gave a smile and came in, acting like the queen of Black Sands. She looked around Reg's little cottage, chin lifted, smile set firmly in place. Reg went to the kitchen to put on a kettle for tea, an action that had become habitual since she had moved to Black Sands and started seeing clients for psychic readings. A cup of tea always went over well with someone who was about to take a foray into the unknown. And Reg could read the tea leaves in the bottom of the cup if they were so inclined. Reg would go with whatever psychic reading method they preferred.

"This is real nice," Norma Jean told her.

"Yeah." Reg wasn't in much of a mood for conversation. It was just a cottage in the back yard of Sarah's big house, but it was better than anything else Reg had ever had on her own. Clean and neat and furnished in Sarah's breezy Florida style. Certainly better than anything that Reg had ever lived in while she was still with Norma Jean, a series of flophouses, shelters, and cold nights on the street.

She watched the kettle intently, hoping that it would take all day to boil.

Norma Jean wandered around, looking at the decorations and furnishings. She touched the leaves of the plant that Fir had given to Reg when he told her that she needed living things in her environment. It did perk the place up a bit, giving the cottage a more homey feeling. Fir said that plants had feelings, and maybe Reg was sensing the warm feelings of the houseplant itself. Or perhaps it just looked good on the little side table.

Eventually, Norma Jean settled on the wicker couch and waited for Reg to make the tea and bring it over on the tray. She helped herself to one of the cups, and they both gave their attention to their tea, Reg studiously ignoring Norma Jean, until it was no longer possible, because Norma Jean was talking, forcing Reg to acknowledge her existence.

"They took you away from me when you were still real little." She took a tentative sip of the tea but didn't look like she enjoyed it. Reg couldn't remember Norma Jean ever drinking tea. She would probably have preferred the Jack Daniels in Reg's corner cupboard. "I didn't have any say in it. I would have kept you if I could."

Norma Jean had been destitute and addicted, completely unable to care for a child. The times that she had ignored Reg had been the best. Better to be ignored than abused. It was a wonder that it had taken child services four years to apprehend her.

"You couldn't be a mother."

"No… I guess I couldn't," Norma Jean admitted. "I needed to take care of myself and deal with my own problems before I could be responsible for someone else."

Taking care of herself was all Norm Jean had ever done, self-serving and focused on her own gratification. How long had it taken for her to get straight after Reg had been removed? Ten years? Twenty?

Reg played with one of the red box-braids that hung down next to her face. It had taken Norma Jean twenty-five years to make contact with her daughter again. How much of that time had she been clean and sober?

"I'm sorry that you had to grow up in foster care. I would have gotten you back if I could have. But they wouldn't even talk about letting you come back unless I cleaned up my act. And…" Norma Jean wavered, "after I was off the drugs, I decided it was probably best if you stayed there. I needed to figure things out… learn how to support myself. I recognized that I didn't have what I needed to take care of a kid."

"Good for you."

"I've been looking for you. Once you were old enough to look after yourself, I kind of looked around… tried to find out where you might be… but I couldn't find you. They wouldn't give me any information, of course; those government agencies act like they're so superior and won't tell you a thing. I thought… that maybe you might be looking for me too. Once you aged out of the system, then you could go wherever you wanted to and you could look for me."

Reg shook her head. Of course she had never searched for Norma Jean. She had known exactly where Norma Jean was. Dead and lurking in a corner of Reg's brain. She had tried to banish the voice, not to go back there. Her life with Norma Jean had never been a happy place. She hadn't liked the instability of foster care, but she had rarely wished she was back with Norma Jean again. "They told me you were dead," she told Norma Jean flatly.

"What? Why would they do that? They knew I wasn't dead!"

"Well, that's what I thought."

Norma Jean shook her head angrily. "I should sue them! I cannot believe that they would lie to you like that. We could have been reunited years ago."

Reg sipped her tea, not answering. She wouldn't have wanted to have reunited with Norma Jean.

Or would she? In the timeline where Norma Jean had not been killed, had Reg yearned to be back together with her again? If she'd known that Norma Jean was alive, would Reg have gone back to her once she was sixteen or eighteen and had a mind of her own? At least there would have been someone in her life who was a constant, even if Norma Jean wasn't able to provide the care of a parent. It would have been better than being out on the streets, as Reg had been several times since her graduation from foster care.

There was a soft thud, and Reg turned her head to watch Starlight come out of the bedroom to see who was visiting.

Norma Jean looked at the tuxedo cat with the mismatched eyes and white spot on his forehead, her eyebrows drawing down in puzzlement. Starlight went to Reg's side and, after surveying Norma Jean for a moment, jumped up into Reg's lap. Reg put down her tea and petted him, stroking the longer fur down his back and scratching his ears and chin. Norma Jean shook her head.

"Where have I seen that cat before?"

Reg knew very well where she had seen the cat, but thought it interesting that Starlight would seem more familiar to Norma Jean than her own daughter. Did she not remember the woman who had been with the cat? Or had her drug-addled brain lost that detail or morphed it into something else?

"Maybe you saw a cat that looked like him," Reg said. "This is Starlight."

"You always wanted a cat. I don't know how many times you dragged some stray in and tried to convince me that you would take care of it."

"Did I?" Reg didn't remember that. But she didn't remember a lot of specific experiences from when she'd been with Norma Jean. She had, after all, only been four. A lot of people didn't remember anything before they were five, not just traumatized kids taken into custody after a parent was murdered. Maybe Norma Jean remembered only that one time when little Reg had met Starlight and hugged and cuddled him and asked if she could keep him. Maybe that had become 'dragging home random strays and asking to keep them.' Parents did that sometimes. Blew one little incident up into something the child 'always' did.

Reg put her face against the top of Starlight's head and breathed into his fur. It was always very calming to hold Starlight. He gave out good vibes. He had chosen Reg when she went to the animal shelter, rather than her choosing him, and she was glad that he had.

"So, tell me all about your life." Norma Jean leaned forward. "I want to know everything. When you were little, where you've been, and what you've done. If you have a boyfriend. What you're doing all the way in Black Sands."

Reg disliked sharing information about her past. She particularly didn't want to give Norma Jean any ammunition. Who knew how she might use it.

"Nothing to tell. This is just where I moved. Now I try to make a living… doing personal consulting."

"Personal consulting," Norma Jean tasted the words. "What exactly is that? What kind of consulting?"

"Life planning. Making decisions about the future. I help people to... look ahead in their lives. Or sometimes, to take a look back at the past and make their peace so that they can move forward again."

"That sounds very interesting." Norma Jean was impressed. "How do you get all of your business? You must make good money to live in a place like this."

Reg cleared her throat. "It isn't as much as you might think. My landlord helps me get some work; she's really... tuned into the community. I advertise, mostly locally, put posters up on community bulletin boards or places they might frequent. It's picking up steadily."

She always worried about how long it would last, and wished that she'd discovered a treasure like gold or jewels instead of Weston. Why couldn't it have been gold?

"Maybe you could help me. I'm always so confused about where to go with my life... I guess I don't have very much direction. I don't have any big talents. You must have gotten an education, to be able to do that kind of life planning for people."

"All self-educated. I didn't have any money to go to college. Nowhere to live. No one to cosign a loan. I didn't do great in school, so there were no grants or scholarships."

"Yeah. That's the trouble with foster care. I've heard it's really hard."

She'd heard it. Too bad she hadn't lived it. She might not be so sanguine about it.

"What about you? What are *you* doing?" Reg turned the question back on Norma Jean. She had enough money to buy a plane ticket across the country. She looked well-fed and focused. Not gaunt and wretched and scattered, unable to conceive of how to make it from one day to the next.

"I do a little of this and a little of that... just whatever I can pick up. That's why I said I should have you give me one of those consultations."

"You pick up what kind of work? Cleaning? Cooking? Outdoor work? Hooking?"

Norma gave a shocked laugh. "Oh, not that! Yes, sometimes cleaning or outdoor stuff like mowing lawns. Some retail stores. Just... positions that don't require any experience. I don't have much on my resume. Employers don't think much of that."

The same kind of jobs as Reg had hopscotched between until she had happened onto the psychic gig. That had worked well enough that she'd been able to give up the back-breaking, footsore work.

Reg got to her feet and put Starlight down. She moved around restlessly. She didn't like having Norma Jean there. It made her anxious. She was too anxious and restless to sit in one place and chat as if they were old friends.

She went to the window and looked out into the yard. The grass was all neatly trimmed around the paving stones that made up the pathway. She couldn't see the main garden from that side of the cottage, but she could see well-maintained bushes, trees, and lawn. It had looked nice before, and since Sarah had hired Forst as a gardener, everything was looking lush and bright and happy. He had done an excellent job.

A movement in the corner of her eye caught Reg's attention, and she turned her head to look at it, but as soon as she did so, it was gone. She watched for a moment to see if it came back. Maybe a bird or the wind blowing a tree. She waited for the movement to repeat itself but she didn't see it again.

"What are you looking at?" Norma Jean inquired.

"Nothing. I'm just looking." Reg moved away from the window again. "So, how long are you here? What are your plans? I use the second bedroom as my office, so there is nowhere here for you to stay overnight."

"Oh, I would never impose on you," Norma Jean assured, her voice earnest and smooth. Reg didn't believe it for a minute. Norma Jean had been hoping for an invitation, or failing receipt of an invitation, to be able to talk her way into staying in Reg's cottage while she was in town. Reg hoped that she couldn't find anywhere to sleep and had to go back home right away.

Reg drifted into the kitchen and cleared a few dirty dishes away. Norma Jean watched and didn't offer to help. Not that there were enough dishes for her to help with. By the time she got to the kitchen, Reg would have been done.

There was a quick tap at the door, then the handle turned and Sarah bustled in. "Good morning, Reg. Isn't it a lovely day out there today? Oh." Her eyes settled on Norma Jean. "I didn't know that you had company."

Reg didn't have quite what it took to say 'she was just leaving' to get Norma Jean out of the way. "This is… Norma Jean." Reg swallowed and tried to think of how much information to share. "My mother."

Sarah looked stunned. She put a hand over her heart. "Your mother? But I thought your mother—"

Reg waited for Sarah to say "was dead," but she trailed off, not finishing the thought.

"Apparently not. That's what they told me, back when I was little, but I guess it was just a lie."

"Well, this is quite a shock." Sarah landed heavily in the chair that Reg had recently vacated. "That's amazing news. How… wonderful for you." Sarah smiled at Norma Jean, turned her head and looked at Reg, and the smile on her face faltered.

"I was so excited to be able to track Reg down," Norma Jean gushed. "And you must be her friend…?"

"Sarah." Sarah stuck out her hand to Norma Jean and shook vigorously. "Yes, I'm Reg's friend and her landlord."

"Oh, so this is your place."

Sarah nodded. "Well, I own it, but it's Reg's for as long as she wants to live here. I needed someone stable to take it for me. Reg has been a lifesaver for me."

Did Norma Jean know she was being lied to? Reg didn't do anything for Sarah but pay a minimal rent for the cottage. Sarah came and went, keeping everything clean and tidy, feeding Starlight when he insisted he was hungry, lining up clients for Reg, delivering her mail and flyers, and telling her about the community events coming up. She was like... a mother to Reg.

Maybe Norma Jean sensed this. Her mouth was a straight line, lips pressed together. She didn't like this interloper in Reg's life.

But to Reg, Norma Jean was the interloper. Who did she think she was, showing up on Reg's doorstep without any warning and expecting to be invited in and even being allowed to stay with her for... however long Norma Jean was planning to stay? Reg bit her lip, worrying about that. Norma Jean hadn't said anything to indicate that she had ties back home. She might be planning to move to Black Sands permanently. A choice that would make things very difficult for Reg.

"It's very nice to meet you," Sarah told Norma Jean pleasantly. "I'm sure Reg will have the best time while you are here."

Norma Jean gave a broad smile, which to Reg looked utterly fake. She nodded vigorously. "Oh, yes, we are going to have the best time, aren't we honey?"

Reg didn't try to match Norma Jean's smile. The answer was no; they were not going to have the best time. Reg looked around, trying to figure out some way of getting out of the situation. She looked back at Sarah, wondering whether she could see the panic in Reg's eyes.

"Did you... need something, Sarah?"

"Well..."

"Did you need me to do something for you? Norma Jean can go, I'm free if there's something that you wanted..."

"No, no. It's not that. It's just that I needed to do some maintenance here. I know I haven't given you the proper forty-eight hours' notice, so I really shouldn't spring it on you like this, but I was going to see whether you were going to... be out for part of the day. and then if you are, I could come back then to work on it."

"Oh." Reg looked around. "Well, you gotta do what you gotta do. Norma Jean, we're going to have to vacate, so..."

"Are you going to go out to lunch?" Sarah suggested. "You could take her to The Crystal Bowl. Maybe go out shopping for a while or go for a walk in the park. Then by the time you are done, I'm sure I'd be mostly finished here."

"Oh, yes, let's!" Norma Jean jumped in. "That sounds like fun."

Reg glared at Sarah. "I don't think that I can fit that into my schedule today."

"You can make time for your mother who you haven't seen in years," Norma Jean pouted. "It's my treat. I don't know the restaurants in the area, so you'll have to tell me what's good, but I'll take you out and we'll have a nice time."

"Go," Sarah encouraged, making a motion to shoo Reg out of the room. "You go on. Have a good time. I need the space to work."

Reg shook her head. "What about Starlight?" she grumbled. "Do you need me to lock him up? What are you going to be working on?"

Sarah looked at the cat. She was not a cat person and would probably prefer that he weren't underfoot, but she was always good about it and didn't make a fuss. "Oh, no. He'll be fine. I'll only have the door open for a few minutes, and I'll keep an eye on him to make sure he can't get out."

"And he won't be in your way? You know how he has to get right in the middle of whatever you're working on."

"He won't bother me. The two of you go ahead, go have a nice lunch together."

Reg fetched her purse, moving slowly, still trying to think of an excuse to get out of it. She could tell Norma Jean that she had somewhere else to go. A competing appointment. But Norma Jean was going to know that something was up. And she would keep persisting until she got her own way. At least if they were going to lunch together, there was a natural break point where they could each say their goodbyes and go their separate directions. She only had to put up with Norma Jean for an hour or two.

That sounded like a very long time.

★ CHAPTER TWO ★

WHEN REG GOT BACK from lunch, it was quite late. She had intentionally given Sarah a couple of extra hours to finish whatever she was working on at the cottage. Norma Jean had pouted and whined about Reg having to take care of other matters, but she couldn't have expected to have all of Reg's time. Reg was running a business. Norma Jean had grudgingly accepted this, and though she had tried to get Reg to let her stay at the cottage, Reg had been firm about that. She didn't have a second bed and Norma Jean wasn't sharing Reg's.

"When are you going back north? There isn't really anything for you to do here."

"What do you mean, there isn't anything for me to do? I am here to see my daughter. I want to know all about you. Really get to know you. We've lost so many years."

"Norma Jean…" Reg held up her hand in protest. "I told you not to come here. I think I've been pretty nice to let you into my house and to go out to lunch with you, but you have to understand, you're not a part of my life. And you're not going to be."

"You can't *not* be my daughter. I gave birth to you and nothing is going to change that."

Reg wasn't sure that either of those statements was true. The more she discovered about the magical world, the less confident she was of anything. Maybe Norma Jean had given birth to her in the usual way, or maybe Weston, being an immortal, had somehow created Reg in a different way. And just because something had always been one way, that didn't mean that it couldn't change. Norma Jean had been dead for almost Reg's whole life, and now she wasn't. If that could change, anything could.

There were lights when she approached the cottage. Reg was surprised that Sarah would have left them on. She should have finished earlier in the day when it was not dark, and wouldn't have thought to leave the lights on for her. Reg hung back from the cottage, looking things over, hesitating about what she should do.

She was being silly. What did she think? That there was someone else in her cottage? That someone had broken in? Or that Norma Jean had arrived back ahead of her, refusing to listen to Reg's refusal to let her stay for the night? If Norma Jean was there, Reg was going to call the police. She'd had enough of her mother's nonsense and wanted to make it clear that she was not welcome there. She could go back north and do whatever she wanted to, as long as it was far away from Reg.

A shadow passed across the window. Not Starlight. Definitely a person.

Reg heard the faint tinkle of bells, which didn't seem like they came from inside the house. Maybe a neighbor had recently installed new wind chimes. Reg couldn't remember hearing them before then.

Was it Norma Jean? Or another intruder? Should she call the police? She didn't want to have any more dealings with the police in Black Sands and didn't need to attract any attention to herself.

Reg crept up to the window and tried to peek inside without exposing herself. If it was just Norma Jean, there was nothing to be afraid of. But if it was some other person or shadowy creature, she wasn't about to go barging in and get herself eaten or cursed.

She watched for the intruder, waiting for them to cross back across the window again. She was at a bad angle and couldn't see inside very well. She could go around to a window with a better view of the interior, but then she would have to contend with the horizontal blinds.

The intruder came closer to the window and, straining her neck for a better angle, Reg finally relaxed. It was just Sarah. Still there after so long? The maintenance must not have gone the way she had hoped.

Reg went to the door and hesitated, wondering if she should knock before entering so that she wouldn't startle Sarah. But knocking on her own door? That didn't seem right. Reg opened the door, jingling her keys, and went in.

She stopped, stock still, her mouth open, as she looked around at the changes to the cottage.

"Holy cow! What happened here?"

Sarah beamed at Reg. "Do you like it?"

Reg didn't know where to look first. There was what she was pretty sure was holly, with shiny green leaves and red berries, and another plant with white berries. There were strings of twinkle lights and a wide assortment of candles flickering in jars around the room. There was an evergreen tree in a bucket and wreaths, pinecones, and garlands everywhere. It seemed like every surface was covered with some new decoration.

"Is this for Christmas? It looks like a department store blew up in here!"

"For Yule," Sarah corrected. "Isn't it lovely? I love decorating for solstice."

"Yule," Reg repeated, looking around. "I thought Yule was Christmas? Yuletide greetings and all of that. Isn't that right?"

"Christians may think that Yule and Christmas are the same things because they borrowed so many of the symbols and traditions from Yule, but they are not the same thing. This is for our holy day. Little Jesus couldn't have been born in December. Not if sheep were lambing in the fields."

"Uh… oh. Okay. I don't know much about the origins of either of them. I mean I've been forced to watch or read the Christmas story enough times, with all of the different foster families who wanted to educate me as to what Christmas was really about, but I never really saw the connection between a baby being born and Christmas and all of the rest—gifts and Santa Claus and…" She looked around, "…this."

"That's because there is no connection. It is a bunch of traditions cobbled together in an effort to keep the pagan converts happy hundreds of years ago. Christmas today is a chaotic mishmash of Christian legend and pagan symbolism and Coca Cola and Clement Clarke Moore. Hallmark and commercialism. Nothing like Yule." She folded her arms and looked around at the decorations adorning every surface with a contented smile. "I love the simple symbolism and stories of Yule. They have barely changed during the time that Christianity was trying to get a foothold and build its empire. Still the same symbols and rituals that have always been part of the season."

Reg indicated the garlands of twinkle lights. "Nothing has changed?"

"Well, if you want to bring modern technology into it. It is a little easier to string lights than it is to try to fill the house with candles. Most of these…" Sarah indicated one of the many candles flickering around the room, "are actually electric." She reached into one jar and pulled the fake candle out, not burning herself. "I get them at the dollar store by the case."

Reg laughed. "Well, you wouldn't want to burn the house down."

"Yule is a time of light, so I always try to provide lots of extra inspiration. You do want a few real candles to practice meditation and healing, but most of them can just be electric."

Reg picked up another of the fake candles and looked at it. She put it back down. "Healing?"

"Fire is a powerful element. It can hurt and do devastating damage, but it can also heal."

"I'll have to take your word on that one."

"If you want to learn about it, I am more than happy to share."

"Yeah… why don't you tell me about the rest? Are you telling me that the Christmas tree is really a Yule tree?"

"Yes, it is," Sarah laughed. "Evergreen trees and branches were a symbol of life for long before the Christians borrowed them. They stay green all winter with the promise of reawakening in the spring. How could that not be a powerful symbol in any pagan culture?"

"Well, I guess." Reg looked around. "Not that anything turns brown in December here. It's sort of funny to be somewhere green all year long."

"It is paradise," Sarah agreed. "I have had enough of cold nights, snow, mud, and miserable weather. Florida is the perfect place."

"As long as there are no hurricanes," Reg suggested.

"Well." Sarah shrugged, conceding the point. "I'd still rather be warm all year. My old bones do not like the cold."

Reg supposed that if Sarah were hundreds of years old, as she claimed, she was entitled to complain about aching bones.

"When is Yule? Is it the same day as Christmas?"

"It is winter solstice. December twenty-first. But it is traditionally held for twelve days, so—"

"The twelve days of Christmas?"

"You didn't ever wonder where that came from?"

"Uh… no."

Reg had always had more pressing concerns around Christmas time. Was she living in a home where she was expected to give gifts? That could be a problem, especially if it was supposed to be paid for out of her own money, something she rarely had.

Was she going to be staying with her foster family for Christmas, or would they be visiting extended family and she would be required to go to respite care for the holiday, where the parents would know nothing about her?

Would she be forced to sing? To perform? To sit through mind-numbing hours of preaching? Or would it be a family that didn't celebrate Christmas and was sneered at by the kids at school and other people in the neighborhood? Many years, she had wished that she could just skip Christmas. She had never once been tempted to research Christmas traditions and to find out where they had come from.

"I'll tell you more about it later, then. We have plenty of time. I wanted to get the decorations up early to get plenty of usage out of them. I'm not one to put them up the day before Yule and take them down again the day after."

"Sure, that makes sense. You may as well enjoy it all."

Sarah clearly did, or she wouldn't have been decorating the cottage as well as her own house. Reg assumed that it was not a Yule tradition to decorate other people's homes.

"Are you going to decorate the tree?"

"You and I can do that over the next few days. I'm afraid I'm out of energy today. The well has run dry."

"Okay." Reg might have fun decorating a tree. But she couldn't make any assumptions as to what they would be putting on it. She was pretty sure that round Christmas baubles and an angel on top of the tree would not be part of the prescribed decorations. "Well, thank you for all of this. It's lovely. I didn't expect anything. I thought when I came home, and the lights were on that… it might have been burgled."

Sarah laughed heartily. "No, just an old lady who doesn't know when to stop. I'm going to get something to eat and hit the sack. I will not be out partying tonight."

★ CHAPTER THREE ★

WHERE IS STARLIGHT?" REG looked around. Usually, Starlight wanted to be right in the middle of it if strange things were going on in the house. He seemed to think that everything was done for his sake and he needed to supervise and ensure that it was done correctly. Even if Starlight hadn't been interested in the decorating being done, he should at least have come out when he heard Reg's voice. He always greeted her and wanted to be fed, even if there was plenty of food in his dish. "Did you end up having to shut him up after all?"

Sarah looked around. "He was over by the tree, last I saw."

Reg walked to the corner, looking for the cat. Starlight was, in fact, underneath the tree, and he didn't look happy. When Reg bent down for a look, his eyes were as round as saucers. When she extended her hand to touch him, he put back his ears and hissed. Reg jerked back, surprised.

"Whoa. What's got into you?"

"Cats don't like change," Sarah said, as if it were a well-known fact. "He's probably just disgruntled by the decorations."

"He's never behaved like that toward me before."

"Give him some space. I'm sure he'll be just fine. It will wear off, and he'll be back to his usual self again."

"I hope so." Reg watched him analytically. "You'd better be on your best behavior tomorrow, since Nicole and the kattakyns are coming by for a visit."

Sarah cleared her throat loudly. "Reg, about that…"

Reg looked away from Starlight, hearing the sternness in Sarah's voice. "What is it?" Her stomach clenched like it used to when she was in school and would be called before a teacher or principal to explain something she had done wrong or to get a dressing-down.

"Having all of those cats in here… I don't like it. We didn't discuss cats before you moved in here, so I conceded the point about Starlight. But you know my stance on cats now… and I don't like all of those mischievous creatures running around here."

"They'll be fully supervised and they won't be outside the house. We've been very careful not to let them damage anything."

"Even so…" Sarah eyed one of the chairs, and Reg wondered how she could possibly know that Nico had been clawing it the last time they were over to visit. There wasn't any visible damage. "I would much rather you took

Starlight over to Francesca's house after this. I'm sure she would be much happier with that anyway. It can't be easy to bring all of those kittens over here at once, especially as they are getting bigger."

Reg couldn't argue that fact. But Francesca liked to get them out of her house for a few hours. Reg had a talent for settling them down and helping them to work through their problems. Francesca wanted them properly socialized and prepared to go to their new homes as they identified suitable matches.

"I'll have to talk to Francesca about it."

"I don't want them here. They get hair and dander everywhere, even if they don't claw the furniture. And I worry about them attracting other cats into the garden. I don't want those filthy beasts using it as a toilet."

"I don't think that's going to happen…"

"But that was why Nicole came here in the first place. Because of Starlight sitting in the window. I don't want more cats coming around here, Reg. Really."

Reg sighed. She was getting a great deal on the rent and everything else that Sarah did for her. Sarah didn't really ask for much in return. "Okay. I'll talk to her in the morning."

Starlight wouldn't come out from under the Yule tree when it was time for bed. Reg had been enjoying the lights and candles and the peace she felt being surrounded by the other decorations, but it was strange not having Starlight to cuddle with during the evening. And he always bugged her for food when she started making preparations to go to bed. He knew it was his last chance for hours and, poor starving creature that he was, he couldn't go that long without fresh food and water. She stood in the kitchen, putting her dishes into the dishwasher and watching the Yule tree, waiting for Starlight to come out.

"Are you just going to sulk under that tree all night?"

He didn't answer or come out.

"I know cats don't like change, but this is a little ridiculous, don't you think? There's nothing here that's going to harm you. And after Christmas—Yule—it will all be going away again. It's just for the month. You can deal with it."

He still didn't leave the shelter of the tree. Reg shook her head, feeling foolish about trying to reason with a cat. If he wanted to hide under the tree, what harm was there in that? Maybe he was pretending he was in a forest, like a kid playing in a tree fort. Or perhaps he was just sulking and letting her know how displeased he was with the changes. Or it might have been something to do with Sarah. Reg always suspected that Starlight understood far more than he should, and maybe he was displeased that Sarah had put her foot down about Nicole and the kittens coming over to visit. He always had a soft spot where Nicole was concerned. Reg would be glad when they had found appropriate magical homes for all of the kittens and it could be just Nicole again. It wouldn't be so hard to smuggle only one cat into the cottage without Sarah knowing about it.

"Okay, I'm going to bed," she tried once more. "Last call."

He didn't come darting back out to show her that even though he was still mad at her, he was hungry too and she'd better keep up with her duties. Reg gave a shrug and didn't touch his bowls. If he wasn't going to insist that she change the food and water, then why make more work for herself? It wasn't like he would starve overnight even if he decided he didn't want them.

In the morning, Reg was used to being awakened several times by Starlight before she finally conceded to start her day. She was up late nights with seances and readings, so she slept quite late in the morning, and Starlight took offense to this and thought she should rise early. But she'd slept through. She looked at the windowsill, where he liked to sit and watch the birds in the garden. It was empty; he wasn't there. Reg rubbed her eyes. The bed was cold; he wasn't sleeping curled up against her. He wasn't on the bed at all. After the months of being harassed by a furry feline when she wanted to sleep longer, it was very disconcerting.

Reg got up and used the bathroom and rinsed out her mouth. She pulled her braids back behind her shoulders, looking at herself in the mirror, then walked into the kitchen.

She saw the tip of Starlight's tail behind the kitchen island and was relieved.

"You finally decided to come out of the tree?"

His tail didn't twitch. Reg rounded the island and gasped.

★ CHAPTER FOUR ★

STARLIGHT WAS LAYING ON his side, unmoving. He was so still, she couldn't even see him breathing, and she reached out and touched him, sure he was going to be cold and stiff. Tears were already running down her cheeks, and she was breathing with her mouth wide open, trying to stifle sobs and get enough oxygen.

"Starlight? What happened? What's wrong?"

He was still warm and soft. She put her hand over his throat and chest and could feel shallow respirations. She looked all over his body, what was visible, for any sign of an injury. What had happened? He had been just fine the night before. Had he been up on the counter and fallen the wrong way? Had he gotten sick in the night? It didn't make any sense. He'd been in perfectly good health.

The only change in his behavior had been in hiding under the Yule tree the night before. Animals, cats in particular, often isolated themselves in dark corners when they were very sick. That was what one of the videos on cat care on YouTube had said. If your cat started hiding in dark corners, he might be seriously ill, and a trip to the vet was strongly recommended.

Starlight had never been sick since she had bought him. He'd complained, but he'd never been sick. Reg gathered him up in her arms, crooning to him. There was no response to her words or the fact that she was manhandling him. Reg held him close and kissed the top of his head.

"Come on, Star. Don't be sick. Don't let this happen."

She closed her eyes and tried to feel his spirit, his consciousness. But she couldn't sense him. Only an aura of sickness and destruction, something left behind by someone else. It was so strong that it made her feel sick. She focused on building a wall around Starlight like she had done before to protect herself from Corvin. If there was some menacing force that had resulted in Starlight's unconscious state, then she needed to protect him from further harm. Another hour or two in that malevolent environment and she wouldn't be able to get him back.

She wrapped layer after layer of protection around her furry friend until she was so exhausted she could do nothing more for him. Then she wrapped him in a soft, clean bath towel and took him out to the car to transport him to the vet.

The veterinary assistant who hustled Reg into one of the examining rooms with Starlight stood beside her with a clipboard as the vet examined her comatose familiar.

"Do you have any idea what he might have eaten?"

"He didn't eat anything unusual. Just his usual food. Maybe some leftovers."

Reg knew very well that Starlight had eaten leftovers; he always begged for human food and only ate a little of the food that was scientifically engineered to suit an active cat's nutritional needs. She racked her brain, trying to remember what he might have had in the previous twenty-four-hour period.

"He usually begs for food when I'm going to bed and he didn't do that last night. He was just hiding under the tree and wouldn't come out."

"Under the tree? He was outside?"

"No, no. He's an inside cat. He's only been out once. He was hiding under the Christmas tree." She hesitated, wondering if she should correct herself to say Yule tree, but they might have no idea what that was, and they did know what a Christmas tree was.

"I see. Do you have other Christmas decorations out? Anything that might be harmful to a cat? Plants?"

"My landlord decorated. I... I have a plant that someone gave me, and he said not to let Starlight eat it, but he's never shown an interest in it. He doesn't eat plants."

"You never know when they might get it into their heads to eat something they shouldn't. You should be careful not to have toxic plants in the environment. What kind of houseplant was this?"

"I... don't know. I guess I could find out."

"It might be important." The veterinary assistant scribbled notes on the clipboard. "That's the only plant?"

"Aside from the Christmas decorations, yes."

"What Christmas decorations do you have?"

"Well, I guess they're not actually for Christmas, they're for Yule. That's what my landlord celebrates. I don't know what they all were."

The woman holding the clipboard raised her eyebrows, waiting for more information. Reg looked down at Starlight, still unmoving as the vet poked and prodded and made his examination. She swallowed hard and pictured her living room after Sarah had decorated it.

"Lots of evergreen boughs and wreaths, with pinecones. Uh... I think holly. And something with white berries."

"Probably mistletoe. White berries are almost always poisonous. And so is the holly, by the way."

"If he ate one of those or the other plant, you can still do something, can't you? How bad is it?"

The veterinary assistant didn't answer. The vet stroked Starlight and grimaced at Reg. "Our little friend isn't in very good shape. You need to be prepared that he might not make it. I'm not sure what he got into. We'll do some blood tests, stomach contents, see if we can figure out if he ate something. We'll give him fluids and do what we can to clean him out. But…" he shrugged apologetically, "the damage may have already been done."

Tears ran down Reg's face. She wiped at them with her hand. "I wouldn't have left him with all of those plants if I had known… I thought… he's never tried to eat anything like that; I don't see why he would now."

"There are other household items that can be toxic to pets as well. Antifreeze, for example. We sometimes see cases where pets were intentionally poisoned. You don't have a boyfriend or neighbor who doesn't like him, do you?"

Reg thought about Sarah's complaint just the night before, not about Starlight, but about the other cats and not wanting them around. She shook her head slowly. "No, I don't think anyone would have hurt him intentionally. I live alone. It's not like he does anything to bother anyone."

"Well, we'll do what we can for him. But he's in pretty bad shape."

Reg gave Starlight one final pat and ear scratch, her throat aching and tears streaming down her face in earnest.

Reg returned to her house in a fog, unsure of what to do next or how to deal with the crisis. She couldn't just go on as usual and hope that Starlight recovered, but what could she possibly do about it? It was too late to take action after he'd been poisoned. She felt like just climbing under the covers and going back to sleep, but she tried to coach herself into facing the problem and not hiding from it. She was a grown-up. She needed to act like one. The loss of her familiar would be devastating, but animals did die, and people too, and she had managed to carry on before. Her loss of Starlight, if he didn't manage to pull through, couldn't possibly be more catastrophic than the loss of her mother when she was four and the dark years that followed. She still had a house to live in, clients who would want to see her, and friends who would be sympathetic. If worse came to worst, she could get another cat.

Reg sobbed as she drove. "I don't want another cat! I need Starlight! He's not just a cat; he's a… he's really important to me." Her voice broke and she coughed and sputtered, trying to see properly through her tear-filled eyes. She probably should not be on the road. She wasn't exactly in any shape to be driving. But what else was she going to do? She needed to get home. She could pull over to the side of the road and try to get her composure back, but chances were that if she did, she would completely break down and wouldn't be able to go anywhere.

So she kept going.

When she finally reached the house, she parked the car and walked in. The Yuletide wonderland gleamed around her. All kinds of festive greens and lights. And she didn't want any of them. She found a storage box in the closet and started to throw all of the greenery into it. The doctor had not said that the evergreen boughs were a problem, but she didn't want to take any chances. If Starlight came back home, she wanted it to look just like it always had, and not to have anything around that could harm him.

Just what kind of a pet owner was she? She figured that watching a few videos on YouTube on caring for pet cats made her an expert? She hadn't had any idea that the plants could be a problem. He'd never eaten plants before. She had thought that all she needed to do was feed Starlight and clean his litter box. Take him to the vet when he needed his shots. He was an indoor cat, so he wouldn't be in any dangerous situations.

So she had thought. And she had almost lost him. Might still lose him.

Sarah came in while Reg was dashing around the room, pulling down all of the decorations. What about the lights? Could he strangle on the strings? Burn his whiskers on the real candles; or worse, knock them over and light the house on fire? Reg didn't even see Sarah until she spoke.

"Uh, Reg…?"

Reg whirled around and looked at her. She looked down at the box full of decorations, thrown haphazardly together without any regard as to whether it was something important to Sarah or not. She froze for a moment, not sure what to say. Sarah's eyes were hurt. She thought that Reg was taking down all of the decorations because she didn't like them or had something against Yule or against Sarah herself.

Reg put down the box and swallowed.

"Starlight is sick. He might have been poisoned by this stuff."

Sarah's eye went wide with shock. "What? What happened?"

"When I got up this morning…" Even though Reg had been crying all morning, the tears came again, and she could barely talk around the lump in her throat, "he was lying on the floor in the kitchen. I thought he was dead."

"Oh, my dear!" Sarah moved toward her, holding out her arms. Reg was not usually a physically affectionate person, but she fell into Sarah's embrace, sobbing loudly.

"He's unconscious. The vet doesn't know if he's going to make it or not. They're not sure what he ate, but they said that all of this stuff is poisonous."

"Oh, Reg! I would never have brought it over if I had realized that! I didn't intend to hurt him."

"He might die. I'm so scared he's going to die."

"We'll find a way to save him. What did the vet say? Does he need surgery? Dialysis? What are they going to do?"

Reg couldn't remember any of the details. "They're going to try to get the poison out of his system. But he says… the damage is already done, and he doesn't know whether Starlight will make it or not." Reg gasped for breath and wept into Sarah's shoulder. "What am I going to do? I miss him so much! I don't know if I can do… all of the psychic stuff without him. He was always there if I needed him to give me a boost. And having someone around the cottage, so I wasn't all by myself. It just won't be the same. I don't know if I could ever live with another cat."

Sarah rubbed her back. "Don't get ahead of yourself. You don't know yet that he isn't going to make it and you'll have to get a replacement. You don't know the future. Just live for today. Think about what you can do today."

"I can't do anything. He's at the vet's… I had to leave him there… I don't know if I'm ever going to see him again."

"You will. You will," Sarah assured her. "Oh, Reg, I'm sure it can't be as bad as all of that. Starlight is a young, strong cat. He'll fight it. He'll recover."

Reg shook her head. "I don't know that, and neither do you. We don't even know how old he is. Harrison said that he was a very old friend. I don't want to lose him. I can't lose him, Sarah."

Sarah moved Reg over to the couch to sit down, holding her tightly to keep her from collapsing.

"What's going on?"

Sarah looked toward the door she had left open in her haste to help. Reg didn't look up. She knew that voice. She had ignored it for so many years it was practically second nature.

"Oh, it's your mother," Sarah said, looking awkward. She shifted her position, not sure whether to get up and offer Norma Jean her seat or not. Reg grabbed onto her and kept her from getting up. She did not want to be hugged and comforted by her mother. Sarah had never been anything but good to her. Unlike Norma Jean, who had failed on every level.

"Reg's cat is sick," Sarah explained when Reg didn't rush to give Norma Jean an explanation for what was going on. "She had to leave him at the vet, and she's very worried about him."

"What's wrong with it?"

Reg did raise her head then and looked into her mother's eyes. Cold, empty eyes. This was the same mother who had refused to let her have a cat when she was a little girl. The same mother who looked at Starlight suspiciously when she had come into the cottage, commenting about how familiar he had seemed. She couldn't have done anything to Starlight, could she? Reg didn't remember leaving her alone there. She couldn't have poisoned Starlight without Reg seeing something.

"He was poisoned," Reg told Norma Jean evenly, watching her face carefully for even the slightest change in expression. She was good at reading people. Really good at it. Scary good.

Norma Jean looked away immediately. She patted her hair and scratched her nose, keeping her gaze averted from Reg's. "Who would poison your cat? Did you let it outside? Maybe it ate something it wasn't supposed to."

Reg looked at the box, nearly filled with the Yule decorations. "No, he didn't go outside. And I don't know whether it was something he got into and didn't know would harm him, or if someone gave him something intentionally. If someone did poison him on purpose… all I can say is, they'd better get out of town before I find out."

Norma Jean still didn't look at her. Reg wondered if that was her answer. Well, she was serious. If Reg found out someone had intentionally harmed her familiar, they had better disappear at the first available opportunity. She wasn't going to go easy on them.

"I didn't do anything to hurt your cat," Norma Jean said sullenly. She looked at Sarah, clearly hoping she would leave. She thought it was her place to be there to comfort Reg.

But Norma Jean was wrong. Reg didn't want her there. "I can't entertain right now. And I don't think I'll be able to in the near future. So why don't you just go back home?"

Sarah made a little noise. "Reg!"

"I didn't ask her to come here, and I don't want anything from her. She can go back home and do… whatever it is she does now."

"But she is your mother," Sarah murmured, looking at Reg searchingly.

"She is not my mother. Giving birth to me does not qualify her as my mother."

Sarah didn't have anything to say to that.

Norma Jean drew herself up, raising her chin and standing very straight. "Fine. If you don't want me here, I will leave. I'll be back when you are feeling better and are ready to be civil to me."

Reg wiped her nose. "That's not going to be for a very long time."

★ CHAPTER FIVE ★

S ARAH STAYED WITH REG for quite a while, not speaking, but rubbing her back and keeping her company and trying to make her feel better. Eventually, Sarah stood up and continued with the work of collecting all of the plants that could have hurt Starlight and putting them into the box. Reg sat with her elbows on her knees and her face in her hands and tried to keep herself calm.

It had felt good to explode at Norma Jean. To lash out at someone, whether she deserved it or not. And she did deserve everything Reg had said. It was all true. Norma Jean was not the kind of person she would want taking care of a child. Reg wiped her eyes and watched Sarah. She indicated the potted plant on the side table.

"Take that too. Fir said not to let Starlight eat it, so I guess that means that it could hurt him too. I shouldn't have accepted it in the first place, but he was so nice, and he wanted to give me something for helping him get out of jail and get his garden space back." Reg sniffled. "What kind of a useless pet owner doesn't do any research to find out how to cat-proof her house? I didn't know that any of these things were poisonous. He's never eaten anything like that before. He just wants me to feed him my food. I didn't think he'd eat anything that would hurt him."

"He is a remarkably intelligent animal," Sarah agreed. "And he obviously has some knowledge or instinct for the properties of herbs, or he wouldn't have brought you the yarrow when you were hurt. I find it very strange that he would eat anything harmful."

"Yeah. I hadn't thought about that." Reg got up and went to the kitchen. She picked up the dishtowel and dried her face, then tossed it into the hallway so that she would remember to put it into the laundry. "Does that mean that someone intentionally poisoned him? If it couldn't have been an accident…"

"It still might have been. You never know what cats will do. You don't even know what people are going to do. They still make mistakes and do stupid things. How are we supposed to figure out animals' behaviors when we don't even understand human behavior?"

Reg was still sniffling, though she was trying to stop. She felt wrung out, empty of any more tears.

"I guess you'll want me to take the tree too," Sarah suggested, looking up at it.

Reg wondered how Sarah had gotten it in there in the first place. She must have had some help. Maybe Forst, though he was so small he might not have been much help with such a large tree. Sarah looked at her watch.

"I'll have to come back for it. Is it okay if I do that tomorrow? Starlight isn't home right now, so there isn't any more danger in leaving it one more day…"

"Yes. That's fine," Reg agreed. "Are you going out tonight?" Sarah had been seeing a lot of younger men lately. At her age, practically all of the men in the community were significantly younger, but the men that she had been dating looked it, too.

"I am." Sarah looked at her watch again and picked up the box, now heavy with the ornaments, garlands, and wreaths. "He will be here to pick me up any minute, so I need to go freshen up. Will you be okay, Reg? I can call him and tell him I need to cancel tonight. If you need someone here with you…"

"No, you go ahead. I think I'm going to put on a movie and fall asleep in front of the TV."

"That's not a very healthy way to sleep. You won't get the rest you need sitting in front of the TV."

"It will be more than I'll get lying down and trying not to think and worry about things. I need something to occupy my brain without having to think about it. I'll binge-watch some rom-com. You go out and have a nice time." Reg shook her head at the incongruity of telling the older woman to have a nice date. She forced a smile and a lift in her voice. "Don't stay out too late and don't let him get fresh with you."

Sarah laughed merrily, carting the box of decorations toward the door. "Oh, I don't know about that, Reg. Didn't you say you wanted me to have a nice time?"

Reg chuckled and watched Sarah go. She shut the door and shot the bolt. She didn't want any more visitors. Especially not Norma Jean.

A few minutes later, she saw Sarah walk past her kitchen window, which Reg could see from her living room. She was changed, all dolled up for the dance or wherever it was she was going on her date. Reg wished she knew what kind of practical magic that was. She would love to be able to look beautiful and polished within two minutes. A few minutes later, she felt Sarah's presence fade, and knew she had been picked up for her date. Reg was left completely alone to spend all night worrying about Starlight.

The night was drawing on and, despite Reg's determination to watch mindless pap on TV until she fell asleep, her plan wasn't working. She was so tired she could cry. But she couldn't go to sleep. She surfed channels, looking for something to occupy her attention, but she wasn't getting very far. She had a cup of Sarah's sleepy tea in hopes that it might help but was still feeling just as restless and empty as ever. She needed her cat. She needed his furry cuddles and his peaceful aura and the way he had of looking at her as if he had human intelligence—or greater than human intelligence—and could understand when she was trying to sort something out.

The tea hadn't worked, so Reg got up one more time and poured herself a slug of Jack Daniels to see if that would work. Just one; she wouldn't allow herself any more than that. It would take the edge off just enough to settle down and sleep without her cat.

She'd slept her whole life without a cat? How could that have changed so completely in the few months she had lived in Black Sands?

She sat down with the Jack and watched the TV while she sipped it, trying to stretch it out and make it last since she knew she would not be going back for another. She was all cried out. Her eyes felt as dry as a desert, and she had a headache and congested sinuses. She had called all of her appointments and advised them that she wouldn't be able to do a reading that night because she wasn't feeling well. She was sure they could hear her congestion, and no one complained about it. There were no emergencies; everyone just rescheduled. Reg wondered when she would be able to do them. What if Starlight never recovered? She couldn't exactly tell them she couldn't do any more psychic readings because her cat had died. People would expect her to recover and move on, to get back down to business.

Reg fiddled with her phone, bored with everything on TV. Maybe she could be distracted by a game. Or maybe she could call someone and talk until she got tired enough to fall asleep. She flipped through screens, looking at the icons, checking in on a couple of social networks to see if anything was going on.

Eventually, she ended up on her contact list and stared at the list of Black Sands friends.

Sarah was on a date, so she was out. She would probably not be back until quite late. Detective Jessup was being too much of a cop and Reg was still kind of irritated with her. So she was a maybe. There was Francesca but, although another devoted cat owner might seem like the perfect conversational companion, Reg had previously lectured Francesca on how she needed to keep Nicole indoors where it was safe, and she hated to admit that Starlight had been harmed while inside the house. Besides, if Francesca was too sympathetic, she might set off the waterworks again, and Reg didn't want to take the chance of crying anymore. She'd cried quite enough. But she needed someone who could take her mind off of Starlight, lying in a cage at the vet's office, the life slowly draining out of him, because Reg had been too ignorant to take care of him properly. Starlight had done his best to take care of her, and she had let him down.

Damon? She wasn't sure where their relationship was going to go after their last encounter. Damon had been horribly jealous since their one failed date, and she wasn't sure she was up to dealing with him. He was a nice guy, attractive, fun to be with if he weren't trying to convince her that she wanted to go bowling. But he could also read her and tell when she was lying, and he could put visions in her head, and she did not like people messing around inside her head. Even though she had told him not to, he continued to do it, telling her that he couldn't help himself, it was just the way that he naturally communicated.

No, probably not Damon. She didn't have the energy to try to sort out his emotions as well as her own.

There was always Corvin. The warlock that she knew she should not talk to or see, but was inevitably drawn toward. He was too dangerous. His powers had grown immensely and, despite all that Reg was learning about her powers and ability to resist his charms, he was still stronger than she was and, in her exhausted state, she wouldn't be able to build the psychic barricade that she needed to keep him from charming her and stealing her powers. He had done it once before when she was naive and had no idea what he could do to her, and she wasn't going to let it happen again, no matter how hard he continued to push.

But that didn't mean she couldn't talk to him on the phone, did it?

She wouldn't let him come over. She wouldn't go out for a late meal or drink. She would just chat with him on the phone. See how he was doing, and let him distract her from her anxiety. He couldn't do anything if he weren't in the same room with her.

Just a conversation. That wouldn't be so bad. He would be sympathetic, but only superficially. He didn't like cats. Starlight, in particular, was a thorn in his side. They did not like each other and always had words if Reg allowed Corvin into the cottage or took Starlight out with them on a case.

Hardly even thinking about what she was doing, Reg tapped Corvin's name and watched the screen as the call started to ring through.

She heard him answer, far away and tinny, and she lifted the phone to her ear.

"Hi."

"Reg." His voice was warm and full, like an embrace. "How unexpected. How are you doing?"

"I'm… having a tough night. Just needed… to talk."

"Sure, of course. What's going on? Some sort of metaphysical conflict?"

"No… very physical. It's Starlight. He's sick."

He grunted. "Sorry to hear that. Are you going to take him to the vet?"

"He's already there. I'm all alone." Not something that she should have revealed to him, but he would have guessed it anyway. "I just needed to hear someone else's voice. In the time that I've lived here, I was only ever alone here that first night. Then I got Starlight at the shelter, and… he's been with me since."

"Do you want me to come over? Keep you company?"

"No. Don't come here; I won't let you in."

"Come on, Reg. I could help. I could make you feel better."

"You making me feel better always ends up with my powers being in peril. I don't think so."

"That's not true. You know I have helped you in the past. Given you strength when you needed it. Given you companionship. Helped you with some of your tricky cases. Don't make it sound like I am just a predator."

"You *are* a predator."

"Yes, but not *just* a predator."

Reg couldn't help but laugh at this. His tone was half humorous and half peeved. He knew what he was, but he didn't like to be classified as an animal. He wanted everyone to recognize what a powerful and intelligent warlock he was. He wanted them to forget the rest of it, how he could seduce and steal powers. He had been strong enough to overcome the Witch Doctor, sucking most of his powers right out of him. If he could do that, he could do pretty much whatever he wanted, whether the Council and the community allowed it or not. They were fooling themselves if they thought their silly rules would have any effect on him.

"So if I can't come over there to provide you comfort, what can I do?" Corvin asked in a husky voice.

"Just talk to me. I need someone to take my mind off of things."

"I could do that so much better face to face."

"Not going to happen."

"Okay," he conceded. "So what does the cat have? Some feline flu?"

"No… the vet thinks that he ate something poisonous. I don't know what; he was going to do some testing to figure out what it was, but I haven't heard anything back from him. It could have been the plant that Fir gave to me, or it could be the Yule plants that Sarah decorated the cottage with. Or the vet's assistant said that it could be something else around the house, or that someone might have done it intentionally. I just can't believe that someone would try to kill him."

Corvin was silent for a few seconds too long. Reg had to wonder if he were looking for a diplomatic way to say that *he* could understand someone trying to kill the annoying beast. He would have done it if he thought he could get away with it.

"Has there been someone in the cottage?" he asked. "He hasn't been outside, has he?"

"No. He's just been at home. So it would have to be something here."

"Then who…?"

Who could have had the opportunity to poison him? If it was intentional, then how had the perpetrator done it?

"Well… Sarah was there, of course, and all of the poisonous plants were hers. I don't think that she intentionally made him sick, but she could have. Or she could have fed him something else. She was there alone with him for hours, and she can come and go as she pleases when I'm not there. She had every opportunity."

"But you don't think it was her."

Sarah had insisted that she wouldn't have brought the Yule plants into the house if she had known that they were harmful to cats. She had seemed sincerely sympathetic. She might not like cats, but Reg couldn't see her trying to kill one. At least, not while she was in her right mind, and she had seemed perfectly sane the day before.

"No. I don't think that it was. She seemed… really sorry that it had happened. It's just that she was talking about cats earlier, and how she didn't want any extra cats around the house or yard. She said that Starlight was okay, but not any other cats."

"And you wonder if she changed her mind and decided that she might not want him around either."

"Wouldn't she tell me that, though? Give me a chance to find a new home for him?"

"If she knows how attached you are to that animal, she would have a pretty good idea that if she gave you an ultimatum, you would be looking for a new place to live. And I think that she likes having you there, even if she does have to put up with Starlight."

"Yeah."

"And no one else has been around the house?"

"Well… of course there has been. I have clients in and out, doing readings. I had three or four people here last night. But none of them would have any reason to hurt Starlight. He wasn't in anyone's way, and none of them were people that I know very well. I can't see anyone having a grudge against him or me."

"Well, then, I'm not sure who else could have poisoned him intentionally. It must have been an accident."

"I guess so." Reg should have felt better about that conclusion, but she didn't. She still had the nagging feeling that someone had done it on purpose. Maybe she just didn't want to take the responsibility herself. Because if someone else hadn't done it, then that meant she had poisoned her own cat, and she couldn't bear to think of him at the vet's office, dying all alone.

"But, you wanted to be distracted from this, not to talk about it," Corvin reminded himself. "So why don't you tell me what else is new. Have you had any interesting clients recently? Any exciting readings? Read any good books lately?"

He probably knew her well enough to know that she didn't read books. She hadn't read a single book since she had left school, and had probably not read a full one even when she was in school. She had done everything she could to avoid books. She liked to watch the movies instead, but the teachers knew the differences between the books and the movies and always caught her. Reg didn't know why reading was so important. There were so many other ways to learn and communicate. Multimedia was the way to go. Face-to-face interviews or teleconferencing. Live broadcasts. Books were antiquated. But then, so was Corvin.

"No good books," she told him. "And there's nothing on TV. I don't want to say too much about my clients; I like to think that we have a sort of confidentiality between us, like with a doctor or a priest. They tell me some pretty personal stuff, and it wouldn't be right for me to break their trust and share it with someone else."

"You're not making this easy. How about Sarah? What's she up to?"

She was about to ask him why he didn't talk to Sarah himself. But she already knew why. Because his coven was shunning him and, even though Sarah was in a different coven, they were shunning him as well. He didn't have any contact with anyone who was in the established covens in Black Sands. Only people like Reg, who was not associated with any organization. Lone wolves like Damon. But Damon and Corvin were not friends.

"Sarah... well, she's out on a date."

"Again?"

"Always. She's always out with someone these days. You'd think she was a teenager again."

"With the amount of energy she has now, she might as well be. She doesn't have a steady guy?"

"No, I don't think so. Always someone new over there. She's just having a good time, doesn't want any commitments right now."

"That would just slow her down."

"Exactly. If she has to stick to one guy, settle down, get married, she's going to be bored."

Reg stretched and turned her head back and forth, trying to release the tension in her neck and shoulders. It was no wonder she couldn't settle down when her body was so knotted up. She gazed out the window into the dark yard. Lights were twinkling, and she tried to focus on them. Twinkle lights at Sarah's house? Lightning bugs? She couldn't seem to focus on them. As soon as she tried, they vanished and appeared somewhere else.

★ CHAPTER SIX ★

"ARTH TO REG?"

"Hmm?" Reg brought her attention back to the phone. "Sorry. There are lights outside, and I was trying to figure out…"

"Lights? What kind of lights?"

"I don't know. I was trying to figure that out, but whenever I try to focus on one…"

"Maybe I should come over and check it out."

"You get points for persistence, that's for sure."

Corvin chuckled. She could imagine the smug smile on his face. He was just so darn handsome. Even when she was just thinking of him, she felt flushed.

Unless he was closer than she thought. It wouldn't be the first time that he showed up when she thought he was too far away to be a danger to her. She tried again to make out the lights. Was he out there? Was he the one who was causing them? They didn't look like anything man-made. She had heard of foxfire lights in the swamp, but she didn't think they could be anywhere else, like in her yard.

"What are you doing tonight?" Reg asked, hoping for reassurance.

"I have been out collecting some plants and am just preparing them now. Chopping, drying, freezing, the method of preparation depends on what plant it is and what they are being used for."

"What do you do with them?"

"A wide variety of things. Some are used in potions; some are burned during rituals. Some are used in healing poultices. It all depends. There are many beneficial plants and herbs in this area."

"What did you find tonight?"

Corvin listed off several plants that Reg had never heard of. He could be making it all up, and she would have no idea. But she didn't feel like he was trying to deceive her. She usually had some sense if he was lying to her. It wasn't like he was usually subtle. If Corvin had something on his mind, she usually knew about it pretty quickly.

Even so, she tried to see him. She had been able to before, when he was in danger. This time, she could be the one in danger, so it should come to her easily. She tried to envision him preparing his leaves, roots, and berries. Was he in his kitchen, or did he have a special potions room in his house? Damon had once referred to Corvin's house as his lair. Was it some dark, underground laboratory? Or was that just figurative, and he lived in a bright, modern home with white cupboards and gleaming marble countertops?

She had never been to his house, of course. That would be putting herself in unnecessary danger. He could do whatever he wanted if he were on his own property instead of Reg's, which was protected with Sarah's wards.

He was still going on, giving a lecture about what plants he was working with. He taught classes sometimes, and Reg didn't have a hard time imagining him lecturing at the front of a class. He had no trouble pontificating on his pet topics. Usually history and politics in the magical community, but apparently herblore was right up there on his list too.

The vision came to her gradually, not all at once. She stared into her crystal ball, trying to remain focused. It wasn't easy without the magnifying influence of Starlight and with the effects of grief, exhaustion, and Jack Daniels on her brain.

She could see him in his kitchen. Just a regular kitchen, not an underground lab or a stone temple with a sacrificial altar. And he was doing just what he said he was, chopping up his various herbs, which were laid out in piles on his counters. There were bowls and jars and all kinds of other culinary equipment. Like some grandma on jam-making day. She enjoyed watching him remotely when he couldn't see her or know that she was watching him. Her heart sped, and she felt that warm flush again.

His cheeks, ordinarily clean-shaven, leaving just a neat goatee around his mouth, were dark with whiskers, all stubbly and rough. He was wearing a black cloak and had the window open, the cool night air washing through the kitchen. His dark eyes were intent on what he was doing, his hair just a little too long in the back, making him look like a knight in a medieval castle. Or in the crusades. Or something.

His phone was on the counter in front of him, on speaker phone so that he could chat with her while he continued his preparations. He paused in his lecture.

"You still there, Reg?"

"Mmm. Yes, I'm still here."

"You sound tired. Do you want to go to bed?"

"I want to, but I can't. That's why I called you."

"I could help with that."

"I'm sure you could." She remembered the one night they had been together, before she knew what it was she was agreeing to, what it was he could do to her. The physical intimacy had been amazing. She felt an electrical buzz whenever she touched Corvin, and to be that close and intimate had been incredible. Her body thrummed with heat just thinking about it.

But she wasn't about to let that happen again. Not when the price was the loss of her powers. Waking up in the morning with all of the voices gone and a silent, flat world around her instead of the chatter she was used to had been devastating. She never wanted to feel that lost and alone and powerless again. And that was why she could never yield to him again.

"You are helping," she told him. "Especially droning on about your plants. That could put anyone to sleep."

"You know me. Always happy to oblige."

Reg's eyes wandered to the lights again. Sarah must have put a couple of strings of lights out there, and Reg just hadn't noticed them earlier. Or maybe she had invoked some twinkle-light spell to make it look more festive.

"What are you doing for Christmas?" she asked Corvin. "I mean… whatever it's called…" Her mind was getting too fuzzy to remember what it was Sarah was celebrating.

"Winter solstice? Well, I'm sure you know that it's a day of celebration and renewal. Normally, I would join my coven for some rituals. This year…" he sighed, "I guess I'm on my own."

Because of Reg, he had been shunned from his coven. She hadn't thought about him missing out on special holidays like that. She felt a little bad that he would have to miss the celebrations. It was like being sent away for Christmas. Reg knew what that was like.

But he wasn't shunned because of Reg. It was because of what he had done. Because he had broken the rules, even after he had repeatedly promised not to harm her. He'd resorted to more than just trickery to get her in his thrall. He had broken the established rules of the community. Rules that were utterly inadequate to protect the women in the community whose powers he desired. He'd broken his promises to her and his promises to abide by the rules of the community.

She hadn't even been the one to bring charges against him. She was so embarrassed by the whole thing that she would have preferred to fade into the woodwork and not bring attention to herself. The hearing in front of the tribunal had been humiliating.

"How about you?" Corvin prompted. "Your first solstice in Black Sands. You must have something special planned."

"Well, no, I don't, actually. I didn't even know about this Yule thing until yesterday. I just thought… everybody celebrated Christmas. I mean, not in a religious way, just… exchanging presents, enjoying the season. Celebrating something."

"And we do. It just happens to precede Christmas. Even the Christians think that Christmas has become too commercialized. Too much about buying the best presents or getting the best deals, making a turkey dinner that will put everyone into a food coma, and racing from one end of the state to the other visiting all of their family and friends without the opportunity to really enjoy each other's company. Yule or solstice is much simpler and quieter. Much more about our connection with nature than about elaborate gifts or meals."

"I don't know. I guess I'll do something. I can buy some pre-cooked turkey for me and…" Reg suddenly remembered, and her words trickled off. There was no Starlight. Not unless he miraculously recovered. She was going to be alone for Christmas or solstice. All by herself. Like she had been for so many other Christmases past.

"Have hope, Regina," Corvin murmured.

Her eyes welled with tears again, as she had known they would if she were subjected to too much sympathy and understanding. Corvin's voice was kind, and she wished that he were there and she could cuddle up against him and take his warmth and strength for herself. He would tuck her into bed and…

Reg gave herself a sharp mental 'stop!' not allowing the images to go any further. She wasn't looking for comfort from Corvin. He was supposed to be the distraction, the one person who wouldn't make her feel worse about Starlight.

"How can I?" Reg wiped her eyes. She had thought that they would be dry for a week after the amount she had cried already. "The vet didn't think he had much chance. He's the expert. How could I have been so stupid? I would never have done anything to hurt Starlight intentionally. How could I not have even looked up what things around the house could hurt him? Are they like dogs? Could chocolate poison them? I don't even know! I didn't even look it up!"

"But you didn't give him chocolate. You didn't give him anything that would harm him. He got into something he wasn't supposed to. It wasn't something you fed him. You take excellent care of him, that's obvious to anyone who sees the two of you together."

Seeing Corvin in her crystal, she saw his nostrils flare, his mouth twist into a sneer, and he shook his head. He did not like Starlight. But he didn't allow that dislike to creep into his voice.

"I know you don't like him," Reg said, "but…"

He glanced over at the phone. "I didn't do anything to harm him. I haven't been around your house in days."

★ CHAPTER SEVEN ★

R EG FOCUSED SHARPLY ON Corvin's words. Why did he get defensive when she hadn't accused him of anything? Was it a case of protesting too much because he was guilty? She reviewed the last few days in her mind. Was there any time he could have come by the cottage without her knowing it? Even if he had, there was no way he could have had access to Starlight. Starlight was inside the house, and Corvin was still prevented from entering by the wards Sarah had placed.

Unless Corvin had grown powerful enough to overcome Sarah's spells.

There was no telling how strong he was. Harrison had said that Corvin was not yet in control of his new powers. As Corvin grew more skilled and comfortable with those new gifts, he would be able to do many things that he hadn't been able to before. Opening locked doors and getting past protective wards did not seem like much of a stretch.

"You haven't been around here," she repeated.

"No, I haven't. Just because I don't like the beast, that doesn't mean I would do anything to hurt him. You don't go poisoning everyone you don't like, do you?"

Reg allowed herself a smile at that. If she did, there would be a long trail of bodies behind her. "No. I haven't poisoned anyone recently."

She saw his lips curl up at her words. He chopped a root into fine dices. "Do you need someone to go with you to the vet tomorrow?"

Reg felt a warm rush of gratitude at his question. "Actually, yeah. That would be really good. I don't really want to go by myself, and coming home today... I had a real tough time and probably shouldn't have been driving."

"What time do you want to go over?"

"I'll have to check their hours. Probably late morning."

"Sure. I'll make some time for it. You can call me when you know what time for sure and I'll drive you over."

"Thanks. That would be a really big help."

"You know I'm always happy to help you, Regina."

At some point, Reg finally did fall asleep in front of the TV. She was restless, waking up several times in the night and staring at the TV, which was tuned to a shopping channel with a too-excited host talking about the latest technology in ladies' tights. It was enough to put anyone to sleep.

Morning dawned and, with the light streaming in the window, she was unable to go back to sleep. She could go to her room and lie down in bed, pulling the covers up over her head, but she wasn't going to be able to sleep in there either, thinking about Starlight and how he wasn't sitting in the window and wasn't going to be trying to wake her up to feed him breakfast.

So she got up and made a cup of coffee and stood sipping the piping hot liquid and considering whether there was anything that appealed to her in the fridge. There wasn't. She deeply missed the little fur-ball winding himself around her legs. It ached like a hole in her chest. How could she go on without him?

Reg was on tenterhooks waiting for Corvin to confirm that he was on the way, and then for him to get there. She sensed as soon as he pulled in front of Sarah's house and she left the cottage without waiting for his call or text to indicate that he was there. Or for him to show up at her door. She didn't need him coming in to get her.

As soon as she slid into the seat beside him in the car, she was enveloped in a warmth that wasn't coming from the car's heater or the sun beating down on her. It was a warmth that reached right inside her and helped her to feel calm and prepared for what was ahead. Reg eyed Corvin appreciatively. She wondered if he understood how much it meant to her to feel strong facing the return trip to the vet's office.

Corvin smiled and nodded at her. "Reg. All set?"

"I guess I am. Let's go."

While he was driving, he rested his hand on her leg. She would normally have found this too intimate a gesture and shaken him off, but she could feel the flow of strength from him.

It was what she needed. But on the other hand, she had to be careful not to let down her guard. The moment she did, he would ensorcel her and she would easily slide into his power in the fragile state she was in. She said nothing, watching out the window and gathering her thoughts the best she could.

She was scared to death that the vet would tell her that Starlight had passed away in the night. The receptionist had Reg and Corvin sit down, and Reg watched the other people with their sick or hurt pets, her heart aching. She needed to hold Starlight again and to know that he would be well.

Eventually, the vet called them in. There were a couple of chairs snugged up against the examining table in the tiny room, and Reg and Corvin sat down. Reg waited in trepidation as the vet looked through Starlight's charts on his clipboard as if he didn't know what the cat's status was. Surely he had seen Starlight already that morning and had reviewed any of the tests that had come in overnight.

Eventually, the vet looked back at their faces. He shook his head slowly, expression serious. "I wish I had better news for you. I did warn you that he was in serious condition, but sometimes animals can surprise us and bounce back much earlier than we would have predicted. Unfortunately, such was not the case here. Starlight is hanging on, which is the only good news that I have for you. He is a fighter. He hasn't yet succumbed to the poison, whatever it was."

"You still don't know?" Reg asked. "I thought you would have identified it by now."

"Real life isn't like you see on TV. You can't just pop a sample in the machine, and have it spit out the poison and how to treat it. We can test for the top few poisons, but we have to know something about what to look for if it isn't one of the usual suspects. I can't just put a leaf in a machine and have it tell me that he was poisoned by a lily. We don't have that kind of ability here."

"But you do think it's a leaf? A plant?"

"He had several leaves in his stomach. But they are too masticated to tell what they are. It doesn't appear that it was anything in the lily family, or holly, or mistletoe. But that still leaves a wide variety of options." The doctor tapped the end of his pen on the clipboard. "I haven't seen a case like this before. The properties of this plant are… strange to me. With poisoning, we expect to see vomiting, diarrhea, maybe seizures. A recognizable constellation of symptoms. But he is quite… he doesn't have many symptoms, other than being unconscious and having a very slow heartbeat and respiration."

"Something is depressing his system," Corvin offered. The doctor looked at him, frowning.

"Yes."

"But you don't know what it is. Could it be… could he have also gotten into someone's medication? A Valium or something else that affects the respiratory system?"

The doctor raised his eyebrows at Reg, asking the question silently.

"No," Reg said immediately. She didn't take tranquilizers. She didn't take anything that would make her sleepy. And no more psychiatric meds. They never helped, and always had annoying side effects. "I don't have anything like that around the house. No prescriptions. No illegal drugs." She shot a glance at Corvin to express her displeasure at being accused in front of the doctor of taking something that would have harmed Starlight.

"What about Tylenol? An herbal tea?"

"It's not Tylenol," the vet said, shaking his head. "A tea… it could be, depending on what it had in it and what its properties were. Do you know what is in your teas?"

"He didn't drink my tea," Reg protested. She couldn't give him any explanation. Starlight was, she supposed, just as likely to have licked the remains of her sleepy tea or some other concoction out of her teacup as he was of chewing on Fir's plant or a Yule decoration. Just because she didn't think it was likely, that wasn't proof.

"I don't know." The vet sighed. "I guess we're just going to have to watch and wait and hope that he recovers."

"You think his symptoms are unusual," Corvin said, giving Reg a meaningful look.

"Yes, they are unusual. Not wildly bizarre, but not what I would have expected."

"And you need to identify the poison before you can treat for it."

"I'll keep doing what I am, trying to get on top of it and turn him around. But right now, he is not responding to treatment."

"That's unusual," Corvin said, again emphasizing the word.

Reg tried to figure out what he was getting at.

"Is there any way we could see him before we go?" Corvin asked.

"He's settled in a bed; I don't like to move him. Best if he stays put where he is."

"We'd really like to see him before we go. We don't know if it might be the last opportunity we have."

Reg swallowed a sob, trying to keep her composure. The doctor was hesitant, then nodded.

"Let me check on things. I'll see whether it is easier to bring him in here or to take you into the kennels. We don't usually allow owners back there."

He left the room. Reg looked at Corvin. "What's all that about? I don't understand what you're trying to do. Why would you care about seeing him? You don't even like him."

"The fact that the symptoms are unusual doesn't bring anything to mind? It doesn't mean anything to you?"

Reg shook her head. What had she missed? What was she supposed to understand?

"If they are that unusual, maybe it's because it wasn't just a natural poisoning," Corvin pointed out.

"Which means what?"

"Maybe it was part of a spell. Maybe there is a magical component, and that's why he is not responding to medical treatment."

Reg inhaled sharply and held her breath. "Yeah… maybe."

"That's why I want to see him. I might not be able to tell anything looking at him or being near him, but I can try. And you and I can both see whether there is anything we can do to help him."

"Okay." Reg breathed out slowly. She couldn't think of anything that she would be able to do to help Starlight, but if Corvin thought there was something he could do… She'd seen him work before, helping Sarah when she had been so close to death. He was able to give strength when he wanted to and maybe, if there was some spell for him to counteract, there was some hope for her kitty.

★ CHAPTER EIGHT ★

T WAS SOME TIME before the vet's assistant came to the examination room and nodded to Reg and Corvin, her eyes gentle and sympathetic. "We've got kitty settled in another room for you. Come this way."

She led them through the back door of the examining room, the one that the vet used, which led to the rooms that were off-limits to customers. They walked past laboratory benches and a bank of cages with sick, sad-looking animals resting in them. One dog on the bottom row barked and growled as they went past, but all the rest were quiet. Much too quiet.

The veterinary assistant smiled again and gestured to a door. "This way."

Reg entered first, with Corvin behind her. Starlight lay on a towel on the examining table, completely still and unaware of their presence. Reg felt the tears flood her cheeks again. How could she bear it? How could she keep seeing him and saying goodbye, knowing that it might be the last time that she would ever see him alive? He seemed to be even farther away from her than he had been before, getting smaller and more faded, his body just a shell that used to hold the bold, vivacious spirit of her companion. Corvin put a hand on Reg's shoulder. Electricity jolted her. The warmth of his hand seeped down into her shoulder and, without any effort, she was suddenly on a different plane. She couldn't explain it any other way. It was like when she had been banished to the pixies' unseen world. She was still in the same place that she had been physically, but everything had changed.

"Reg?" Corvin murmured, his hand tightening slightly.

Reg waited for the vet's assistant to leave the room, pulling the door closed behind her. She turned and looked at Corvin.

"What happened?" he asked.

"I thought it was you. Wasn't it?"

"No… I don't think so. Though it's hard for me to tell. You do things to me that no one else can."

She ignored his claim, which was probably intended to make her feel sorry for him. She looked at Starlight on the examining table. There was a halo of light around him. His aura or his spirit. She led Corvin a couple of steps closer to the table. He released his comforting grip on her shoulder, and Reg took his hand in hers, not wanting to break the connection they had made. She looked at Starlight, then closed her eyes.

"Show it to me," she breathed. "I don't know what I'm supposed to be seeing here. What do I look for?"

She didn't know whether she was talking to Corvin, or just making a plea to the universe in general.

"I'm not sure if you and I are seeing the same thing. I see light around him, do you?"

"Yeah. All around him. What am I supposed to do?"

"Let's look for any changes in the light. Places where it is dimmer or more diffuse."

Reg studied Starlight, turning the picture over in her mind, manipulating it and trying to come to a conclusion. "I think… around his head and eyes, it's darker. And inside… I can't really see inside. I think… He's bleeding in there. But how could I know that?"

"Don't question it. Just accept it. If you think he's bleeding inside, then we should probably stop that. Do you know how to do it?"

Reg shook her head. "I don't know anything about any of this."

Corvin worked his hand out of Reg's grip, and positioned both hands over Starlight, as if warming himself by a log in the fire. But Reg had seen him do that before, healing and providing strength to the subject. He'd done it to Sarah and Damon, and he'd done it to Reg on occasion as well. But what about cats? Was it all the same for cats? Or did he have to have an affinity for them in order to heal them?

Corvin stayed in that position for a long time, then shook his head. "I'm not feeling anything. I don't think it's having any efficacy."

"You can't heal him?" Reg's voice choked up.

"I don't think so. I've given him as much strength as I can, but that's all I can do. I can't initiate the healing process."

"Is it because he's a cat? Or because it's magic? Or something else? I don't know what to do."

"You can try it yourself. He knows you and his body may respond differently to you. Just pet him and talk to him, like you normally would. I know I'm not doing that, but most subjects prefer I don't actually touch. The cat knows your touch. Try to give him more strength and to make him whole."

"I don't know how to do that." But Reg petted him anyway—long, soothing strokes, followed by cuddles and ear scratches and loving words whispered into his ears. She focused on that warm transfer of strength that she had felt from Corvin. If she could take it from him, she could give it too.

She rested, her hands still on Starlight. She breathed in and out and tried to relax her whole body and brain. If she were going to heal him, it was going to take a lot of energy, and she wasn't sure whether it would 'take.'

"You protected him before," Corvin said, talking while she rested.

Reg was surprised. "Well… I tried when I found him, and he was so sick. I wanted to stop him from getting any worse. But I don't think it did anything.

It was already too late at that point; he'd already taken—or been given—whatever made him sick by then."

"I think it has helped. I think that's probably the only reason he's still with us."

"You think so?" Reg felt a little heartened by this. She hadn't known what she was doing, she had just gone on instinct, but maybe it had helped.

"I do," Corvin agreed. "And I think he recognizes that you are here, trying to help him."

"I don't… feel his presence at all," Reg confessed. "I don't think he's conscious."

"No, I don't mean that… but I think he still knows that you are here, deep down inside. Whether it's a coherent thought or not."

Reg shook her head. She remembered Harrison's comment when she had asked him whether Weston was still alive. That humans had funny ideas about life and death that he couldn't comprehend. As an immortal, he didn't have to deal with death and the unknowns that came after. Not if he really was immortal, and not just long-lived. Reg wasn't sure whether the immortals even understood the difference. Humans talk about death, but then life after death, and reincarnation, and so many other opposing theories, Harrison wasn't sure what they meant by death.

"He's not dead, is he? Is he out of his body? Is that why I can't feel him?"

"No, he's still here. I'm sure we wouldn't be able to see the light if he wasn't."

"Yeah?"

Corvin nodded. Reg took a couple more deep breaths and then tried again, trying to locate the bleeding that she could see in her mind and to tell the body to heal itself. In spite of the bleeding, there was not a lot of pain. Reg hoped that much was true. She explored his stomach, which is where she thought the poison must have come from, and explored for damage that radiated out from it. She'd seen pictures of neurons, little dark blobs with spidery legs stretching out from them, and thought that was the best visual description for what she could feel. Multiple spots of damage, with branching blood vessels or nerves radiating out. Reg focused on each one in turn, hoping that she could do something to heal them and make them whole again.

It was a long time before the vet entered the examining room. Reg opened her eyes and looked at him, exhausted from her work, unsure what to do next.

"Miss Rawlins, we really should be getting Starlight back on his IV and settled in his room. I don't think it is doing either of you any good to spend so much time with him. He needs his rest, and frankly, you look like you do too."

Reg nodded. The vet looked relieved that she had agreed. He looked at Corvin to see if he had any objection, but Corvin said nothing.

"We'll do our best for him," the vet promised, "Keep praying; that's all you can do at this point. And if you can figure out what plant he might have eaten… do let me know."

"Should I… bring you samples of the plants that were in my house? Other than holly or mistletoe?"

He nodded. "That might be helpful."

"And your tea," Corvin suggested.

"It wasn't my tea."

"You can't know that."

"If you have the ingredients list for any tea or other substance that you think he might have consumed," the vet said. "Don't bother to bring me the tea leaves, I won't be able to identify them any better than I can what was in his stomach. Whole plants, I might be able to identify from their appearance, but not dried and crushed leaves."

"I don't have the ingredients… I'll have to talk to Sarah. She's the one who makes the tea."

And Reg had also given her Fir's plant. Reg hoped she hadn't destroyed it.

She prepared to leave, petting Starlight one last time. "He's bleeding," Reg told the vet.

The vet stared at her, then looked over at Starlight. He made a quick physical examination and shook his head. "He looks just the same. There's no blood."

"But he's bleeding inside." Reg put her hand over the location. "Right here."

"How could you know that?"

"I… I'm a psychic. It's what I do."

He refrained from rolling his eyes, but Reg was sure he'd heard this line before. He couldn't practice in a town like Black Sands without running into practitioners who had no qualms telling him that they were witches, psychics, or some other kind of magical practitioner.

"I see."

"Please check. If you can stop the bleeding… I don't know. Maybe he'll survive."

The vet nodded. He palpitated Starlight's stomach gently. "We'll do some imaging. See whether I can see any bleeding. I don't believe in this stuff… but I've seen it be right often enough that I know I'd better not discount it."

★ CHAPTER NINE ★

REG WAS QUIET AS she and Corvin walked out of the vet's office and back to Corvin's car. It was a good thing that he had driven her, because she wasn't sure how she would have gotten home otherwise. She was too much of a mess to be responsible for driving herself. What was she going to do? Had their visit done any good? It just reinforced in her mind how precarious Starlight's health was. Even with all that she and Corvin had done to try to give him strength and healing, she wasn't sure it would do him any good or prolong his life more than a day or two. Even if the vet could figure out what he had eaten and stop the bleeding, she wasn't sure that would help. Especially if there were magic involved. The vet was clearly not a magical practitioner, so he wouldn't be able to reverse the effects of any spell. They would need someone skilled in healing arts. The only person she knew who had such skills was Corvin, and he hadn't been able to heal Starlight.

Maybe he didn't want to. Maybe he would rather have Starlight out of the way. He might have only been putting on a show for her.

But if he had put a curse on Starlight, then why would he bother telling her that? It would make more sense for him just to let the curse and poison run their course without telling Reg anything about it.

Reg caught a movement out of the corner of her eye and turned her head to see what it was. She couldn't see anything that would account for the movement she had seen. But she had seen something; a shadow, a surreptitious movement. Something that she couldn't quite identify.

Corvin noticed her look. He raised his eyebrows. "What?"

"I... saw something."

"What?"

"I don't know. I thought there was someone there. But there isn't."

Corvin stared in the direction she was looking. "I don't see anything."

"No... I don't know either."

"Just a trick of the light," Corvin said with a shrug. "Maybe a shadow or a bird."

"But it was..." Reg tried to think of the words to explain that it had seemed like a person. She hadn't seen it well enough to be able to say more than that, to describe it in terms of height, build, or gender, but she had seen something there that was not a shadow or a bird. "I don't know."

"You're distraught. Let's get you home."

Reg fumed silently at his dismissal. She wasn't seeing things due to grief. Being upset didn't make her have hallucinations.

But even as she thought that, she had to wonder. She had been treated in the past for seeing and hearing things that weren't there. Since she had come to Black Sands, she had come to believe that the psychiatric disturbances in the past were not mental illness, but a manifestation of her psychic abilities. She saw and heard spirits. She could see things that other people couldn't, hear them and feel them as clearly as she could see Corvin standing next to her. She'd been able to see the pixies when they had turned invisible. Not well, but their shadowy shapes. There was no reason for Corvin to suggest that just because he didn't see something, it wasn't there.

"Maybe it was a spirit," she said as she got into his car.

Corvin looked at her, confused for a moment before he caught up to her line of thought. "I suppose it could be," he admitted. "Do you have a spirit attached to you these days?"

"I always have spirits attached to me." He knew that from when he had held her powers. For Reg, it had never been difficult to see or hear the spirits around her. The challenge had been to filter out the voices so that she could listen to them one at a time or be able to think her own thoughts without the other voices crowding in.

"Is this one that you know? Is it trying to communicate something to you?"

Reg settled herself in the seat and looked back to where she had seen the movement. She reached out psychically, trying to isolate it and figure out who it was and what they wanted from her. But the presence shifted and withdrew. It seemed not to want to communicate with her. Reg shook her head.

"I don't think it wants to be seen. I don't know."

He looked at her, waiting for more, but Reg didn't have anything. She didn't know what to tell him about the movement she had seen. It had been too quick, just out of her sight, and now that she was looking for it, she couldn't see it. A lot of good psychic vision did in a case like that. She didn't know what the shadow wanted, if it even wanted anything from her. Perhaps it had just been watching her by chance and hadn't expected to be seen. Then it had withdrawn when she tried to reach out because it didn't want anything from her.

Reg sighed and pressed her fingers to her temples. "I can't deal with this right now."

"You don't have to. You saw something. You turned your head and it wasn't there. That kind of thing happens all the time. If whatever it was isn't trying to communicate with you, then ignore it. I'll get you home, and you can rest and relax."

"How can I relax when Starlight is in there…" She couldn't bring herself to say the word *dying*. Putting it into words was just too much.

"We've done everything we can for the cat. Now, we'll have to wait, and hope that the vet is able to do something for him."

"But you know he's not going to be able to. Not if it was because of a spell or curse. He can't treat for that. And sitting around at home waiting for something to happen isn't going to help. I can't just sit around waiting. We need to figure out who did this to him and why they did. If we can figure that out, maybe we can find out how to make him better."

Corvin started the engine. He pointed the nose of the car toward home. For a few minutes, he just drove in silence. "Of course I'll help you however I can," he promised. "But I'm not sure it will make any difference. You might make yourself crazy, trying to do something that you have no control over. What help will that be to him? It's better if you just… focus on other things and let nature take its course."

"You think I should let him die?" Reg's voice came out in an indignant squeak. She couldn't believe that he would even suggest such a thing.

"That's not exactly what I said. We've done everything we can for him. He's in the best hands. At this point, you turn it over to… fate. We can't fight against what is intended to happen."

"I sure as heck can!"

He shrugged. "You can… but you may be risking your own sanity. There is only so much that we can do. If you keep fighting after the struggle is over, you are harming yourself."

Reg pressed her lips together. There was no point in arguing it with him. It wasn't his cat that was in peril. He couldn't know how it felt. She would fight to her last breath to save Starlight. She wasn't going to stop just because someone else thought she should.

Reg stared out the window at the passing scenery without seeing any of it. She tried to make a list in her head. Her foster sister, Erin, was always a great one for making lists. Even as a young teenager, Reg could remember Erin sitting down and pulling out a notepad and balancing it on her scraped knees. "We just need to make a list…"

It had always made Erin feel better to have a plan, and Reg had been jealous of that. She wanted to feel better too. But her plans always remained tangled up in her head and things generally spun out of control. Maybe making a list would help Reg to keep a logical sequence in her head, but it had never come easily to her.

Reg needed to talk to Sarah to get the plant from Fir and the ingredients to the tea, and to find out what other plants had been in her house other than holly and mistletoe that could have poisoned a cat. She should ask whether Sarah had seen anything unusual around the yard or the cottage too. There had been a lot of odd feelings or occurrences over the past few days, and Reg didn't know how to explain them. Maybe Sarah could.

What about an animal healer? There were all kinds of gifted people in the magical community. There had to be someone skilled in healing cats. Witches and warlocks had to have somewhere to go when one of their familiars fell ill. Somewhere other than to a vet who didn't know the first thing about magical curses or healing.

Who would want to poison her cat? If there had also been a magical curse involved, then it wasn't just a random neighbor, it had to be someone who was a practitioner and who, for some reason, didn't want Starlight around. Was it to clear the way to get to Reg unimpeded? Or was it to prevent her from using his psychic powers to boost her own?

All of Reg's meditations were dashed from her head when they pulled up to the house.

★ CHAPTER TEN ★

R EG SAW A WHITE car in front of the house and knew immediately who was sitting there waiting for her. She swore and hit the dashboard with the heel of her hand. It smarted, but she was angry, so she didn't care. Corvin looked at her, eyebrows raised, wondering what was wrong.

"Norma Jean," Reg snapped. She pointed to the car. "Sitting right there."

"Norma Jean?" Corvin's tone was incredulous. "When did this happen? How?"

He had held Reg's powers, heard Norma Jean's spirit in his head. He knew that the Witch Doctor had tortured and killed her. In the other timeline.

"She's alive," Reg stated the obvious. "When Harrison went back, he must have prevented the Witch Doctor from killing her. So now she's here, wanting to be all buddy-buddy. I do not need this today!"

"But if she didn't die, then what does that mean to you? Did she raise you? And why would we be able to remember the way the timeline unfolded before?"

"Child Services took me away from her. Because she was a terrible parent. So no, all that stuff is still the same. Fate, I guess. It was going to happen to me whether she lived or died."

"But we shouldn't be able to remember what happened before. That creates a paradox. We should only be able to remember our own timeline."

"Don't bother me with theoretical nonsense. A bunch of scientists speculate on the results of time travel. They don't know. They haven't done it!"

Corvin's eyes widened at her outburst. He nodded. "Of course." He looked toward the car. "Would you like me to get rid of her?"

Reg settled back in her seat. "Yeah, do you think you could?"

"Sure. When I go talk to her, you get out and go to the cottage. I'll distract her and get her to come with me."

Reg hesitated. "How will you do that?"

He smiled, and she could smell roses and feel his power sweep over her, an overwhelming attraction to someone she knew very well was a danger to her. She braced herself against the door and the dashboard.

"Stop that! You can't charm her."

"Why not?"

"Because..." Reg tried to marshal her thoughts, already foggy from his magic. It wasn't like Norma Jean had powers Corvin could steal. He would just be tempting her, enticing her away from Reg. What was wrong with that? There would be no harm done.

"I just... I guess I'm just worried. You won't... you can't..."

"I'll just take her for coffee." He shrugged. "Surely you can't object to that?"

"Well... no... I guess not."

Corvin raised a brow at Reg and waited for her to confirm that she was really okay with it. Reg sighed and shook her head. "Why not. There isn't any harm in it, is there? If you're just going to take her to coffee?"

Corvin opened his door and got out. Reg watched him approach Norma Jean's car and, once she figured he had blocked Reg from Norma Jean's view, she got out of the car and headed toward the back yard. But she couldn't help stopping to take a quick look at how things were progressing. Corvin was leaning on the car, radiating charm. Reg could feel the heady mix of magic and pheromones even from where she stood. There was no way that Norma Jean would be able to resist him.

She still felt guilty about letting Corvin do that. She kept repeating to herself that there was nothing wrong with it, he was just helping Reg out by chatting up Norma Jean; but she had spent a lot of time and energy denouncing his use of magic to seduce Reg in multiple attempts to take her powers again. And he wouldn't be giving them back a second time. That had been a one-time deal, to save her from torture.

There was a movement behind Corvin's car. Reg turned her head to see who had arrived. But there was no one there. There was only empty street behind his car, when she was sure someone had been there just a fraction of a second earlier.

"I am losing my mind!"

She said it aloud, trying to jolt her brain into working properly. Why was she suddenly hallucinating everywhere she went? Was she having a breakdown because of Starlight? The stress was too much for her, and she was going to have a complete nervous breakdown because she couldn't handle it?

"There's nothing there. Quit worrying about everything and go home. Make something to eat. Have a nap." Reg muttered to herself as she walked the path back to her house.

She took a look over her shoulder to make sure that no one was lurking nearby as she fit her key into the lock and let herself in. She hadn't managed to convince herself that there hadn't been anything there. But whatever it was hadn't followed her to her door. She wasn't letting it in by unlocking her door and letting it trail in behind her. Keys were powerful, Harrison had told her. They held their own special kind of magic.

She closed the door behind her and locked it. But only the handle, not the bolt or the chain. Sarah could still come in if she wanted to. Reg was used to Sarah looking in and checking to make sure that Reg had everything she needed. She frequently brought nourishing food or invitations to community events, intent on keeping Reg healthy and happy.

But how could she be, without Starlight?

Reg wandered around the empty house, feeling Starlight's absence keenly.

"You need to eat something, Reg." Sarah clucked over her, tidying up the cottage and checking out Reg's fridge to see what she could heat up. "You're not doing yourself or Starlight any favors by not eating. You need to keep up your strength."

"I can't eat anything right now," Reg objected. "I'm not feeling well. I'm not just... avoiding eating because I'm sad. I really can't."

"Surely you could get something down. I can even go out and get you something. What about..." Sarah considered what might appeal to Reg. "Ice cream?"

That gave Reg pause. She hesitated. "Uh... maybe. I don't know."

"What's your favorite kind of ice cream?"

"I'm not picky. I'll eat anything."

"Any kind? You don't have a favorite? Rocky Road? Chunky Monkey? Mint chocolate chip?"

"No. Any kind is good for me."

She had always had a bit of a sweet tooth for ice cream. She didn't think Sarah was going to be able to introduce her to any new flavors that she hadn't tried yet.

"That's what we'll do, then."

"Can you get me that list of tea ingredients first?" Reg had already told her about how the vet was trying to figure out what Starlight had eaten, and needed to see the plant and know the ingredients to any teas Reg had had out the day before Starlight had gotten sick.

"Of course, dear." Sarah looked at her watch. "But the vet will be closed soon. It will have to wait until tomorrow."

Reg hated to wait one more day. Why didn't the vet have extended emergency hours for patients like Starlight? He needed to provide better service than that.

"He needs to figure out what's going on, and I'm just sitting around here, doing nothing."

"You've been recovering. You can't be expected to be bouncing around here like usual when your cat is in the hospital."

Reg didn't think that she bounced around normally. She wasn't a bouncy person.

"That doesn't help Starlight."

"Being calm and finding your center will always help, even if you can't see how."

Reg rolled her eyes, but Sarah didn't catch her doing it.

"Has there been… anything unusual going on lately?" Reg thought about the half-glimpses she had been catching over the last few days.

"What do you mean?" Sarah got down on the floor to pull some miscellaneous objects out from under the TV entertainment stand. Probably things that Starlight had hidden away. He was often batting little bits of paper or plastic milk bottle caps around the cottage, chasing them and pretending that they were mice or some other kind of prey, until they rolled underneath the fridge or a piece of furniture where he couldn't get them back out.

"I mean… I keep seeing or hearing things. Just for an instant. And then they are gone when I look more closely."

"I'm sure it is nothing. The unseen world is all around us. Things slip through the veil from time to time. It is almost solstice, and the boundaries separating worlds become thin."

"So… that happens all the time?"

Sarah shrugged. "I would imagine it happens to some people more than others. You are psychic and very sensitive, so it would not surprise me that you see more than most people do. I wouldn't think it was anything to worry about if it isn't accompanied by… a feeling of menace or darkness."

"Like I had with the Witch Doctor."

"Exactly. When he was working his magic here, you knew something was going on. Little shifts in the veil and chance glimpses of the other side… that doesn't sound like anything worrisome."

"I guess not," Reg agreed. Sitting on the wicker couch, she drew her knees up to her chest and watched Sarah, too tired and sad to move, but also too keyed up to eat or sleep. "You don't think anyone is following me, then?"

"Do you think someone is following you?"

"Well, I saw something before Corvin and I got into the car, and then after we got here. Was that just a coincidence? Or was it the same… person or force each time?"

Sarah shook her head. "I can't understand why you would be spending time with that warlock. You know how dangerous he is and how much he desires your gifts. If it was me, I wouldn't have anything to do with him."

"But you do. You don't avoid him. You've asked for his help, had dinner with him, why can't I?"

Sarah pursed her lips. She shuffled through Reg's mail and flyers on the kitchen island. "It's different for me. An old woman, it's harder for him to tempt me than it is for someone like you, simmering in a stew of hormones. I'm past the age when I can be influenced by a little charm and a handsome face."

"Oh, sure you are! I've seen how you react when he influences you. Why is it different for you? Do you think that it's just because he wants my gifts so badly? I don't get why he wants them more than anyone else's. I know he compared them to having dessert, that they are particularly sweet to him, but… I don't know. I think he's obsessed. Over the top. One day, he'll probably go off on some other woman and forget all about me."

"Not any time soon. Was that your mother I saw him with earlier?"

"Uh…" Reg cleared her throat and tried to think of a way to deny it. She looked at the face of her phone to see what time it was. She had expected to hear from one of them hours ago. Corvin saying that he'd just left and giving her an update on whether Norma Jean was still trying to connect with her daughter in a meaningful way. Or Norma Jean knocking on her door again, telling her what a nice break she'd just had with the very handsome warlock. But there had been silence from both of them. No calls, no knocks on the door. She wanted to call Corvin to find out what had happened, but she didn't want to know.

And she did.

"Yeah… Corvin was running interference for me, so I didn't have to talk to her. It's nothing. Just… a favor."

"Just like him going with you this morning?"

"We just went to the vet," Reg protested. It wasn't like she had gone to a restaurant with him, out dancing, or to something more daring. "He was just there to help me get through seeing Starlight again and to see if there was anything he could help with. He was really nice about it."

"You know what he wants, and it's not a casual relationship."

"I think we can still be friends. I know he's made wrong choices in the past, but I think he's really trying. Would you ever have thought before that he'd suggest driving me to the vet's? Mr. Chivalry he is not."

"Exactly. He will do whatever it takes to worm his way into your life. Today you're going to the vet with him, and tomorrow you're inviting him home." Sarah gave her a sideways look. "Don't think that I don't know you brought him back here that night."

"What night?" Reg's heart was beating fast and she knew she couldn't hide her reaction from Sarah for long. She was going to have to come up with a cover story double-quick, something that made sense.

"You know very well what night. I thought I was going to have to come over here and break things up with a baseball bat before Harrison showed up."

Harrison.

He had saved Reg from her own stupidity that night, for sure. Reg wouldn't make that same mistake again, letting Corvin take the keys from her to let her into the house. Give him the keys, and you give him permission, Harrison had told her. She had thought she was being careful, but she still didn't know all the rules to the game.

"I, uh, didn't know that you saw him here," Reg said, squirming in embarrassment.

"I see a lot more than you think I do. These old eyes still don't miss much."

★ CHAPTER ELEVEN ★

SARAH DID SEE A lot more than Reg would have liked. It was too bad she'd seen Norma Jean with Corvin earlier. Sarah sounded quite sure that there was something more going on than just Corvin doing a favor for Reg. And maybe there was. Reg had been watching the clock all afternoon. She didn't like Norma Jean, but she hadn't intended to put her in harm's way, either. Maybe letting Corvin take her out for coffee had been a stupid idea. It had been a spur of the moment decision. One she probably should have stopped to think about.

"But your mother doesn't have any powers, does she?" Sarah asked.

"No."

"So he can't take them from her. The most he could do is… show her a good time."

"He wouldn't do that."

"Why not?"

"She's old. I mean, maybe not old, old, but she isn't in her prime. She looks nice enough now that she's had all of that work done, but she's not a young woman anymore. Corvin is…" Reg trailed off. She had no idea how old Corvin was. Like with Sarah, Reg had been told that he was older than he looked. Decades older than Reg. So he was closer in age to Norma Jean than to Reg. Maybe he had been interested in Norma Jean, and not just taking a hit for Reg. "Oh, I don't know. I don't know how you all do it, remembering how old everyone is and making appropriate matches. I don't understand the way any of this works."

"It's just like the rest of the world, dear. If you are interested in someone or find them attractive, then see if they have similar feelings. You don't have to be the same age… or even the same species." Sarah shrugged. "Our community is much more understanding about differences than the rest of the world."

"I suppose that's why it doesn't make a lot of sense to me. I think of the old mythology stories, and it sounds like anything goes. But you still have some social structure, and rules about how the different races interact with each other, and what Corvin is allowed to do with his powers. There are *some* rules."

"Just like anywhere," Sarah agreed.

Except that Reg wasn't sure she knew what all the rules were or what would happen if she violated them.

It was a long night.

Reg devoured a bucket of buttered pecan ice cream, scraping the bottom with her spoon and licking around the top edge for as far as her tongue could reach.

She considered calling Corvin several times, but couldn't bring herself to do so and show herself to be concerned about Norma Jean's welfare. Norma Jean was an abusive monster and Reg didn't want to admit to caring what happened to her. She went to bed, but couldn't sleep. She sat in front of the TV, but that didn't work either. She looked at her phone and considered calling Detective Jessup or Damon. But what would she tell them? That she was worried about her missing mother, who she hadn't cared about until then? Or that she was worried about her sick cat? They would think she was just a crazy cat lady. She especially didn't know about Damon. Several times she tapped his name and then stared at his headshot, finger hovering over the phone icon, trying to muster up the courage to call him.

And talk about what? What exactly was she going to tell him? The last time she had spoken to him, she had been angry about the jealousy between him and Corvin. The two warlocks had fought, and Reg was done with that scene. She didn't want to continue to encourage their jealousy by seeing them both, even as friends.

So she and Damon had to be finished.

If Corvin had decided he wasn't interested in pursuing her anymore, then she could see Damon. But not calling Reg back after his coffee date with Norma Jean did not mean that Corvin had given up on her. It just meant that he didn't see the need to call her after a casual cup of coffee. Like Reg had told Sarah, he was doing her a favor. Just something casual. It didn't mean anything.

Reg looked at Francesca's icon too, but by that time it was so late, she was worried that anyone she called would be asleep, and she didn't have the kind of relationship with Francesca where they could call each other at all hours. Reg had no idea what time the woman went to bed, but she seemed like a very normal, business-oriented woman, and that meant she probably kept regular hours and was in bed by midnight.

Reg wandered to the window in the bedroom, sitting on the low windowsill where Starlight often perched, watching the garden. There were fireflies out again. Having seen them once before, she knew that they were nothing to worry about. Just little bugs with a "flare" for fashion. She watched them spark on and off and breathed in the cool, salty air that blew in through the screen.

Starlight should have been home enjoying the sights and smells and sounds. He should have been there with her.

The sleepless nights eventually caught up with her, and she woke up on the floor under the window, where she had apparently either passed out or had lain down, unable to make it a few feet to her bed. Her cheek was wet with drool and there was a crack in the corner of her mouth that send out darts of pain whenever she opened her mouth or moved it the wrong way. Reg rolled over and eyed the bed, trying to decide if she had the energy to climb into bed and go back to sleep where it was more comfortable. Her bones and joints ached from lying on the floor.

She managed to prop herself against the wall and waited for her body to wake up. She needed to use the bathroom, so she wasn't going to be getting back to sleep until she had taken care of that necessity. Afterward… maybe she would slide under the covers and try to sleep for a few more hours.

Once she managed to get to her feet and visit the bathroom, though, she knew there would be no getting back to sleep. Her head throbbed, her mouth felt like something had died inside it, and her stomach had a tight knot. She couldn't identify whether it was illness or too much ice cream or just dread of the coming day.

Her brain started to click through the things she would have to take care of, just as if she were Erin making a list. She had to get the plant and the information from Sarah to take to the vet. She should visit Starlight again and see whether there was any improvement. Only this time, she was going to have to go alone, since Corvin hadn't checked back in with her.

She wasn't sure how she was going to face it alone.

Eventually, Reg made it to the kitchen and, after deciding that her stomach could not handle any food or coffee, she found herself calling Detective Jessup. She just couldn't get through the day without someone's help, and Jessup seemed like the best option. She probably wouldn't be able to drop everything to rush to Reg's side. She would be on shift and have duties to attend to. But Reg called her anyway.

Jessup answered after just a couple of rings. "Reg? Hey, how are you?"

Reg let the words hang in the air at first, not sure what to say to that. How was she? She didn't even know how to begin.

"I'm… hey… I'm wondering if you're working today, or if you could…"

"No, I'm off." Marta Jessup's voice was curious. "What is it? Is something wrong?"

"Yeah. It's Starlight. He's pretty sick. I don't know what to do. I didn't know who to call."

"Well, didn't you take him to the vet? You should find out what's wrong with him."

"I did. Yeah. I did that. He's been at the vet for a couple of days now. I need to go over to see him today, take the vet some information… see if Starlight is doing any better. If he's still… okay. You know."

"The vet doesn't know what's wrong with him?"

"He was poisoned."

Jessup gasped. "Poisoned? Are you sure? Who would do that?"

"I wish I knew. Somebody… I think he might be cursed too. It might have been a magical potion. It's something really bad."

"I'll come over. You must be feeling awful. I'm so sorry. I'll come right away, okay?"

Reg found herself nodding. "Yes," she agreed with relief, hot tears prickling her eyes, "that would be good."

"I'll be right over."

Reg hung up. She stood for a long time at the island in the kitchen, absorbing the silence of the house.

She needed Starlight. She needed him to come home so that she could be whole again. She hadn't understood before she had brought him home how important he would become in her life and how much he would help her with her psychic vision. He seemed like the missing piece in her brain, the one that made her almost normal. He stopped her mind from jumping haphazardly from one thing to another and helped her to focus. She imagined that was how everyone felt, all of the normal people who didn't have ADHD and learning disorders and who couldn't hear voices or see things from another plane.

All her life, they had been trying to find the drugs to tame her brain, when what she needed was a cat. Not just any cat. She needed Starlight, with the white spot between his eyes that Sarah called his third eye, the old soul who happened to inhabit the body of a cat. She had been looking for him for her whole life.

Or at least, since she had been four.

Reg looked out the living room window to see if Jessup was there yet. How long would she take to get there? Had she been at home or with someone else? Would she use her lights and siren to get there faster? That was probably against department policy. Reg went to the door and unlocked it. She opened it and stared out into the yard. It was lush and green despite being December. Since Forst had started working for Sarah, it was practically vibrating with life, and Reg imagined that when he walked into it—or appeared in it, since he always seemed to come out of nowhere—that his living plants greeted him excitedly, like a spaniel rushing to see its master at the end of the day.

She sat down on one of the deck chairs near the door, which she hardly ever used. She closed her eyes, feeling the nature around her and, without realizing she was going to, fell asleep again.

⋆ CHAPTER TWELVE ⋆

RE G H E Y R E G , I ' M here. Are you okay?"

Reg woke up groggily and, even though she could only have been asleep for a few minutes, she felt like it had been hours. Like she had been sitting there waiting for Jessup all day. She gave an involuntary start and immediately looked at her wrist, where she had never worn a wristwatch, then looked for her phone to check the time. She was sure it must be late in the day. Afternoon or evening. She had missed her chance to get to the vet and give him the information that he needed to take care of Starlight properly.

Jessup put her hand on Reg's arm. "It's okay. What's wrong?"

"What time is it? How could it be so late?"

"It isn't late. Relax."

Reg couldn't find her phone.

"Your door is open," Jessup pointed out. "Do you want to go back in?"

Reg looked at it and couldn't remember why she had left it open. Had she been waiting for someone? Had someone gone into her house while she was asleep? She couldn't just leave it wide open for anyone to walk in. What if Corvin had shown up for a visit while she was asleep there? He could walk right in. Or could he? Would the wards keep him out if she left the door open? If she didn't give him the key, would he still be prevented from entering?

Reg rubbed her eyes, trying to clear her brain and think straight. "Is Corvin here?"

"Corvin? I don't think so." Jessup poked her head in the door and looked around. "Hello? Anyone here?" There was no answer. Jessup shook her head. "No, I don't think so. Was Hunter supposed to be coming over?"

"No. I don't think so. But I haven't heard from him since yesterday when he took Norma Jean out for coffee. I don't know what happened to him."

"What happened to him? Why, have you tried to get him? Has he disappeared?"

"No... I don't... I don't think so. But he hasn't called me back. I thought he would call me once he was finished coffee to let me know that she might be on her way back again." Reg pressed her temples, trying to get her train of thought back on the rails. "That was a really weird nap. I feel all addled."

"You're probably just short on sleep and I woke you in the middle of a REM cycle. You'll feel better in a few minutes. Should we go inside and get some coffee?"

"Yes."

"Now, exactly what happened?" Jessup asked as they both stared at the coffee maker, waiting for the coffee to finish brewing.

"I don't know. He's been out all night. I was worried that…"

"Hunter can take care of himself."

"No, I mean… Norma Jean… he was with her. I am kind of worried—I don't need to worry about her either, I know, but… I can't help it. I know what he did to me, and I said it was okay for him to take her out. Was that the wrong thing to do?"

"Isn't Norma Jean your mother?"

"Yes."

"I thought she was dead."

"Long story. She's not."

"Sounds like a rather short story to me. So Corvin decided to take her out?" Jessup's lip curled. "Why would he do that?"

"It was a favor to me. I couldn't face her after being at the vet's and dealing with this stuff with Starlight, so he said he would take her out to coffee and take her off my hands. Only… I don't know what happened after that. I thought he'd let me know when he was done, but he didn't call me."

"That doesn't necessarily mean he's been out with her since then. Did you call him? He has probably just been working on other things and didn't think he needed to report back to you. Did he say he would call you after?"

"No."

"Well, there you go. He just didn't realize you'd be waiting for his call."

"Then where's Norma Jean?"

"Is *she* missing?"

"I… don't know. I thought that she'd turn around and come back here after she was finished with him. I thought I'd just get a little bit of time to myself; I didn't think she'd be gone all afternoon and all night."

"Do you want to see her?"

"No."

Jessup rolled her eyes. "Then why does it matter that she didn't show up here? Maybe Corvin did you another favor and managed to talk her out of coming back to see you. So you could have a longer break from her. Why don't you want to see her?"

"Because she's an awful person."

"Okay…" Jessup cocked her head and waited for more, but Reg didn't feel like detailing any of the ways that Norma Jean had been negligent or abusive all of those years ago, or what it was like having Norma Jean in her head for all of those years, always telling her what to do.

Reg stared at the coffee maker. The coffee was dribbling into the pot, almost done. Then she'd be able to have a cup of coffee, and her brain would come into focus, and she'd be able to have a sensible conversation with Jessup instead of making Jessup look at her like she was half crazy.

They both watched it in silence for the last few drops. Then Reg grabbed it off the hot plate and poured a couple of mugs. They drifted over to the seating area in the living room and settled themselves.

"So Corvin and Norma Jean are missing, only they're not actually missing. You don't want to report them missing, and you don't want to see them, you just want to know what happened when they got together yesterday?"

Reg thought this through. It all sounded right. "Yeah," she said with relief. "I think you nailed it."

"Okay. Great. Well, why don't you give Corvin a call then? Assuming that he is the least objectionable party to call."

"Yeah, I guess so."

Reg's phone had been on the counter in the kitchen when she stepped back inside. She looked at it uncertainly, then back at Jessup. "I actually don't want to talk to him. I guess… I'll just wait until I hear from him."

"Okay, then. Feel better?"

Reg sipped the piping hot coffee, knowing that she was going to regret scalding herself later. She couldn't wait for it to cool; she needed the shot of caffeine right away if she were going to be able to think straight and carry on a sensible conversation. It hurt when it hit her stomach. She wondered if she had an ulcer. It really hurt. Reg put the coffee mug down, feeling out of sorts. Betrayed by the coffee that was supposed to make everything better, and instead just lit her stomach on fire.

"Are you okay?"

"Yeah. I'm fine." Reg brushed the inquiry away. "I'm wondering about Sarah."

Jessup sighed. "What about Sarah?"

"She's been gone all night. Why is everybody staying out all night? They don't usually do that."

"How do you know Sarah's been gone all night?"

Reg didn't answer. She wasn't sure what she should respond. She knew that Sarah wasn't back at the big house yet, she could sense Sarah's comings and goings if she paid close attention. Sometimes even when she wasn't trying to tell, she knew. But she also wasn't sure why it mattered that Sarah wasn't home. It didn't mean there was anything wrong. Sarah and Corvin and Norma Jean were all free to come and go as they liked without reporting to Reg. She had never wanted to hear about their comings and goings before.

"Are you worried about Sarah?" Jessup pressed.

Jessup was more likely to care about Sarah's absence than anyone else's. Sarah was an older woman, and she and Jessup seemed to be pretty good friends. They all felt more responsible for Sarah. She had nearly died once, and they liked to keep track and make sure she was okay. It was what you did in a community.

"No. Not really. It's just… unsettling. It feels like everybody was gone to a party except me."

Jessup chuckled. "Well, maybe they did. There might have been some sort of Yule ceremony going on. It's early yet, but sometimes there are Yule mixers or Yule craft days, to get everything ready before Yule. It's nice to have a community where everyone is celebrating. For a lot of witches and warlocks around the world, it's a bit isolating, celebrating Yule when everyone else is getting ready for Christmas. They'll participate in Christmas stuff, but it's not quite the same." Jessup took a sip of her coffee.

"So you think she was probably just out at some craft club? All night long?"

"Not handicrafts. Witchcraft. And yeah, a lot of them go overnight, or everyone crashes somewhere after instead of going home."

"Oh." Reg thought about that. Was Sarah just off at some witching ceremony with her coven? She tried to remember if Sarah had been alone when she left. Reg had just jumped to the conclusion that she was out on a date, but maybe that was because Sarah always seemed to be on a date lately.

★ CHAPTER THIRTEEN ★

B UT NORMA JEAN AND Corvin wouldn't have been at any Yule celebration or ritual," Reg said suddenly, raising his eyes to Jessup's, feeling a scowl crease her forehead.

"No, that's right," Jessup agreed, sounding surprised. "I guess I forgot about him being shunned. He wouldn't be able to participate in any community rituals this year. That will be weird."

"And Norma Jean doesn't have any powers."

"Doesn't she?" Jessup cocked her head. "I thought that was who you got your powers from."

"No. Not from her." Reg didn't explain any further. For that, she would have to tell Jessup all about Weston, and it was much too long a story to be trying to tell Jessup now. It would have to wait. Since Reg had called Jessup, she supposed that meant they were friends again, and she would end up telling Jessup all about it some other time, when she wasn't worrying about Starlight. When Starlight was healed and back together with Reg again.

If that were ever going to happen.

Tears sprang to Reg's eyes, and she tried to hide them by taking another drink of the coffee, which again caused further shots of pain radiating out from her stomach. She wasn't going to be able to drink any more of it. She would have to take an antacid and hope that would settle her stomach down.

"Not feeling very well?" Jessup sympathized.

"No. Everything is wonky."

"Sorry about that. When did you want to go over to see Starlight? You said you had some stuff to take to the vet?"

"Yes, I need to get him the plant and the ingredients to the tea that Sarah gave me." It wasn't until then that Reg realized that she still hadn't gotten that information from Sarah. Sarah had promised it to her, but then she had been gone all night and hadn't returned to the house. "I need to… maybe she left it in the big house. I'll have to go over and check."

"Do you want me to come with you?"

Reg eyed Jessup. In spite of Jessup's helpful tone, Reg couldn't help feeling like Jessup was worried about Reg doing something if she went to the big house on her own. Even though Reg hadn't been the one to steal Sarah's emerald, she felt like there was still a cloud of suspicion over her head. Jessup knew something of Reg's past and maybe knew that she had previously been accused of theft. Reg couldn't very well say that it was unfair, since she had, in fact, walked off with certain possessions of value in the past to survive through rough times. She was untrained and barely had a high school education, so she needed to take her opportunities where she could. She had honed her ability to con and steal, sharpened them the best that she could. If that was the only way she could survive, that was what she was going to do.

"I don't need you to come to the house with me," Reg said firmly.

Let Jessup stew about what other mischief Reg might get into at Sarah's house. If she was going to be a suspicious person, then she deserved the anxiety that would go along with it when Reg refused to cooperate. Reg *wasn't* going over to steal anything from Sarah. If she did, it would mean having to run before she was discovered, and she had a good gig in Black Sands.

Sarah was worth far more to her as a landlord and friend than she was as a mark.

Reg left Jessup in her cottage while she went to Sarah's big house. Jessup couldn't do anything about it unless she admitted that she thought Reg was going over there to steal while Sarah was gone. She had offered to help, and Reg had declined.

She hoped that she would find the plant and a list of ingredients on Sarah's table, where she had left them intending to take them to Reg in the morning. But when she entered through Sarah's back door, she was disappointed. The box of Yule decorations was near the back door, but there was no sign of a list of ingredients. Reg dug through the box to find the plant from Fir. It was looking a little worse for wear after being thrown into the box with everything else.

"Sorry," Reg apologized to the little plant. It wasn't the plant's fault that Starlight had been poisoned. If Starlight had eaten some of its leaves, that was on Reg, not the plant. She felt guilty for not taking care of it the way Fir would have wanted.

She set it on the table while she looked for a list of ingredients. There was nothing left out for her. Reg started looking through cupboards. She found a supply of handcrafted teas in one cabinet. Each jar had a label indicating what kind of tea it was, but none of them listed what herbs were included. Reg scowled and shook her head. "Come on, Sarah… how hard is it to list the ingredients?"

Maybe the ingredients varied from one batch to the next. Did Sarah even know what the exact ingredients of the tea were? She had said she would give Reg a list, but maybe she couldn't.

Reg finished her inventory of the cupboards without any luck. They were bursting at the seams with various culinary and medicinal herbs, but she couldn't find a recipe book or box.

"Where did you put it, then? On a computer?"

At first, she thought that Sarah probably didn't even have a computer, but then she remembered Sarah talking about ordering herbs on Amazon and selling items on Etsy. So she must have a computer somewhere in the house.

"Okay, where is your office…?"

She hesitated for an instant before resuming her search. Going into Sarah's kitchen while she was gone was one thing. It wasn't really an intrusion. In a community like Black Sands, walking in someone's front or back door was not unusual or unexpected. It was small-town hospitality. But going through the rest of the house was not so usual. If Sarah returned home while Reg was searching her house, could Reg explain or justify herself? Would Sarah be upset? Would she, like Jessup, think that Reg had let herself into the house just to help herself to any valuables that caught her eye?

Maybe it didn't matter what anybody thought. Reg wasn't there to lift anything, and Sarah wasn't going to charge her. Reg was there for Starlight. What anyone else thought was irrelevant.

Having made her decision, she left the kitchen quickly to look for Sarah's computer. When she found it, she was going to have to figure out how to get past the password, but she had a few tricks up her sleeve. She closed her eyes partway, focusing on the computer, trying to let it guide her to her destination. It was a big house, and she didn't want to have to check every room or take the chance of Frostling, Sarah's African gray parrot, attacking her.

It should have come as no surprise to Reg that Sarah's house was decked out in the finest of the Yuletide season. Twinkle lights and green boughs everywhere. Reg followed her instincts and went up the stairs to check out the bedrooms in that part of the house. Sarah probably had an office next to her bedroom, or had a computer in her bedroom, though Reg didn't remember seeing one there when Sarah was sick. But she had only had eyes for Sarah at the time, worried as she was about her friend. Reg walked down the hall, trying to remember which room housed the emerald necklace that was guarded by Frostling. She did not want to open that door. She'd been attacked by the bird once, and she didn't want to experience it again.

"Just the computer," she murmured. "I just need to take a peek at the computer to find the recipes for the teas, and then I'll be out of here. No one will be any the wiser."

She hadn't been prevented from entering by any of Sarah's wards, as she would have been if she had entered for sinister purposes. Sarah's magic obviously recognized that she was not there to steal anything or to harm Sarah in any way.

Why hadn't Sarah returned home? Was it just a Yuletide celebration, as Jessup had suggested? Jessup would have a pretty good idea if there were anyone in town targeting older women. But that didn't mean that nothing could happen to Sarah.

She'd be in trouble for going into Sarah's house if anything actually had happened to her. But then, so would Jessup, for letting Reg go inside unsupervised. So maybe Jessup would think it wise to stay quiet.

Reg opened the door she thought was Sarah's bedroom, and was rewarded with the familiar furnishings. First guess. She looked around the room but didn't see a computer or laptop anywhere in evidence. What about a tablet? That could be tucked away in a bedside table or bookshelf, much less visible.

Reg decided to check the other rooms quickly, and then to return for a more thorough search if it didn't turn up in one of the other nearby rooms.

She ducked into the next room and found it to contain clothing — racks and racks of every imaginable kind of outfit. Whatever Sarah needed, she had it on hand. It was no wonder she had been able to dress Reg up for the dance Reg had attended with her. Reg had been to boutique stores that had half the amount of merchandise on the racks.

But Sarah's computer wasn't going to be in her dressing room. Reg went on.

Reg tried the next door and found a spacious bathroom, white marble sparkling in the morning sun. Not a smudge or fingerprint on anything. Reg kept going. At the end of the hall was a large, unoccupied bedroom that she thought must function as the guest bedroom. She started on the doors at the other side of the hall, the pain in her stomach growing as she knew she was running out of options. Maybe Sarah had kept her computer closer to the kitchen so she could record recipes close at hand. Or maybe it was a tablet, and Reg had overlooked it in her quick scan for a desktop or laptop computer. Sarah wouldn't just rely on her phone, would she? Her older eyes would need the larger screen for anything detailed.

She probably should have stopped and called Sarah when what she wanted wasn't just in the kitchen waiting for her. Checking the cupboards for a list of ingredients or recipe book was one thing, but checking the rest of the house for a computer she could hack into and search for the recipe? Sarah probably didn't even keep the recipes on a computer. She had probably memorized them.

Reg stood in the hallway for a minute, frustrated with herself and unsure what she should do next. Go back downstairs and out to her cottage without checking the rest of the house? When she might have found what she needed in one of the last rooms?

Keep going even when she had decided it was a violation and she shouldn't be there?

She couldn't just stop what she was doing. She needed to know whether the information was there. She needed to figure out how to help Starlight.

She decided to open the last few doors, and if the computer weren't obvious, she would go back to the cottage. She'd call Sarah to see if she could tell Reg the ingredients. If not, she at least had the plant to take to the vet.

Holding her roiling stomach, Reg peeked into the last few rooms. Another guest bedroom, this one with an ensuite, another room full to bursting with clothing. And directly across the hall from Sarah's bedroom, her craft room.

Not a craft room like Reg would have thought of a year ago, before she knew that there were real practitioners of the magic arts living in Black Sands.

The craft room was full of items of every description. Jars and jars of herbs, roots, mushrooms and other fungi, and jars that Reg decided held pickles which she didn't want to look at any more closely. There were candles, pots, salvers, tweezers, tongs, measuring spoons and cups, and bunches of dried flowers tied together. There were pieces of clothing hung on pegs. Cloaks and hats and gloves and whatever else Sarah needed to perform her magic spells. And there was a computer.

Reg held her breath, looking at it and wondering if she dared enter the craft room. There would probably be additional wards there to keep it safe and she might be prevented from entering the room. Or something bad might happen to her once she did. There was no telling. She'd twice been trapped by spells when entering a room without permission, and it probably wasn't a good idea to be stuck there when there was no one to help her to get back out again. Though at least Jessup was close by and would know something was up if Reg didn't return.

★ CHAPTER FOURTEEN ★

JESSUP RAISED HER BROWS when Reg returned to the cottage carrying the little plant. "Find everything you needed?"

"No. But I'm going to have to wait until she gets back. If she has the recipe I need written down somewhere, it is probably on her computer." Reg shrugged. "I checked for a recipe book or box in her kitchen, but there wasn't anything, so I thought I'd better leave it at that. At least I can take this to the vet."

"Do you think he'll know what it is? Think that it will help?"

"I don't know. If there was a spell involved, then… it might not make any difference. He can try as much doctoring stuff as he likes, but Starlight isn't going to get better if there isn't some way to counter the curse."

"Corvin went over there with you?"

"Yeah."

"And he couldn't do anything? Didn't he try to reverse the spell and heal Starlight?"

"He did his best. Or what appeared to be his best, anyway. And I tried to talk to Starlight and do something for him. I don't know what else to try right now. Do you know any magical vets? Is there such a thing?"

"I don't know. I think most people take their pets to the regular vet. And supplement with spells and charms at home, when they can. I don't know if there is anyone experienced in removing curses from cats."

"There has to be someone in a community like this…"

"You would think so," Jessup agreed. "You might want to ask around. I don't know anyone, but that doesn't mean that there isn't. Just that you need to ask someone better qualified. I've never had a pet, so I don't know…"

"He's not just a pet," Reg snapped. "You keep saying that."

"Well… okay. He's not just a pet. But he is still a pet too. I know that he helps you with some of the psychic stuff, but how much of it is him and how much of it is you? Are you sure you're not just… assigning him some power that he doesn't have? Like a placebo effect? You think that he gives you a signal boost, so you're able to do more?"

"No," Reg said flatly. She quickly discounted the idea. She knew that Starlight often knew things before she did. That he had herblore, since he had brought her the yarrow when she needed it to treat the festering wound in her hand. He had fought pixies beside her. There was no way that he was just a cute cat who gave her more confidence in herself.

Jessup nodded. "Did you want to go to the vet right away, then?"

"Do you mind going over with me? I know it isn't any fun, but… I could use the support."

"Of course! Why do you think I came over here? Besides, I'm off today. If I didn't help you, I'd have to stay home and do things like clean the toilet, which I would rather not do."

Reg smiled. One of the problems of being independent and living in a house was that there was suddenly a whole list of things to do to keep the house clean and take care of her possessions. Sarah did a lot of them without Reg ever asking, and Reg was still trying to navigate her way through being an adult and taking care of all of the things that a responsible adult was supposed to do. She was used to living in hotels, flophouses, shelters, or on the street, and then she didn't have to do anything but get her next meal or wash up at a sink. Living in a house where she had to keep up appearances was a whole different ball game. She was happy that Jessup didn't seem to think much of the chores she had to do either. Better to visit a sick cat with a friend than to have to stay home and scrub toilets.

"Thanks. Do you mind driving?"

"You bet." Jessup headed toward the door. "Do you need anything else? Did you want to put that coffee in a 'to go' cup?"

"No." Reg wrinkled her nose. "I think there's something wrong with it. It's really bothering my stomach."

Jessup frowned down at her empty mug. "It seemed okay to me."

They walked out to the car together. Reg took a look around, watching for any of those little peeks through the veil that Sarah had referred to. *Was* she being watched? Was it just a glimpse of another plane and they weren't even aware of her?

Again, there was a shadow just outside her field of vision, which disappeared when she turned her head and tried to pinpoint it.

"Did you try calling Sarah?" Jessup asked. "She's usually an early riser, so I don't think you need to worry about getting her out of bed at this hour."

Reg looked at her phone, but already knew it was past eight. Sarah had probably been awake for several hours, even if she was up until the wee hours of the morning.

That was another reason she was starting to worry. If Sarah had been up for a few hours, then why hadn't she returned home? Why hadn't she given Reg the information she needed by the time the vet's office opened? It was so unusual for her to be away from her home at night, Reg didn't know what to think of it. It was worrying.

"I don't know. Do you think I should? I didn't want to interfere with her life, to act like I was monitoring the hours she was out like I was her mother. She's a grown woman; she can certainly keep whatever hours she likes."

"At this point, I don't think you need to worry that you're hanging over her. You don't even have to say that you know she's been out. You can say that you were wondering if she had the recipe that you needed before you head over to the vet."

Reg nodded slowly. She sat down in the car and selected Sarah's number. As it started to ring, she looked around, trying to spot the shadow again. It seemed to be following her, too interested in her comings and goings to be a coincidence. She trusted her instinct when it came to being time to get out of a situation, and she had the uncomfortable feeling that she was going to have to leave Black Sands. What if it wasn't something supernatural on her tail, but a federal agent with a warrant? What if they were watching her to see what her scam was this time, just waiting for the right time to swoop in and make a bust?

Sarah's voicemail kicked in. A pleasant, grandmotherly voice telling her to leave a message and she would call back. Reg chewed on her lip and tried to decide whether to leave a message or not. She rushed at the last minute, wanting to get her message in before the voicemail timed out.

"Sarah, it's just Reg. Looking for those ingredients, you know? For the vet? I picked up the plant, but I couldn't see the recipe anywhere. Would you let me know if you have it? Thanks. Call me. Please."

Jessup nodded her approval. Reg had a sneaking suspicion that it had been a test to see if Reg were telling the truth. Now she was satisfied that Reg's story was consistent. Although Reg could have dialed anyone she wanted to on the phone and left that message. Or called no one at all. She was good at misdirection.

Reg slid her feet into the car and pulled her door shut. Jessup started the engine and made sure she knew where she was going.

"And… you're sure Starlight was intentionally poisoned?" she asked tentatively.

"I don't know. The vet said there are a lot of household things that could have poisoned him accidentally, but if there is a spell involved too, that means that it wasn't just an accidental poisoning. He didn't just chew on this plant," Reg looked down at the potted green plant in her lap, "or get into something else that he shouldn't have. That means it was intentional, and I can't understand anyone doing that! How could they poison an innocent creature? And not just poison him, but curse him so that he couldn't get better?" Reg sniffled, trying to hold back the tears. She shook her head impatiently at her own emotion and lack of control. "I have to figure out who did it so that we can figure out how to counter it."

Jessup watched the road ahead of her, thinking about it. "You haven't reported it to the police?"

"What could the police do? Would they take the poisoning of a cat seriously? It would go on the back burner. No one would care about it. They wouldn't go out and question anyone; they'd just wait for me to provide evidence as to who it was. Right?"

"Yes, probably. But if you had some evidence, they might go out and talk to people. They might be able to make some progress on it. And if there was magic involved, you really might want to do that. Magic means that it was intentional and targeted."

"But if there is magic involved, then the police can't handle it because so few of them are practitioners. They'll roll their eyes at any of the magical stuff."

"But you can't expect them to do anything about it if you don't tell them."

"No. I'm not expecting them to do anything." Reg glanced over at Jessup. "I called you as a friend, not as a police detective. Can't you just be a friend for once and forget about your job? You said it was your day off."

Jessup's lips pressed tightly shut, thinning out into a straight line. "Yes. I didn't realize I was doing anything wrong."

"You're not. It's just… this isn't an official investigation. I don't know what to do, but inviting the police into it and trying to justify myself to them isn't even on the list."

"Right." Jessup was silent for a couple of minutes as she drove. "Do you mind if I ask… non-official questions about it?"

Reg rolled her eyes. Even when she asked Jessup not to be a police detective, she still couldn't help herself.

Jessup took her silence for consent and proceeded. "What benefit would it be to anyone to poison and curse Starlight? Who would want him out of the way?"

"I don't know. I've been thinking about it. But I don't think that anyone would do that. I mean… I know some people don't like him or don't like cats in general, but would they hurt him just because of that? That takes… a certain kind of person."

"But you can't always tell by talking to someone if they are that kind of person. Psychopaths are usually very charming, very friendly and good at getting people to trust them." Jessup opened her mouth, then closed it, not saying what she had been about to.

"I know plenty about psychopaths," Reg said dryly.

She didn't care whether Jessup thought she was one or not. Reg herself had given up on trying to figure out if there were something wrong with her brain, or whether it was just a combination of her supposedly psychic gifts and the traumatic events that she had been through as a child. It wasn't that she didn't care about anyone else. But she had been hurt and had to protect herself and to lie, cheat, and steal to survive. She had to put herself first, no matter how it might endanger anyone else. If she didn't take care of herself, no one else would. If that made her a psychopath, then she would wear it like a badge of honor. And if not, she had still dealt with enough people in her life who were evil and showed one face to the public and another to their victims. She knew how charming they could be.

"Who were you thinking of?" Jessup asked. "Who did you think of who doesn't like Starlight or want him around?"

Reg stared out the window at the street ahead of them. "Corvin, of course. He hates Starlight and won't even call him by name. Starlight hates him and hisses at him and yowls and gets angry if I let him into the house."

"If you let him into the house? Why would you do that?"

"Sometimes it has been accidental…" Reg squirmed uncomfortably.

"But you don't think that Hunter did anything to him, because…"

"For one thing, I don't think he's had the opportunity. Starlight has only been in the house. Corvin hasn't been, not in the last few days, when Starlight was poisoned. So how could he have done it? No opportunity."

"Are you sure he doesn't have the ability to get into the house? You said that he has been in there by accident."

"I don't know. I don't understand all of the details of how wards work and when they don't work and if Corvin is powerful enough to break them."

"So he is still a *maybe*."

"But he went over to the vet's with me and tried to heal Starlight."

"And you know he could very well have done that just to mislead you and make you think that he was sincere about helping and didn't have anything to do with him getting poisoned and cursed in the first place."

Reg let out her breath. "Yeah."

"So he's on the list. Who else?"

"Sarah doesn't like cats. She puts up with Starlight, and she talks to him and feeds him when she comes over. She was there putting up all of the Yule decorations when he got sick. There were a lot of things that were poisonous to cats. Holly and mistletoe, I don't know what else. I packed it all up, but not until after Starlight was poisoned."

"And you think she dislikes cats enough to have poisoned him?"

"No, I don't. But like you said, you can't always tell. People lie to you. Pretend that they care and are kind and loving when they aren't. Do I think Sarah is that kind of person? No, but that's just what I would think of a very successful psychopath. I don't think she would poison him just because she doesn't like cats. But she *has* been complaining about the other cats coming over to visit and is kind of paranoid about them being around the house or in the garden. She thinks that too many cats in the cottage will attract more cats, like when Nicole first came to see Starlight when he would watch her out the window. Even though he was an inside cat, he still attracted a cat who was allowed to roam. Sarah was worried about being overrun by them and of them catching birds. And she does like birds."

"Yes, she does. Okay. So Sarah is on the list. She had lots of opportunity and some motive. And she hasn't given you the list of ingredients in the tea that you want for the vet."

"Yeah. But I think she still will. I don't think she's intentionally holding that back. We wouldn't have any way of knowing if she gave us the wrong information. If she did poison him intentionally, she wouldn't tell us what she used. I don't think he was poisoned by the tea. That was Corvin's idea, and I don't think it's what happened."

"You think he's trying to cover up how he gave Starlight poison?"

Reg considered. "Maybe," she admitted reluctantly.

"Corvin and Sarah. Who else?"

Reg thought about it. There weren't a lot of people in her life who had reason to dislike the cat. Most people liked him or even loved him. "There are the fairies and the pixies. They don't like cats."

"No. But would they come to your house to poison him? Why would they do that?"

"I *don't* think they would. But you're asking for a list of possible suspects, and the fairies and pixies have to be on it. The pixies don't like cats and they don't like me because I took Calliopia away from them. And then Ruan left to be with her too. They could get up to the house through the sewers, and then… I don't know how they could get into the house, but they are tricky. Maybe they could find a way. Or they could cast a spell on him from outside when he was sitting by the window."

"Okay. I suppose. And the fairies? They have helped and protected you. I don't think they would do anything against your cat."

"I don't think so. I haven't done anything to hurt them. It's just that… some things I have seen lately made me think that maybe they are around lately, in the garden, watching the cottage. And if they are… maybe they didn't like Starlight being there or thought he was a danger to them. I don't know. They've said that they won't hurt me because I'm protected by Calliopia's blood. But that wouldn't stop them from hurting my cat, would it?."

"Right." Jessup pulled into the vet's parking lot but made no move to get out. "So the fairies are a possibility… but probably not as likely as the other suspects."

"Yeah."

"Anyone else?"

Reg was silent for a minute, thinking before she brought up the one that had been bothering her. "My mother."

"Norma Jean? Why would she want to hurt him?"

"I don't know, exactly. But she's the kind of person who lashes out and hurts people. She might apologize afterward or say it was just because she was high or drunk or tired, but that doesn't stop her hurting people. She might actually enjoy it."

"What was she like when she came to see you? Why did she come here?"

"Apparently, because she's turned over a new leaf. She's all cleaned up and wants to reconnect with me. But I don't believe people can change that much."

"It's been a lot of years."

"Yeah. But she was in my head for a lot of years too, and she didn't change then. She would act sweet as honey one minute and then be cursing and threatening the next. If I didn't listen to her, she'd be screaming and ranting. That kind of person doesn't change to permanently sweet. She can pretend, but she can't do it forever."

"And would she have any reason to hurt Starlight? She didn't even know that you had a cat before she came here, so it isn't like he did something to hurt her."

"He's very smart. The way he reacts to people... it's a good guide for what kind of people they are. He's intuitive that way. And he didn't like her. She certainly didn't like him. And she had met him before, even if she didn't know he was my cat."

"How would she have met him before?"

"When we..." Reg realized that Jessup didn't know any of what had transpired with Weston and Harrison and tried to think of the best way to explain it briefly. If she didn't, they'd be sitting in the vet's parking lot all day while Jessup tried to get caught up. "Let's just say... we kind of went back in time and saw her. Back to when I was four and she was still alive. So she saw me then and saw Starlight. And the little me, the four-year-old Reg, she wanted to keep Starlight. So maybe Norma Jean was jealous of him. Maybe he came to represent all of the things that her child demanded. I don't know. But she knew him, and she recognized him when she came to see me. She was... suspicious of him. Didn't know what to think of him."

"And do you think she could have poisoned him? You said she doesn't have any powers, so she couldn't have been the one who cursed him."

"No, but Weston could have."

"Who is Weston?"

"He's... an immortal like the Witch Doctor."

"And he knows Norma Jean?"

"Yeah. They were... very close. I thought that he had gone away and didn't have anything else to do with her after we went back in time, but I don't *know* that. He's an immortal. He could have done anything, right? He could have poofed himself into the cottage, poisoned Starlight, cursed him, and gotten away, and no one would be any wiser. I saw the way that he flirted with Norma Jean, even when she was a drug addict on the skids. He would do anything for her."

"Okay. So Norma Jean and Weston in concert. Is that everyone?"

Reg thought about it. "Yeah... I think so. But... there's been someone following me, too. I don't know who, and I don't know what powers they do or don't have. But someone has been… showing up at the edges of my vision and then disappearing…"

"Like a pixie?"

"Like that, but I don't think that's what it is. I thought it was bigger, like a human, but I've only caught glimpses out of the corners of my eyes. Sarah said that the veils between the worlds are thin around solstice. She thinks I'm just getting accidental glimpses through those veils. But I don't think so. The pattern seems too deliberate."

"What is the pattern?"

"It's whenever I leave the house. Whenever I go out or come back."

"Is it following us now?" Jessup squeaked, immediately turning her head back and forth to scan for something that couldn't be seen.

"Yeah. I saw the shadow again before we left the house. I don't know if it has a vehicle or some kind of teleportation. But I saw it here before when I was here with Corvin and at the house a few times. It obviously wants to know where I'm going."

"That's a bit creepy. You should file a restraining order—"

"Against who? Or what? I can't go to a judge and say that I saw a dark shadow out of the corner of my eye, and I want him to make it stop following me."

Jessup nodded. "No… I suppose not."

"I can't do anything about it. I keep watching for it and trying to figure out who or what it is. It hasn't tried to attack me."

"You lead an exciting life, Reg Rawlins."

"I kind of wish I didn't."

Jessup opened her door, and Reg followed suit. She led the way into the vet's reception area and approached the receptionist to explain why they were there. The young woman recognized her and nodded a friendly greeting. She didn't rush in to tell Reg that Starlight was alive or dead. She just gestured toward the chairs. "If you want to sit down for a few minutes, I'll see when the doctor will be able to see you."

★ CHAPTER FIFTEEN ★

REG SAT IN THE waiting area and was again drawn to look at the sad animals of everyone who was waiting in the chairs. She hoped that they were all just regular checkups or deworming, not anything serious. Not people who were going to have to have their animals put down. No one who'd had a pet poisoned as Reg had. It was too much sadness.

She didn't know how anyone could work in a veterinary hospital or anywhere else where there were sick and injured animals or children on a regular basis. It would have taken too much out of her. Being a psychic was bad enough. She didn't like having to talk to people who had just lost family members or who had significant trials in their future. But most of the time, she made people happy by giving them a chance to talk to their loved ones who had gone on before, or she could find something in their future, no matter how small, that she could pick out to help cheer them up about their futures. She liked giving good news and reconnecting loved ones who really wanted to talk to each other. Or finding lost items or making her clients happy in other ways.

She supposed that being a vet would have happy moments as well. Animals healed and made well, new babies, new pets who made their owners happy. It wouldn't all be sad. But she thought that too much of it would be. She couldn't handle that. It would be like being a cancer doctor for little kids.

She shifted in her seat, unable to get comfortable. She wanted the vet or his assistant to come out and tell her how Starlight was, so she didn't have to sit there wondering if he had died and they were trying to clear a room in order to tell her. She reached out mentally, trying to make contact with him. She hadn't been able to since she had found him unconscious, but that didn't keep her from hoping. When she couldn't sense him, it didn't answer her question as to whether he was okay or had passed.

Jessup eyed her and flipped through some magazines and coffee table books in front of them, showing Reg cute pictures and asking her questions about what kinds of animals she would like to own and what she would never have. Reg tried to focus and engage, knowing that Jessup was trying to help.

"I have a foster sister, and her half-sister has a lizard," she commented, looking at the picture of a snake lovingly wrapped around its owner's arms and shoulders. "It freaks her out. My foster sister, I mean. Erin. She doesn't like lizards. She has a cat and a rabbit."

"Yeah? Do they get along with each other?"

"Yeah, they do. It's kind of cool. But they get jealous of each other when they both want her attention. Her boyfriend has a dog, and the cat doesn't like the dog, but the rabbit is okay with him. And the dog is okay with the cat. But he puffs up into a big furball and hisses when he sees the dog."

She was babbling. Jessup didn't care about Erin's animals. Neither did Reg.

Finally, the veterinary assistant came out looking for Reg and directed her and Jessup to one of the exam rooms. "The vet will be right with you."

Reg licked her lips in preparation for asking whether Starlight was okay or not, but she couldn't get the words out. She ended up just going into the tiny exam room with Jessup. There wasn't enough room to pace, but she felt too crowded sitting down, the seats too low for her to look over the examination table. She stood up, thumbs in her pockets, trying to look casual, but Jessup had to know that it was driving her up the wall. The potted plant sat in the middle of the examining table, incongruous.

It was only a couple of minutes before the vet came in, rubbing his hands with an alcohol gel that cut the air sharply with its scent. Reg didn't offer to shake hands with him, wondering what animal he had just been handling and what procedure he had performed.

"Oh, is this something we need to identify?" he asked, hovering over the plant.

"I just had it for a little while before Starlight got sick. The guy who gave it to me said not to let him eat it. And I didn't think he would. I don't know if he did. I never saw him near it, and I don't see any bite marks on it…" She trailed off and shrugged.

The vet inspected the plant, pushing the leaves around, looking at the soil, sniffing it. "I don't recognize the species. I'll have to get to work on the computer and see if we can identify what it is. It may not have anything to do with Starlight's illness, but we can at least check it out."

"Is he… okay?"

He nodded. "I would say… he's doing a little better today. Not enough that I can say he is definitely on the road to recovery, and I don't think he's going to be waking up today, but… a little stronger. You were right about the bleeding, and we were able to stop it. Pulse and blood pressure are up a little bit. That's good news. If we can keep him going in the right direction, there is some hope for recovery."

Reg let out her pent-up breath and felt the tears immediately flood from her eyes again. She rolled her eyes up to the ceiling and tried to convince herself to stop crying, but it was such a relief to have Starlight show even a tiny bit of improvement, she couldn't help herself.

Jessup got up from her chair and gave Reg an awkward hug. "Hey, Reg. It's okay. He's doing better. This is good news."

"I know. These are happy tears." Reg had never understood happy tears before. She'd had parents or teachers tear up when they were happy or relieved about something, but had never understood what it meant. She'd never experienced the kind of good emotion that was strong enough to cause tears. She sniffled and tried to stop the flood without success.

Jessup rubbed her back. Reg squirmed away from her, not comfortable with the contact. It had been better when Corvin had gone with her. She always felt good in his proximity. And when he touched her. She got goosebumps just thinking about it.

"Can I see Starlight? It doesn't have to be for a long time, but I think it helps him."

The vet nodded. "My assistant will be bringing him in in a moment. She's just getting him ready right now." The vet moved the potted plant to the counter. "I hope this gives us some clues as to what we can do to speed his recovery. Right now, I'm afraid all we can do is palliative care and hope that he continues to recover on his own."

"If he does… that would be good."

"Yes," he chuckled. "I would take that."

The veterinary assistant brought Starlight in, snugly wrapped in a towel and cuddled in her arms like a baby. "Here's your mommy," she crooned to him, even though he was still not conscious. She put him down on the table and unwrapped the towel, readjusting him so that he looked like he was in a natural position. Reg moved forward as soon as she could and started to pet him and whisper to him, rubbing his head and scratching his ears and chin. The vet and his assistant withdrew so that she could have some time with him. Reg stroked him and held her hands against his body, again trying to fill him with her strength and to build up the protections she had wound around him when she had first found him unconscious before bringing him to the vet.

"You can do it. You can get stronger. We'll find a way to counter this magic and the poison and to make you better again. I promise. You'll be able to come home again and have some tuna fish and sit in the window and watch the lights outside. I'll make sure there's never anything around the house that can make you sick again. I'll do everything I can to protect you so that no one can hurt you. They won't ever be able to hurt you again."

She knew, of course, that she was making promises she couldn't follow through on. Just like a parent who promised her child she would always be there. Or the cops on TV who promised that they would find the person who had been kidnapped or find the killer of the person who had been murdered. Reg always scoffed at those scenes, at the ridiculousness of the thought that a policeman would ever feel compelled to make promises like that. They would never make a promise they couldn't keep and, obviously, they couldn't keep a promise to bring a criminal to justice. Plenty of crimes went unsolved for years, decades. Look at Jack the Ripper. Had the police on his case promised that they would bring the killer to justice? If so, they had failed miserably. It wasn't something that they could follow through on.

But the words welled up from her heart, and she promised Starlight over and over again that he was going to be okay, even though she had no way of helping him or knowing if he would even last another day. The doctor said that he was getting better, but he still looked the same, and Reg still couldn't reach him when she tried to reach out and touch his mind. He was deeply unconscious.

After a while, she didn't have any more strength to spare. She could barely stay on her feet. She withdrew from him and leaned against the wall, tears streaming down her face again. Tears of frustration this time that there was nothing more she could do for him.

"Are you okay?" Jessup asked solicitously.

Reg shook her head and didn't answer. The vet's assistant returned and wrapped Starlight back up like a burrito. "We'll take good care of him, momma. We're doing everything we can for him."

"I know."

She disappeared through the other door of the room, into the inner rooms, where in the distance a dog was whining and whining and wouldn't stop.

"Let's go." Jessup escorted her out of the room with a supporting arm around her shoulders. "It'll be okay, Reg. They're taking good care of him."

"I know." Reg sniffled and sobbed and tried to catch her breath. "But they can't do anything as long as the curse is still on him. Even if they counteract the poison, they can't do anything about the magic."

"Maybe there is someone who can. We'll find out. We'll figure out what to do."

★ CHAPTER SIXTEEN ★

'M GLAD I CAME with you," Jessup said, taking Reg back to the car. "This would have been really tough for you to do on your own. Are you going to be okay at home? Do you want me to stay with you for a while?"

"I don't know." Reg slumped into her seat, exhausted. "I just don't know."

"Okay. Well, see how you feel. I'll understand if you do. And like I said, I'm okay with not cleaning my toilet today."

Reg smiled and closed her eyes, not wanting to engage. She needed to rest for a few minutes, not to have to have a conversation.

Jessup accepted this and drove her back home without any questions about who might be suspects in the poisoning and cursing. When they got home, Reg sat still for a minute, not getting out. She looked toward the house and could feel that Sarah was home at last.

Jessup looked at her. "Do you see it? The shadow that you were talking about earlier? Did it follow us again?"

Reg continued to look at the house. As soon as she turned her head, the shadow, if it were there, would disappear. She just stared at the house, monitoring the edges of her vision, before turning and looking around. "No, I didn't see anything this time. Maybe it's given up."

"Maybe." Jessup didn't look convinced.

"Sarah is at home."

Jessup looked at the house. "How can you tell that?"

"I just can."

"Well, at least that's one missing person you don't have to report."

"I'm going to the cottage. I don't think I can deal with anyone else."

Jessup hesitated. "Does that mean you don't want me to come in, or do you mean you don't want to talk to Sarah?"

"I don't know…" Reg took a deep breath and tried to sort out her emotions. "You can come in. But I might want to go to sleep. And if I do…"

"It's fine. I'll just let you sleep."

"Okay."

Reg pushed herself out of the car and shuffled back to the cottage. They were barely in the door when Sarah's back door opened and she walked briskly to Reg's door.

"Oh, Reg, you're back. I'm sorry I was so late getting back. I did mean to have everything ready for you this morning." She took in Reg's appearance. "Is it too late, then? Is… did something happen?"

"He's still hanging on," Reg assured her. "Maybe a little better. I'm just… I tried to build him up as much as I could, but this healing thing is not something I've ever tried before. It takes a lot of energy."

Sarah nodded. "Yes, of course it does. I don't know if I would waste my effort—" she cut herself off and changed direction. "I have those ingredients here." She patted her pockets and found a piece of paper, which she handed over. Reg looked down at the scribbled list and nodded. As she had told Jessup, she didn't think that the tea had poisoned Starlight and, if it had, Sarah wasn't likely to tell her what had hurt him anyway.

"Sarah, what about your emerald?" Jessup suggested.

They both looked at her.

"What about my emerald…?" Sarah repeated, eyebrows raised.

"I mean, it is very powerful. Couldn't you use it to heal Starlight?"

"No."

Reg and Jessup looked at her, waiting for further explanation. Sarah just shook her head.

"No. That's not what it is for."

Reg wasn't sure if she meant it wasn't for anyone but Sarah, that it wasn't for healing someone from poisoning or cursing, or if it wasn't for animals. But whichever it was, it was clear she didn't intend to use the powerful crystal for Starlight's benefit.

"Okay," Jessup muttered. "I guess that's not what it is for. What about some other potion or charm? Is there anything you have that might help him? Anything you can think of that might help him to get better faster?"

"I am not a cat healer. You'll have to find someone who knows about cat physiology and what is beneficial to them. It isn't something that I can help with."

"Do you know anyone…?"

"Why would I? I haven't ever had a cat."

Reg was getting irritated with Sarah's unhelpful responses. "You don't really care whether Starlight gets better, do you? You would rather he didn't, so that there isn't a cat over here and you don't have to have one on your property."

"I think I have been very kind to allow Starlight to stay here. I wouldn't want anything to happen to him. But I don't have the skills or the resources to help you."

Reg shook her head. "Fine. I'm going to go lie down."

Reg awoke to knocking on her door. She rubbed her eyes and looked around, disoriented. She tried to remember what day it was and why she was sleeping in the middle of the day, and slowly, the events of the past few days seeped into her consciousness. The pain in her stomach increased as her muscles tightened. She rolled over and sat up slowly, giving her body time to adjust being in an upright position, then wandered out to the door. It wouldn't be Sarah; she would just walk right in. And Jessup would either have stayed while Reg slept or would have gone home and wouldn't be back looking for her again. She would call.

Reg looked out the peephole and saw Damon. She opened the door, considering.

"Hey." Damon looked a little uncomfortable. They hadn't been dating. Reg had told him to take a hike after he and Corvin had a big jealous fight over her. In public. Crashing tables, splashing coffee, it had been a scene, and Reg hadn't appreciated it. Then he'd shown up again later when she was meeting with Davyn about Corvin's sentence. He'd again showed his jealous side, and Reg wasn't going to put up with him being jealous every time she spoke with another man. Big red flag. "I was checking in on you. I heard about Starlight and wanted to make sure you were okay."

Reg stared at him. "You heard about Starlight. From who?"

"Uh… I don't know… it was, I think it was Bill over at the Crystal Bowl."

"How did he know?"

Damon raised his brows. "I didn't ask him how he knew. I guess he heard it from someone else. Bartenders know everything, you know. They hear all of the rumors going around."

"I didn't tell him about it. The only people that knew were Corvin and Sarah."

"Then I guess one of them has been over to the Crystal Bowl." Damon shrugged. "Was it supposed to be a secret?"

"Well, no, I guess not. But it is kind of personal."

He shifted his stance, angling toward the door. "So are you okay? Could I come in?"

"I don't know. I don't like to invite men in here, since Corvin, you know."

"You don't seem to have a problem hanging around with him, and he's the one who is a predator. I don't know why you would have a problem being with me."

Reg grimaced. He was right. When she looked at it from a logical perspective. But her emotions and her attraction toward Corvin were not logical. She couldn't control that. Damon was a nice guy, and he was probably more compatible with her since he wasn't going to steal her powers if they got too close. But she had a hard time getting to know him. The fact that he could tell when she was lying and could put thoughts into her head made her suspicious of him.

"I guess… come in for a few minutes. But it's not a date, and I don't want you putting visions into my mind."

She moved back from the door to let him in. He stepped over the threshold before answering her. "I'll do my best, but have you ever had someone tell you not to think of a thing? I don't know what you're thinking of right now, but what would you think of the minute I tell you not to think about elephants?"

Of course, Reg hadn't been thinking of elephants, but now she was. "I don't know what that proves."

"Just that telling me not to communicate using the part of my brain that shares visions is counterproductive. The more I try to avoid using it, the more it is triggered. I don't understand what your objection is. It's just the way I communicate. It's part of my language."

"I don't like the way that your visions pop into my brain and affect the way I'm thinking. I don't know when I've imagined something, and when it's you. It's unsettling."

He shrugged. "I'll do my best, but I don't have perfect control."

She suspected that he had a lot more than he pretended to. She could control what she said or didn't say out loud; it didn't have to be the same as what she was thinking in her head. So he should be able to control whether he shared a vision or just kept it in his head. If it were just like speaking. And of course, she could be completely wrong.

But right or wrong, she didn't like it, and she would kick him out the minute she thought he was putting thoughts or visions into her head.

She motioned Damon to the couch and he sat down. He had a lot of physical similarities to Corvin; the dark eyes, short beard, and dark hair. But he was nothing like Corvin. She didn't feel the same warmth and attraction when she was near him. She liked him well enough as a person as long as he behaved himself, but she didn't feel the desire to curl up in his arms as she did with Corvin. She got him a tumbler of Jack without asking what he wanted, and the same for herself. It wasn't a 'tea' day.

"So how are you feeling?" Damon prompted. "It must have been a pretty big shock, finding Starlight… sick like that."

"It was awful. And I don't think I've recovered. If he doesn't get better, I don't know what I'm going to do. I never realized how important he would become to me. I thought I was just getting a prop for my business, and he's ended up being so much more. I can't imagine carrying on without him."

"You could get another cat. And even though you don't think so, you would probably get just as attached to a new one just as fast."

"No. Starlight is special. Another cat wouldn't be the same."

"You might be surprised."

Reg hated people who always thought they knew more than she did or what was right for her. She knew a lot more about cats than she used to. She had not just been around Starlight, but also around Nicole and the kittens. She had discovered that they all had different personalities and gifts. People talked about cats as if they all had the same personalities and behaviors, but they were so wrong. Each of the cats and kittens was as different from the others as humans were. They might not have language and communicate the same way as humans, but that didn't mean they didn't have personalities.

She sipped her drink. It felt good going down, but as soon as it hit her stomach, it burned, and Reg's stomach reacted so violently that she almost brought it right back up. She put her glass down. Coffee and whiskey were both out of the question. She needed real food in her stomach, and maybe milk or water. She was going to have to take care of herself, or she would wind up in the hospital herself.

"Reg?" Damon asked, a note of alarm in his voice.

"I'm not feeling very well. I should probably go back to bed."

"You're so pale. What can I get you?" He stood up and went into the kitchen. He looked around, opening cupboards and the fridge. "I could make you some tea. When was the last time you ate? Do you want some toast?" He poked through the takeout containers in the fridge. "Leftover pizza?"

"Maybe… toast. I don't think I could keep anything else down. And maybe some Pepto from the bathroom."

He put a slice of toast in the toaster and depressed the handle. He disappeared into the back hallway for a few minutes—a little longer, Reg thought, than he needed to in order to find the pink medicine—and then he was back, shaking the bottle and reading the dosing instructions.

"I should probably have the toast before the medicine."

Damon nodded. "Whichever you want. It should only take a couple of minutes. Are you sure there isn't anything else you want?" There was a crease between his brows. "You don't seem to have any herbs."

"I'm really not into herbs and remedies. Sarah is the one who knows all that stuff; I don't. Pepto Bismol works for me."

He put the bottle and a tablespoon down on the coffee table for her. "You should see someone if it lasts too long. Is it just a bug, or…?"

"Just worried about Starlight, I guess. I haven't been able to eat very much."

"Sarah could probably prepare you a calming remedy. Something that would help you to be less stressed about it."

"Probably," Reg agreed. That didn't mean she was going to do it.

The toast popped a minute later, and Damon looked in the fridge again. "Do you want butter? Jam?"

"Nothing, just dry toast. Really, I'm not even sure if I'll be able to handle that."

He put it on a plate and took it over to her. He sat back down and watched Reg take an experimental bite. Reg chewed the dry toast and swallowed, then waited to see how it would feel. It didn't bother her stomach too much, so she sat there nibbling at it while Damon looked around the house and searched for a safe topic.

"I gather… you don't know how Starlight got sick?"

Reg turned her eyes to his face, studying his expression carefully to see how much he knew. She hadn't seen him around, but that didn't mean that he hadn't been around without her seeing him. With his black cloak on and the cover of night, he could go pretty much wherever he wanted without anyone knowing about it.

"He was poisoned. And cursed."

Damon portrayed shock. "Really? Who would do that?"

"I don't know." She continued to stare at him. "I have a few suspects."

"It takes a pretty bad sort to poison a pet. You think you know who did it?"

"I said I have suspects. And Starlight is not a pet. He's my familiar. He's a…" she wanted to say 'real person,' but wasn't sure how that would go over. He seemed like one to her, but Damon would think she was crazy. He wouldn't understand what Starlight meant to her.

"Well, I hope you find out who did it. Is he going to be okay? You caught it in time?"

"I don't know. The vet said he was doing better today, a tiny bit better, but I don't know… It's pretty serious. We don't know if he'll recover."

Damon shook his head. "Shocking. I'm so sorry to hear that."

He took another sip of his whiskey. Reg tried to figure out a way to get rid of him quickly.

Later, when she was alone again, she thought about Damon and wondered whether he had been closer than she thought. She hadn't seen him, but he might have been around without her being aware of it. What if he was the one who had been following her? She didn't know the extent of his powers, but she suspected that with his ability to project visions, he could cloak himself, making her think she was looking at an empty street when he was standing right there.

Maybe she had been catching glimpses of him, and he had been hiding himself with his powers whenever she turned toward him. It was odd that he should know about Starlight being sick when it wasn't common knowledge in the community. It wasn't like she'd posted it on her social networks. She'd told a couple of people, and yet word had apparently made its way back to Bill at the Crystal Bowl and Damon. If Damon was telling the truth. Reg knew Bill, but she couldn't imagine him talking to Damon about her personal life. Why would either of them be interested in Starlight?

★ CHAPTER SEVENTEEN ★

WHEN IT STARTED TO get dark, Reg took a walk in the garden. She was feeling restless and she wanted to look around. Were the things she had seen and heard in the yard at night indicative of fairies? If so, why were they there? Were they guarding her? Investigating her? Just there by chance?

Or was she seeing and hearing things that weren't actually there? Maybe she was ill. Perhaps all of the strange happenings were just indicators that she was slowly losing her mind.

The night air was crisp and pleasant. Even in the dark, the garden was pretty and had a feeling of calm. Reg sat down on a large decorative rock and closed her eyes, listening to the breeze blowing through the trees and smelling the salty tang of the ocean it carried. It was such a beautiful, peaceful place.

And then she heard it. A sound that reminded her of the tinkling of bells and of childish laughter. Like the trees were whispering secrets to each other and laughing at their own jokes. There were flickering lights, but she couldn't see the fireflies themselves, just the lights, which didn't seem to move the way that bugs did. Maybe it was some other phenomenon. Not the northern lights so far south. What other natural phenomenon produced light? Ball lightning. In children's movies, pixies lit up like little lights, but they were nothing like the real-life pixies she had encountered, dirty and vicious and cold.

The whispering noises swept past her, as if a group of invisible people had passed.

Reg got up, trying to follow the noise but, as soon as she moved, it was gone. She walked toward the front of the house. She could go for a walk. Or go talk to Sarah. She felt like she needed to do something to help solve the problem of who had poisoned Starlight, but she couldn't think of anything that would actually help. She took off down the street at a brisk pace, and in a few minutes found herself turning and heading toward the Crystal Bowl. Usually, she drove there, but it wasn't far; it didn't actually take much more time to walk there than it would take to drive. And she got the exercise she felt like her body needed, sluggish after so much sleep and sitting around. She pushed open the doors of the Crystal Bowl and walked into the babble of voices. No one turned to look at her. She headed up to the bar, even though she knew she couldn't have anything to drink. Whatever she got would just hurt her stomach.

Bill was not on duty, so that wrecked the idea of asking him where he had heard about Starlight and if he had been the one to tell Damon about it. She didn't trust Damon's explanation.

One of the other bartenders, a tall thin man called Taco, shuffled down the bar to her.

"Evening, Reg. What can I get you?"

"I can't really drink anything."

He raised an eyebrow.

"My stomach. I'm not feeling well."

"Oh," he nodded. "Milk or water? Ginger ale? Ginger is good for sick stomachs."

"Okay, I'll give it a try."

He poured her a glass and set it on a napkin in front of her.

"Has Damon been in here today?"

"Damon? I only just started my shift, but I don't usually see him around here."

"He said that he heard about my cat here."

"Your cat?"

"Starlight. About him being sick."

Taco shook his head, bemused. "I don't know. I haven't heard anything. What's wrong with him? Is it contagious? Rabies?" His mouth quirked into a grin, questioning why it would be news that her cat was sick.

"No. He was poisoned and cursed."

The grin disappeared. "Oh. I'm sorry. Why would anyone do that?"

"That's the question. Who would want to hurt my cat? Why would anyone do that? Was it to hurt me? Did he... offend someone? I mean, what does a cat do that he deserves to be killed for?"

"Is it that serious?"

"Yes."

"I guess... I couldn't know that without knowing more about the cat. People talk about trapping or poisoning animals that dig in their gardens or get into the garbage. No one likes to have to clean that crap up."

"No, he's an inside cat. He's not getting in anyone's gardens."

"Well, then, who else would he bother? Someone who came over to your house who didn't like him? A roommate?"

Reg shook her head again. She sipped the ginger ale and looked around the crowd at the Crystal Bowl. It was usually fairly busy. They did good business. "How about Corvin? Have you seen him around?" She couldn't help it that her mind kept going back to him. The way he hated Starlight. The way Starlight hissed and acted toward him, as if they had been mortal enemies in a previous life. Had they? Corvin had suggested that Starlight might be a human reincarnated as a cat. Harrison had said he was an old friend. Maybe they were right. Maybe Starlight knew things about Corvin. Maybe Corvin had something to cover up by killing Starlight; it wasn't just that he didn't like Starlight being around when he tried to get in to see Reg.

"Saw him here last night with a woman. Stranger I didn't know."

"Norma Jean."

"Could have been," he nodded slowly. "We weren't introduced, but they were around most of the night. That sounds right."

"She's my mother. Biological mother, anyway." Though who knew how much of Norma Jean's DNA Reg actually had. Harrison had been very vague about how an immortal like Weston and a human woman would create a child, so she wasn't sure the process was the same as two humans having a baby and the baby inheriting both of their genes. Maybe Reg was a new creature, who did not share in the genetic heritage of either of them. She didn't look much like either one of them. Though who was to say whether Weston always took the same form, or whether he could take whatever form he pleased.

"Your mother?" Taco raised his eyebrows, surprised. "I had no idea."

"I hadn't seen her since I was four. It wasn't like she was in my life."

"Corvin was behaving... very strangely, for him."

"Oh?" Reg leaned in closer to Taco, hoping for more details. He moved farther away from her to serve up a couple of refills, then moved back to her again.

"He was acting as if... the roles were reversed," Taco said slowly. He frowned, trying to decide whether there was a better way to describe what he was talking about.

"What do you mean, the roles?"

"Well Corvin is the one who is always charming the women. He can have a very powerful effect on them." Taco gave an apologetic shrug, doubtless knowing Reg's history with Corvin.

"Yeah, I'm aware of that."

"But this time, he was the one who was acting... a little loopy."

"Corvin?"

"Yeah, I know. They were sitting together, and usually, it's the women who are falling all over themselves, pulled in by his charms. Even the ones that he isn't trying to charm; the ones without powers or who are older. They are still attracted to him, it's natural. But this woman—your mother—she was the one charming him."

"No."

He shrugged, holding his hands palms up. "I don't know how else to describe it."

"She doesn't have any powers."

Taco cocked his head. "Yes, she does."

"No. She doesn't. She's just a regular human. No special gifts."

"Then we're not talking about the same woman."

"Maybe not," Reg agreed, relieved to find an explanation. "He wouldn't have been here that late with Norma Jean. He took her out for coffee earlier in the day. He must have been here with someone else."

Taco nodded, accepting this as the explanation. "It must have been someone else. I'd like to know who she was, though. It was quite something to see the tables turned."

"I'd like to see that too," Reg admitted. "Let him see what it's like, for once."

She felt immediately guilty for even thinking it. She wanted Corvin to have a taste of his own medicine? After all she had said and done to try to make him and the other warlocks understand what the women who were his victims went through? If she didn't want it for the women, then she didn't want it for him either. It would be reprehensible to wish that on anyone. No one deserved to be treated like prey and to have their willpower taken away from them by magical means.

She covered her mouth to hide her frown, then rubbed her forehead. She was still having trouble focusing on anything but Starlight's immediate condition. She worried that her phone would ring any time and it would be the vet calling to tell her that he hadn't made it.

"Well, if you see him…" Reg started, then stopped. If Taco saw Corvin, then what? Did Reg really want to pass a message on to him? 'Let me know if you're okay' or 'Call me and let me know how it went with Norma Jean' or, worse yet, 'tell me what you thought of her.' Ugh. Why did relationships have to be so complicated? Her relationship with Corvin was difficult enough without adding in her relationship with Norma Jean and then mixing them up with each other. Whether it had been Norma Jean that Corvin had been with the night before or not, what right did she have to ask Corvin to look after her? She should have been doing her best to keep them apart, not complicating things by letting them talk to each other. The stories that they might have shared over coffee…

"Yeah?" Taco's brows went up, waiting.

"I don't know. Nothing, I guess. I'll see him when I see him. I'm sure we'll run into each other again, that's never been a problem before."

Taco nodded. He moved away from her, polishing the bar counter with a white towel. Reg sipped a little more of the ginger ale, but it didn't seem to be doing much for her stomach. She should probably go home and go back to bed. Maybe she'd be feeling better by morning.

But she was used to being up late and, since she'd already had a nap, her body was wound up, and she wasn't ready to go back to bed so soon.

She left a tip for Taco with what remained of her drink and headed back out. There were a few stores to browse along the street that the Crystal Bowl was on. She would do a little window shopping and see where it led her. Maybe she'd even stop at the grocery store and pick up something healthy to eat. Like a bag of chips. Chips were vegetables.

She continued walking up the street, looking in the windows of the shops that were still open. Most were closed and dark. If she wanted to buy anything, she would have to start earlier in the day. The stores in Black Sands didn't stay open late, despite the large magical community, which she would have thought would have preferred shopping at night over shopping during the daylight hours. Maybe there was another area of town where the stores stayed open late, but you had to be a local to know about it.

She crossed the street and walked back the direction she had come, down the other side. She saw a drunk slumped in one of the benches along the street, and looked back at the other side, deciding whether to cross back over and avoid the drunk. It wasn't like he was being belligerent, though, he was sleeping. He wasn't going to harass her. She decided to keep walking and pretend she didn't see him, like everyone else was doing.

Until she was a few feet away from him and felt the familiar stirrings inside her. She looked back at the drunk, frowning. He hadn't shaved. His clothing was rumpled and stank of sweat. The hood of his cloak was up over his head and obscuring most of his face. But she knew the warm feeling she had as she got closer to him, it was unmistakable.

"Corvin?"

She said it too quietly. He didn't even stir. Reg got close to try to get a good look at his face. She hooked one finger around the edge of his hood to pull it away from his face for a better view. It *was* Corvin. A Corvin who had clearly had too much and maybe hadn't even gone home since his date with the mysterious woman the night before. Reg poked him a little gingerly.

What did she think? That she was going to catch something from him? Intoxication or a hangover was not contagious. She wasn't going to catch any cooties. She gripped his arm and shook hard. She could feel the buzzing electricity of their contact, just as she always did. Even with him unconscious. That just proved that it wasn't something he had full control over.

"Corvin! Wake up! Corvin!"

It took determined shaking and shouting in his face before he finally began to stir. People walking by were glaring at Reg. Why? It wasn't her fault that he was drunk. No one else had taken it upon themselves to intervene. She was doing what any responsible citizen of the community should do and making sure he was okay.

Corvin's head tipped back, wobbling back and forth. He looked at her through slitted eyelids, not opening them any farther than he had to. "Regina."

"Hey. What's going on? You can't sit here passed out on Main Street. Some cop is going to roust you. What are you doing here?"

He stared at her, not responding.

"Come on. Corvin. What are you doing here?"

"Is she gone?"

"Who?"

"Your mother." His words were thick and slurred. "Norma Jean." He gave a smile and a small shake of his head. "The incomparable Norma Jean."

Reg laughed in disbelief. "Good grief. Don't tell me you're falling for her scam. She's a con artist, Corvin. She was one long before me. Where do you think I learned all the tricks of the trade?"

"She's... such a lovely woman."

"No. She's not. What are you talking about? Everything you see is fake. The hair, the teeth, the body. You should have seen her when she was a junkie. You *did* see her when she was a junkie. So how can you look at her and fall for the image she's trying to project now? She's just trying to lure you in. The only reason she ever cared for a man was when she wanted something from one of them."

Corvin grasped Reg's wrist. The skin-to-skin contact gave her a much stronger jolt of electricity than just touching his arm, with a layer of cloth between them. Reg gasped and tried to steady herself. But he pulled her over so that she fell into the seat next to him on the bench.

"She's gone?" Corvin asked. "Where did she go? Tell me—tell me she didn't go back home."

"Oh, I highly doubt it. But I haven't heard from her. Why don't you tell me what happened yesterday? I can't believe the shape you're in." He was usually so classy. So elegant. Rakish, but well-groomed and always aware of his presentation. "What happened when you took her for coffee?"

"We came here." Corvin looked around to orient himself. "To the Crystal Bowl." He finally focused on the restaurant and bar across the street and nodded to it. "Had some coffee."

"Yes. And then what? Taco said you were there with another woman later. That you were acting..." Reg tried to think of the appropriate word. *Loopy*, Taco had said. *Besotted* would be impolite. "You were... attracted to her."

"Of course I was," he agreed, leaning toward her. His breath smelled awful. How long had he been sitting on that bench? Since the Crystal Bowl had closed? Had he gone home? Gone to Norma Jean's hotel? She shook her head. No, he'd been with another woman after Norma Jean. The powerful, charming woman. "I think I love her, Reg. She's not like any woman I've ever met before."

Reg recoiled. "Norma Jean? Tell me you're not in love with Norma Jean. You couldn't be."

He smiled dreamily. "Norma Jean," he said slowly, drawing it out. "The beautiful and charming Norma Jean."

"No. Not beautiful and charming. You know what she's like under all of that fakery, Corvin. You remember. She's a snake. She was horrible. She's only pretending to be interested in you. She isn't really."

"I love her," Corvin declared to the world.

"Oh, man. I think we'd better get you home. Is your car around here?"

Corvin didn't look for it. Reg looked up and down the street and found his little white compact. Usually, when he went out on a date, he used the big black car.

"There it is. Do you have your keys?"

He patted at his pockets, expression bland, not looking as though he understood what he was looking for. Reg took it upon herself to check through his pockets and was glad to find his keys in the loose outer pocket of his cloak rather than having to fish them out of his pants pocket. "Come on, big guy. I can't carry you, so you're going to have to get there under your own power. Up on your feet."

She poked him and pushed him from behind and, eventually, he got the idea and was on his feet. Reg watched him, making sure he was going to be able to walk. He didn't seem too unstable, so she got beside him and took his arm, encouraging him gently toward the car. Corvin tried to go to the driver's side, and she pulled him harder to the right, forcing him to go around the passenger side and get in there. He looked around the interior of the car, clearly confused. When she slid into the driver's seat, he was looking around for something that he might have lost.

"Seatbelt on," Reg advised, and reached around him to pull it out and lock it into place. "What are you looking for?"

"Someone has taken the steering wheel," he pointed out.

"Oh. Yes, it looks like they did."

★ CHAPTER EIGHTEEN ★

R EG WASN'T SURE WHERE she should take Corvin. She didn't want to take him back to the cottage. It could all be a ruse to make her think he was unable to take advantage of her, and that would quickly change once he was in her door. He was that kind of person. He'd faked illness or fatigue before and almost drawn her in. She shouldn't be fooled by a little bit of wobbling and slurred words. She'd never been to his house and didn't know if it would be any better to take him there. She would still be alone with him, and he would not have to deal with any warding spells at his own house. He could have all kinds of spells that could bind her. He could have his own little dungeon.

She looked around for inspiration. There was a flutter in her peripheral vision, and she turned to catch it, but could not. Again, she was too slow to catch whoever it was following her. Now whoever it was knew that she and Corvin were together.

Was it Damon? He had been jealous of Corvin. He seemed to know things that he shouldn't have known. He could have been the one who had followed her to the vet's office, and that was how he knew Starlight was sick. Not because anyone at the Crystal Bowl had told him so.

Reg dug her phone out of her pocket and tapped through the recent calls until she came to the number she was looking for. She hadn't input him into her contacts, but she had taken a call from him. There was no answer. Reg waited for the call to go to voicemail, trying to figure out what she was going to say. It wasn't exactly her responsibility to take care of Corvin when he was on a bender. But she wasn't sure who else would want to be involved.

"Uh, hello?"

Reg collected her thoughts. "Yeah. It's Reg Rawlins. This is Davyn, right?"

"What can I do for you, Miss Rawlins?"

He sounded a little too formal, which made her wonder about asking for the favor she had been planning on. She hesitated. "Well… I sort of have a problem. I was hoping you could help, since Corvin is in your coven…"

"Corvin is being shunned."

"Yes, but… He's still a member of your coven, right, and don't you have… any responsibility to help him when he needs it?"

"No, I don't. In fact, I am prohibited from helping. What seems to be the problem?"

"He's… kind of in bad shape. I need somewhere to take him, but I can't take him back to my place. I don't want to be alone with him. So I thought… you could help. I could bring him to your place, and he could sleep it off there and make sure everything is okay. Couldn't you?"

"No, I can't. I can't have anything to do with him. What kind of example would I be setting to the rest of the coven when I, as their leader, cannot follow the ruling that was made by the tribunal? I must obey the decision of the council, no matter what I might want to do personally."

"Then who can help me? I don't know enough people in town that I could take this to."

"You would have to pick someone outside of the coven. There are not a lot of practitioners who will have anything to do with him while he is being shunned. Most will heed the ruling of the council even if they are not part of the coven. That is one of the reasons that shunning is such a harsh punishment. It is very isolating."

"And you can't do anything, even if he is in danger."

"What kind of danger is he in? It sounds like you have everything under control."

"I don't. I'm confused and I don't know what's happened to him. I've never seen him like this before. And I don't have anywhere I can take him. What am I supposed to do?"

"Why don't you take him back to the Crystal Bowl? Or to a coffee shop? Sit him down, give him a few cups of coffee, I'm sure he'll be fine."

Reg looked in her rear-view mirror at the Crystal Bowl. She didn't want to take him somewhere quite that public. Rumors would be flying all over town in an instant. She didn't need that and neither did Corvin. Whatever had happened, he deserved a little privacy while he recovered and got his head back on straight. Reg shook her head. *In love with Norma Jean?* He had to be out of his mind. There was no way he could be falling for Norma Jean.

"I guess… I'll try a coffee shop. But I don't know how late they'll be open. Won't they be closing before too long? Then what am I supposed to do?"

"I've given you my advice, Miss Rawlins. If you can't find a coffee shop that is open… you could try the medical center. Or the jail. Call it in as drunk in public, and the police will take care of him for you."

"But I'm not sure he's just drunk." If he had been drinking the night before, that was way too long for him to still be intoxicated. He could have been drinking the whole time, but he didn't smell like alcohol in spite of his unsteadiness and slurring. He acted… loopy, just like Taco had said. Maybe he had been drugged. Or ensorcelled. Taco had said that the woman he had been with the night before had powers and that she had charmed him. She might have taken his wallet, or something else of value, and then left him there, still in an enchanted state. "He might have had a spell cast on him. He's acting weird. I don't want to turn him over to the police, and if I take him to the hospital, they're not going to know what to do with him any more than the vet knows what to do with my cat!"

"That's the best I can come up with. If you want something else… you'll have to come up with it on your own. Or call someone else. I shouldn't even be giving you advice on dealing with someone who has been shunned. I shouldn't even be acknowledging his existence."

"That's pretty hard when you're supposed to be keeping an eye on him and deciding when he is worthy of being readmitted to the coven," Reg snapped.

"You're right, of course. I have to maintain a level of distance and decorum yet still be aware of what he is doing, and that is not a simple matter."

"Well, you're doing a great job of it." Reg pulled the phone away from her ear and tapped the red button. She missed the days of being able to slam the phone receiver down with a loud crash. That was a satisfying way to end an angry phone call. Tapping a touch screen didn't even come close.

"Where are we going?" Corvin asked.

"Coffee, I guess. We'll try to get as much in you as possible and hope you're just drunk. How much did you have to drink?"

"I haven't had anything to drink." He leaned toward her in the manner of drunks all over the world declaring their soberness. "I—am—not—drunk."

"Then what are you?"

His head raised, he gazed toward the stars. "I am in love."

Reg sighed and shook her head. "Did she roll you?" She reached over to pat his breast pockets, hoping that he kept his wallet there rather than in his back pocket. There was a solid rectangular lump. She reached inside his cloak to find the pocket and pulled the wallet out. Everything appeared to be in order. Credit cards, identification, and cash. No empty slots. Nothing was obviously missing. And he'd had his keys. So what had the mysterious woman been up to if she hadn't been after his wallet or keys?

"What did you do last night?"

"We had coffee. And we talked. And we had supper. And we talked. And she was so delightful. And then we came outside, and we sat and looked at the stars… and then…" Corvin shook his head. "Did I fall asleep? Maybe I fell asleep."

"What did she want?"

"She didn't want anything. Just to be together."

Reg snorted. Norma Jean wasn't sweet to anyone for no reason at all. When she had been an addict, she had used men for drugs or money. Now that she was clean, or appeared to be clean, what did she want? She was probably still after money. Norma Jean figured Corvin was a rich mark—and Reg suspected from the way that he wined and dined her that he probably was—and she wanted his money.

But she hadn't taken his wallet or his watch, so she was after more than just pocket change. She was looking for a bigger score. Marry him and get access to it that way? Or convince him to be her sugar daddy? Reg's head hurt with how tight her facial muscles were as she thought through the possibilities.

Then there was the question of why Norma Jean had come looking for Reg in the first place. Did she think that since Reg was in Florida, she had money? Or she wanted to see what kind of a scam Reg was running to either get in on it or to blackmail her?

Reg didn't believe for a minute that she just wanted to see her long-lost baby girl.

"Well, let's see if we can get you sobered up."

The best suggestion that Davyn had been able to offer was a coffee shop, and Reg decided that would have to do. There had to be a few in Black Sands that would be open all night. She wouldn't pick the one that she and Corvin had gone to after the Harbor Port of Call. He and Damon had busted things up there when Damon had happened to show up and caught Reg with Corvin. Reg didn't want to show her face there again.

As she drove, she told her phone to find a coffee shop nearby, and it directed her through a few winding streets to The Witches' Brew. Reg rolled her eyes at the name. Maybe just a little too cute. There was a lit 'open' sign and people inside. And hopefully if it catered to the needs of witches, it would be open late.

★ CHAPTER NINETEEN ★

G ET OUT. WE'RE GOING in for coffee," Reg told Corvin in a stern voice.

He looked around vaguely for a moment before moving to release his seatbelt and get out of the car. She was glad to see that he was awake enough to get out of the car and head toward the door of the coffee shop under his own power. Maybe once he'd had a coffee or two, he'd be back to normal.

"A couple of black coffees to stay, and keep them coming," she told the barista, and steered Corvin to a table. Once he was sitting down, she went back to the counter to pay. The barista, an aging blonde in a long white dress and apron, peered over at Corvin.

"Is he okay?"

"I'm sure he'll be fine when he's had a bit of caffeine."

"Is that Corvin Hunter?"

Reg nodded. She expected that Corvin would be pretty well-known in any of the magical establishments in Black Sands. "Yeah, and if I hear rumors being spread around about this, I'll know where they came from."

The woman's lips tightened. "I would never spread rumors about the clientele."

"Good. Then you don't need to ask any more questions."

The barista poured a couple of black coffees without further comment. Reg took them to the table where Corvin was sitting and put one in front of him. "Drink up. I want to know more about what happened with Norma Jean."

He smiled and picked up the coffee. He had a sip and put it back down. "Is she really your mother?"

Reg shrugged. "As far as I know. Don't know why she would have been raising me otherwise. No reason for her to claim me as hers when she disliked having me around so much."

"It's no wonder I am so attracted to you with a mother like that." He smiled, showing teeth.

"You think she's pretty, huh? Should be, after all of the work she's had done. You think those teeth are hers? She probably lost all of her own to meth use."

"It's too bad you can't see how special she is."

"Oh, she's special, alright. You think it was pleasant having a mother like that?" Reg shook her head. "What's with you and Weston being attracted to her? Even when she was an addict, he was doting on her. Are you men blind?"

"We can see what she's really like. Beyond the surface."

"I know what she's like underneath that veneer. Trust me; she's no princess."

Corvin shook his head, bemused. He had another sip of coffee. He was still looking—for lack of a better word—lovestruck.

"Who else were you with last night? After Norma Jean."

"No one. Just my lady, Norma Jean…"

"Focus here, Corvin. After you had coffee with Norma Jean, you were seen at The Crystal Bowl with another woman. Someone with powers."

"Sweet Norma Jean."

"No, not Norma Jean. She doesn't have any powers. This other woman must have addled you. She's changed your memories."

"You really should give her another chance, Regina. She's a lovely woman."

"No. She's not. I know that better than anyone else. She can't be trusted. Any time she's making eyes at you, you can bet that her real focus is on your wallet. She doesn't care about me or you. Only about herself."

Corvin swirled his coffee in the mug, splashing a little over the edge onto the table. "Oops! Better be more careful. Pay attention."

"Yeah. You'd better. Or you're going to end up in real trouble. Now, look at me." She tried to hold his gaze. If she could connect with him mentally, it would be a lot easier to sort out his confusion and keep his mind on track. "Corvin. Look at me." He met her gaze, but his mind was still meandering, his eyes sliding away to look around the coffee shop as if he'd never been in such a place before. At the rate he was going, he might burst into song at any moment. She touched his arm, careful to keep the fabric of his cloak between her hand and his arm, to at least dampen the electricity that flowed between them whenever they touched. His eyes went back to hers, and she tried to hold his focus. "Let's think this through. Norma Jean doesn't have any powers, right?"

"She is the loveliest creature—"

"No, she's not. But that's beside the point. She doesn't have any powers."

"Yes, she does."

"No." Reg shook her head impatiently. "She doesn't. She doesn't have any powers."

"You don't know the first thing about your mother. Your own mother."

Reg swallowed. Her mouth was suddenly dry. She took a sip of the hot coffee and kept focused on him. "I know her better than you do, and she does not have powers." She tightened her grip on his arm. "Come on, Corvin. Wake up and remember."

The physical contact seemed to galvanize him. The silly, sloppy manner dissolved. His gaze grew sharper. "Regina."

"Yeah."

He blinked at her. "Regina… you really don't know what she is?"

"She's a woman. A junkie. Or a recovering junkie. That's all. She isn't anything special. Nothing magical."

"She is part siren."

"Siren?" Reg remembered the brunette she had seen at the Port of Call with Corvin, a predator working in tandem with a mermaid to seduce and capture a man at the bar. The woman had been beautiful. She hadn't looked inhuman. So how would one even know who was a siren? They presumably would only be near the water because, as Reg remembered it, the sirens lived near the ocean. So it had made sense for one of them to be at the Port of Call, right on the shore. But how else could one tell a siren from a regular human woman? Corvin had clearly not been dragged to a watery grave. Was there some other giveaway? "How could she be a siren? She doesn't even like water. She doesn't have any powers. She isn't… she just isn't anything else. You're mistaken."

"Part siren," Corvin emphasized, "not full-blooded. Or you probably wouldn't be here. And she's on the hunt."

"She's not a siren."

"Saying it doesn't change the facts."

Reg stared at him, shaking her head. But she remembered the way that Weston had hung over Norma Jean, talking and flirting like she was a beauty, even when she'd been a dirty, sickly junkie. Was that why? Could an immortal be affected by a siren? "Is that why… Weston was so smitten with her? Why you're acting all loopy and lovestruck?"

Corvin rubbed his bristly jaw, looking embarrassed. "I… don't recall everything that I might have said or done… you might want to take it with a grain of salt."

"Are you in love with her?"

Corvin cleared his throat uncomfortably. "In love with her…? That sounds so juvenile. It doesn't really express what I feel when I think of her." His eyes slid away from hers, but not because he was distracted this time, because he didn't want her to read the emotion there. Reg waited. "She's a very attractive woman. And she has… sirens have ways of pulling men in. Entrapping them."

"So you realize that she was… ensorcelling you?" She hated the word but didn't know what else to say. She didn't believe that Norma Jean could be a siren, even a half-blooded one. Norma Jean was just a regular person who had become addicted to drugs and made wrong choices. A woman who was hard and cruel, it was true, but because of what she had gone through in her life, not because she was some mythical predatory creature.

Corvin rolled his eyes up toward the ceiling. He took a long drink of his coffee, not answering. It was mostly drained when he put it down, and Reg motioned to the barista for a refill.

"She was very charming," Corvin said finally. "I can't say I've ever been magicked by a siren before, so I don't know exactly how to describe it. I suppose that it is her powers that attract me to her. But what I feel isn't any less real because of that."

"Exactly." Reg answered too quickly, then her face flared with a violent blush. She had been thinking of the way that she responded to Corvin's charms, and he had described it accurately. Even though she knew it was magic and not her own feelings, she couldn't help feeling that way, and it wasn't fake, it was really what she felt.

It was her turn to look away and pretend to drink her coffee as she waited for the flush and the awkward moment to fade.

"How could she be a siren? A part siren, I mean. She's really… hunting men to drown in the ocean?"

Corvin gave a little shudder. Not something dramatic that he was just putting on, but an actual physical reaction to Reg's words. Of course he didn't want her to drag him back into the ocean to drown. He knew that she had charmed him and was powerful enough to affect his behavior.

"The world's siren population is pretty small. You'll note that when Odysseus talks about them, he only talks about one. They tend to be very competitive and need a wide-ranging hunting ground. That means that they will kill each other if they become too overcrowded. I don't know Norma Jean's ancestry or how much siren blood she has. One of the ways that they preserve their territory is that… they tend to kill their own young. So for a siren's progeny to survive, they generally need to be raised away from other sirens."

"You mean like me being raised in foster care, instead of staying with Norma Jean." Reg pictured Norma Jean as one of those species that ate or killed their own young. Like an enormous spider or rat. It was her turn to suppress a shudder.

Corvin nodded. "I don't know. Maybe Norma Jean doesn't have enough siren blood in her to be concerned about her having that instinct. But maybe… it might explain why she treated you the way you say she did."

"You think she would have eventually killed me if I had been left with her?" Reg tried to swallow the lump rising in her throat. "I guess she probably would have."

Corvin shrugged and sighed. He rubbed his eyes as if he were still waking up after a long sleep. Had he been passed out on that bench all day, in a stupor after Norma Jean had ensorcelled him?

"This is a bit much to be laying on you. I'm still trying to comprehend it myself. It was like I could see myself falling for her, but I couldn't stop. Right now, I can think about it logically, tell myself that I wasn't attracted to her because of who she was or any real emotional response… I can think that, but I still want to see her again. I still don't feel like I could ever be complete without her."

"So what about your powers?" Reg asked curiously. "Do your charms work on her? Can you get her to fall for you, so that you're both making the other person fall in love with you?"

Corvin's forehead wrinkled. He rubbed his temples, looking at her. "I have… no idea."

"Well, you must have tried to charm her yesterday when you realized she had powers. Didn't you try to take them from her?"

"By the time I realized she had powers, she had already magicked me. I was helpless to do anything but what she wanted."

Reg raised one eyebrow. "And what did she want?"

"I don't know… I'm at a loss. She apparently left me behind, which makes no sense for a siren. Maybe she doesn't have enough siren blood to have the instinct to drag me into the sea. Maybe she's like an animal raised by humans, so it has no idea how to hunt on its own. Once she had me, she didn't know what to do with me."

"Maybe." Reg felt a little bit better about that. As much as she feared and despised Norma Jean, she didn't like to think that her own mother was that kind of predator. And that Reg might have that blood running in her veins. "So do you think… they were too weak for her to have passed it on to me. These… siren instincts?"

"Inheritance is a weird thing, and when you're talking about powers and gifts, it can be even more unpredictable than other human traits. Throw in some questions about your parentage, and I don't think we can predict what you have or haven't inherited from her."

"You said that must be why you were attracted to me."

Corvin looked like he'd been forced to swallow a pair of dirty socks. "Forget I said that. I wasn't myself. In fact, I'm still not myself." He gave his head a shake. "I feel like I need a week to shake this off. Then maybe I'll be able to think straight and make a reasonable judgment."

"But I want to know. Do you think that I inherited something from her? I don't have her looks. Or Weston's, for that matter. I'm just… my own person. Do you think that I inherited any of her powers? Or her instincts?"

"You should look to your past for that. Do you have a long history of luring men to their deaths? Or luring them and then leaving them passed out on a park bench somewhere?"

"Corvin, be serious."

"I am." He looked away from her. "Or, I'm trying to be, anyway, but I'm not expressing myself very well. What have your past relationships been like?

Do you pull men in and then not know what to do with them once you've got them? Or have impulses to do… inappropriate things?"

"Like drowning them?"

"Perhaps. Even if it's just a fleeting thought. Or… do you like to sing and think you have a particularly entrancing voice? What about children? Do you want to have children? Or is the thought repellent to you?"

"This is ridiculous. You're just making this stuff up. You and Norma Jean got together for coffee, and then you thought, 'why not see what kind of a con we could pull on Reg? Why don't we see if we could get her to believe this bizarre story?' So ha-ha, you got me. You had me going for a while there. You're an excellent actor. You deserve an award."

Reg faked clapping for him. She was angry and frustrated. She didn't know how to respond to Corvin's revelations. But what made the most sense to her was that it was all just a joke. They were gaslighting her. Trying to get back at her for being so impatient with her mother and for constantly spurning Corvin. They wanted to turn the tables and make her see how it felt.

"Reg… I wouldn't do that."

"Sure, you would. You do everything else you can to get me alone, to try to take my powers from me. This was pretty elaborate, but look where you are. You didn't get back to my house, but I nearly took you there. And as it is, you're the only magical one here, as far as I can tell."

Reg glanced around at the other occupants of the coffee shop. Business was slow. Besides the barista, there were only a few other people talking or nursing coffees on their own.

"So if you wanted to, you could start charming me right here, and by the time the night is over, who knows how far you could get with me. Now that you've got my attention and got me alone, you're free to do what you want. And Norma Jean… Norma Jean gets back at me for not being there when I was little. Maybe she thinks it's my fault I was taken away, so she wants to get back at me. Nice job. Really nice work."

★ CHAPTER TWENTY ★

ORVIN STARED AT HER.
Reg looked away, her face hot again. Why was she attacking? Because she felt like she had to defend herself? Because she thought that he was saying she was a predator, when all along, he had been the predatory one?

She had been getting better at protecting herself against him. She had been practicing building up that psychic wall between them to prevent him from charming her, learning how to reflect the heat back at him as a weapon. She had thought that she was learning to control her gifts and that Harrison had been helping her to understand how to use them properly. But had it been her heritage from Norma Jean all along? Was she becoming her mother? She was horrified at the thought. She never wanted to be like her mother in any way.

"Reg, I'm sorry for all of this," Corvin said slowly. "I let things get out of hand. I didn't realize, when I took your mother out for coffee, what it was I was facing. I thought, like you, that she was just a regular human without any powers. I had no way of knowing, before she turned her wiles on me, what she really was."

"It's not your fault," Reg muttered.

"Maybe not… or maybe I should have looked before I leaped. I've gotten used to the idea of being able to work my charms on whoever I like. There are those who can resist, or who do not have a natural attraction toward me, but I've never had someone charm me. I was too sure of myself."

"None of us knew she had any powers. Well… I didn't. None of us mortals knew. I guess Weston knew since she lured him too. Can a siren lure an immortal? Is a siren mortal?"

"Having seen her with him, I would guess the answer is yes. She can. Or at least that immortal in particular. Maybe that should have been a clue, but I missed it."

"Do you think Harrison knew? He must have—don't they know everything?"

"You're mixing up immortal and omniscient again. Just because they are long-lived, that doesn't mean they know everything. They clearly keep secrets from each other, or the other immortals would have known where you-know-who was, even when he hid himself."

Reg blinked. "Are we not saying his name now?"

"I prefer not to conjure him up if I can help it. If he's gone away... I prefer to keep it that way. I don't want to be invoke him by calling his name."

"Okay. What about the other you-know-who? He's not a danger to us, is he? He helps me out."

"I don't know. They are fickle beings. Just because he's helped you out a couple of times, that doesn't mean he will every time. It doesn't mean that his interests won't sometimes be against you."

Reg rolled her eyes. She took a deep breath. "Do you think H knew that Norma Jean was a siren?"

"I expect so. He seemed to be pretty familiar with her."

"But she wasn't interested in him, so he didn't have to worry about being taken in by her charms?"

"I don't know. Do we have proof that he wasn't?"

"That he wasn't...?"

"That H wasn't taken in by Norma Jean's charms. He took an interest in protecting you from the other immortals. Was that just because he liked cute little redheads? Or was he charmed by Norma Jean too?"

Reg rubbed her eyes. Her head was whirling. She tried to remember everything that had happened in the past, but she didn't have enough information to answer all of the questions that sprang to mind. She kept her hands over her eyes, elbows on the table.

"Are you okay?" Corvin asked.

"I guess. Do you know where Norma Jean went after she left you alone? She didn't come back to my house. I thought that as soon as she was done with you, she would come back to see me. She obviously wanted to talk to me again."

"Yes, that's what she said. I'm afraid I don't know what happened next... I don't remember anything past dinner."

"Then where is she? It's been twenty-four hours."

"Maybe she got distracted. Went hunting somewhere else."

"One can hope."

"But she'll come back," Corvin said wistfully, "Won't she?"

Reg sighed. "I'm sure she will."

"Do you mind driving me home?" Corvin asked, massaging his temples again. "I'm afraid I may still be... somewhat impaired."

"Do you promise not to try to charm me when we get there?" Reg countered.

"Regina... I don't think I could even begin to charm you right now," he said, his voice sounding as tired as she'd ever heard him.

"Yeah, I've heard that before. 'I need just a little bit of strength from you, Regina, I'm feeling so tired.'"

"I'm not trying to fool you. I'm being completely open and honest."

"I'm not buying it. But I'm warning you now, you try anything, and I'll invoke whatever names I have to to get you off of me. I'm not dealing with any of your nonsense tonight. I've got too much else on my mind."

"After my recent experience, I can totally relate to that," Corvin declared.

Reg snorted. "Sure, you do. At least she didn't suck all of your powers out and leave you an empty husk, never able to get any back again."

"Well… no."

"So don't tell me you understand what it's like."

"Okay."

Reg studied him suspiciously, not believing that he wasn't going to plead his case or to try to get away with charming her again. He said he couldn't help it, so what good were promises to the contrary? If he couldn't control it, then he couldn't promise to stop it.

"You ready to go home now, then?"

Corvin nodded. "Yes. I think I need to head to bed. You wouldn't think so, since I've been asleep for…" he trailed off and looked at her, eyebrows raised.

"A good twenty-four hours, it looks like," Reg supplied.

"Twenty-four hours. Good heavens. I feel like I've been dancing the Tarantella the whole time."

Reg got up, and the two of them walked together back to the car. Corvin got in and buckled up, and put his head back, sighing.

"It's going to be a while before I dare show my face at The Crystal Bowl again."

Reg looked at him, something tickling the back of her brain. She couldn't figure out quite what it was. Corvin opened his eyes again in a minute and looked at her.

"Reg? Waiting for something?"

"I'm trying to remember…"

"What?"

"What you just said, made me remember something… or almost remember something, and I can't quite grasp it…"

Corvin nodded his understanding. "I've been there. But right now, I can't remember much of anything. I hope I didn't do anything too stupid while I was with that woman. I would never have guessed that I would be so easy to enthrall."

"Welcome to the club."

"Well then… shall we head home?"

"Yeah, I guess so…"

Reg turned the key to start the engine. She put the car in gear.

"I don't know where your house is, so you're going to have to give me directions. Or at least the address, if you can't keep your eyes open."

"Sure." He gave her the address, and Reg entered it into her phone to get directions to his house. Her mind started to replay the conversation with Davyn about taking Corvin home or back to her own house.

Or take him back to The Crystal Bowl.

Reg hit the brake.

"Wait a minute!"

Corvin looked at her sourly. He really was tired and wanted to get home. She would have felt bad for him, but she was too close to figuring it out.

"Back to The Crystal Bowl," Reg said.

"I… don't want to go back to The Crystal Bowl."

"Because that's where you were. But how did he know that?"

"Who?"

"Davyn. How did he know that you had been at The Crystal Bowl?"

"I don't know what you're talking about."

"I called him. Because I didn't know where to take you or what to do with you."

Corvin blinked. He shook his head. "Why would you call Davyn?"

"You were in pretty bad shape. I thought maybe he could help out."

"He couldn't help. He's the head of my coven. If he did that, he'd get booted. He has to be an example of good behavior. Following the rule that the council imposes. I was shunned. He couldn't disobey that."

"Yeah, that's pretty much what he said. I think he still could have helped you. Why listen to a bureaucracy when someone is really in danger?"

"Clearly I wasn't in that much danger."

"No, but you could have been. He didn't know that. He didn't know what had happened to you, what kind of spell you had cast on you. You could be in a magical coma like Starlight. I know how powerful magic spells can be."

"Yes… you do. How is the cat? Any improvement?"

"A little. I tried to give him more strength again, but I don't know if it helped. I wish you had been there to help again."

"I would have preferred that to being magicked by a siren."

"At least she was only a part-siren, or you could have been in much worse trouble."

"Yes."

"So why wouldn't Davyn at least ask more questions to find out if you were really in any danger? And how did he know that you had been at The Crystal Bowl?"

"Maybe he was there when I was there with Norma Jean."

"Did you see him?"

"Not that I recall. But things are a little fuzzy around the edges as far as last night is concerned."

"Even if he was there when you were, how would he know twenty-four hours later that you were still just across the street? He didn't ask where you were. Why would he assume that you were close to The Crystal Bowl? That you had never really left there?"

Corvin pursed his lips, then shook his head. "I don't know. Maybe you're not remembering the conversation correctly. Maybe you did tell him where I was and try to tell him what kind of condition I was in. Or he might have understood more than you think. He might have been there when I was at The Crystal Bowl with Norma Jean, so he knew what kind of shape I would be in later."

"If he knew that you were eating supper with a siren, wouldn't he have been a little more concerned? Because chances were, you wouldn't be asleep on a park bench. You would be in your new digs under the ocean."

"Well… yes… but…"

He was usually more coherent than that. The magic must have really affected him. Reg felt bad about pushing the matter when he was clearly not in shape to be discussing it, but she pressed forward anyway.

"Somebody has been watching me. Following me. I couldn't figure out who it was, because he's never there when I turn and look. I thought maybe it was Damon, but it must have been Davyn. He followed us to the vet and back. He's been watching my house. He knew that you were at The Crystal Bowl. Because he was watching us."

Corvin's dark eyes showed that he was taking it in. "Davyn has been following us. Which of us?"

"Well, me for sure. You've been with me some of the time. I don't know whether he's been following you too or just me."

Corvin shook his head in disgust.

"Why is he doing that?" Reg demanded. "Don't tell me that he's jealous like Damon is? Honestly, I don't know what's wrong with all of you warlocks. I'm not the only game in town."

"Maybe you're the only part-siren."

Reg scowled and opened her mouth to retort.

"I'm only joking," Corvin assured her.

"Then why do you think he's following me? I'm getting tired of this."

"Because of me."

"Why? Because he's jealous?"

"No. Because one of his charges is to determine when I have served my sentence. Until he decides that I can be a productive member of the community. How is he supposed to know that without keeping an eye on me or at least checking in from time to time?"

"He's going to keep following you until he decides that you can be readmitted to the coven? But that could be…"

"It could be a long time. Or, if he decides that I am still breaking the rules of the coven, he could make the opposite decision. He could decide to bring me back before the tribunal for further judgment. They could bind me."

"But they wouldn't. I know, I've talked to Davyn about it a few times. They hate even having you shunned. They don't want to bind you."

"Reg… you don't understand the way that a community like this works. I know that in the real world out there, people get away with breaking the law all the time. They don't think that it's really a big issue. They'll let you off with a slap on the wrists, look the other way if they don't think you are really harming anyone else. But that's not the way it works here in Black Sands."

Reg cocked her head, considering this. She didn't think anything was any different in Black Sands. She had been pleased that they had at least decided to discipline Corvin for his misdeeds, but she didn't think that any of them were that concerned with making sure that he really complied with all of the rules of the coven or the community.

Corvin shook his head. "You don't understand, Reg. Here, with so many different magical folk in one place, we have to follow the rules strictly, or there end up being problems between the races. That can lead to a massacre or an all-out war. If a certain race thinks that they're not getting the protection they need, or not getting what they have been promised, they won't follow the rules anymore. We've worked very hard to get these treaties in place and to come up with rules that everyone can abide by. If you get one person who refuses to follow the rules, then…"

Reg shook her head. "Then what? All they did was shun you. You've tried to take my powers against the rules time after time, and nothing happens to you."

"I have obeyed the rules of the community… mostly. It was just that one time that I lost control. And I have been disciplined for that. If Davyn suspects that I am breaking other rules, or that I am going to break the rules, then he would be within his rights to bring me before the council again. And if he has proof that I'm doing something I'm not supposed to, then they will bind me this time."

Reg stared at Corvin, her eyes wide, trying to see as many details of his expression as she could in the darkness of the car. She tried to read how much he was telling her the truth and how much he was bluffing. She needed Damon there to tell her. Corvin was a very convincing liar.

"But you're not breaking the rules. So you don't have anything to worry about."

He nodded. His pupils were widely dilated to pull in as much of the dim light as they could. They made him look like a cat out hunting.

Reg felt a shift in him. The change from victim to predator once more. He was looking at her, trying to decide just how vulnerable she was and if he dared to make another attempt at taking her powers.

"Corvin."

"He can't be here all the time," Corvin said softly. "And he can't do anything to stop me if he's not here. He can't take me before the council if he doesn't know what happened."

"You're not thinking straight. You're still being affected by Norma Jean's magic."

"Do you think so?" He reached out and ran the back of one finger down her cheek.

Reg couldn't help shivering with pleasure, goosebumps popping up all over her skin. She knew that he was the predator now and she needed to fight back against him, but she couldn't convince herself to do it. She needed to raise the psychic walls again, build a fortress around herself to protect herself from him. But something was wrong. She couldn't seem to find the place in her brain that would do that. She couldn't remember the steps to go through. It was like she had forgotten how to ride a bike. Or even how to get onto one.

"You can't do this," she said firmly. "You were just telling me, they won't let you get away with it again. You can't break the rules again, or you will be bound."

"If they don't know, they can't do anything about it," he breathed, leaning closer to her.

"They will know. Do you think they won't know what's happened when I tell them you took my powers away? Do you think they won't be able to tell the difference?"

"It will be too late," Corvin reminded her. "They can bind me, but they can't force me to give back what I have taken. Once I have what I want, no one can take it away from me. I can only give it back voluntarily. And I won't be doing that again."

"No, Corvin!"

"And if they can't find you, they won't even know what happened. Reg Rawlins has run away before." He licked his lips. "They'll think you've just left town."

His hand slipped down to her shoulder. She knew that she had to push him away and get out of the car. The only way she could protect herself was to run, since her powers seemed suddenly to have abandoned her. But she was paralyzed. She couldn't move. She couldn't fight back against him. The words froze in her mouth, and she wasn't sure she was even protesting aloud anymore, or whether she was just saying the words in her mind, trying to communicate them to him telepathically.

What had come over him? Why was he suddenly so reckless and apparently ready to simply rip her powers from her by force, without even pretending to follow the ridiculous rules that the community had enacted?

"Corvin... stop..."

Tears sprang to her eyes. She could hear screaming in her head. She knew what was going to happen, and so did they. She had been left without the voices once before, completely alone and bereft, and she couldn't handle it again. She didn't know how to stop him, but she couldn't just sit there, frozen, and let him do it.

But she was prevented from moving.

His hand was on her shoulder, not holding her down, but controlling her powers, already starting to drain the energy from her. He put his other hand on her, pulling her closer. She fought against him, but it was all in her mind. Her body did not fight back. She couldn't reach her powers.

He was going to succeed this time. She was going to lose her powers again, and this time nothing would persuade him to give them back to her. Reg closed her eyes. She didn't want to see it happen.

★ CHAPTER TWENTY-ONE ★

THE DOOR OPENED, AND Reg nearly fell out of the car. Her eyes flew open, and she tried to figure out what was going on. A strong hand grabbed her and pulled her out, away from Corvin. When they broke physical contact, she felt both relieved and sorry at the same time. While she knew what he was capable of, her body wanted that contact with him so badly, it was maddening.

"Get out of here!" a voice ordered.

But Reg didn't run. She stood there blinking, trying to get control of her faculties again and to figure out what was going on. The dark, cloaked shape moved quickly around to Corvin's side, before he could get himself untangled from the seatbelt and get out of the car. The two forms collided as he got out, and Corvin was pushed back against the vehicle with a loud thump. He swore and protested, but Reg's mysterious rescuer didn't let him go. The two struggled until Corvin was leaning back against the car, puffing, unable to fight any longer. The stranger's hood came down, and it wasn't a stranger. It was Davyn.

Reg knew it. She *knew* he had been the one following them.

"What are you doing here?" Corvin growled. "You have no right to interfere!"

Davyn shook his head in disbelief. "No right? It's my responsibility to stop you. If I didn't, I would be just as responsible as you for the consequences."

"She was mine!"

Davyn leaned in, studying Corvin's face. "What is wrong with you?"

Corvin pounded his fists against the car in incoherent rage. "She was mine; you have no right to take her."

Davyn held Corvin's head still by pinning his jaw. He stared into Corvin's face.

"What happened?" he asked Reg.

"I don't know. We were talking. Everything was pretty normal, once he had some coffee and I got him to focus. And then everything just… shifted."

"What does that mean?"

"He was talking about how he had to follow the rules of the community. He had to do what you said, or you would bind him. I had just realized that you were the one watching us. Following us. Or me."

He glanced over at her and didn't deny it. How could he, when he had just rushed in to save the day?

"And then?"

"He was looking at me... and I knew he was going to try it again. He said it didn't matter; no one would find out. He said that... I would disappear so I wouldn't be able to tell anyone what he had done." She swallowed. He had never said that before. He had never threatened physical violence against her. He had always insisted that it was a two-way exchange, and had pretended that it was what was best for both of them. Even though he was feeding himself, he still pretended to care how she felt. Reg's throat was tight and hot again. She didn't want to cry in front of Davyn, but it was all so overwhelming.

"Sit down," Davyn advised. He clearly couldn't move from where he was and give Corvin any latitude to move. "On the curb here. Just get off your feet for a minute, I don't want you passing out. You've had a shock."

Reg wobbled over to the curb and lowered herself to the ground. It felt good to get off of her jelly-like legs.

"He wasn't acting like himself," Davyn said.

"No. I mean... he was, for a little while there. When I first woke him up, he was so loopy and silly. Saying how much he loved her. And then when I—"

"Loved her? Loved who?" Davyn demanded.

"Norma Jean. My mother. That's who he was with yesterday. She magicked him. Charmed him, like he does to me. Then she left him there behind, even though sirens usually drag their prey into the ocean—"

"Sirens? What are you talking about?"

"He said she's a siren. Or part-siren. Corvin thought maybe her instinct just wasn't strong enough to know what to do once she had him. So she left him there. And he was really dopey when I woke him up."

She waited for more questions and demands. Davyn just looked at her. Reg went on. "So I gave him coffee, and I... I connected with him, and he went back to normal..."

"What do you mean, you connected with him?"

"I touched his arm and made him look me in the eye... and then he went back to normal. We talked about what had happened, and he told me about her, what she was, and what had happened. He was tired, so I was going to take him home. Then I realized that you were the one following me. And we were talking about that, and how he had to follow the rules, and then he just changed."

"And it was like he was someone else."

Reg frowned. "Well... he was, and he wasn't. Usually, I can fight back when he starts to charm me. I've been working at it, and I'm getting better at protecting myself. But it was like I was paralyzed today. I couldn't do anything, physically or mentally. I was just... trapped like a..."

"Was there anything different about the way he was behaving? Different from when he is usually trying to charm you?"

It all came to Reg in a flood, all of the images at once. She tried to sort them out, to compare Corvin's usual stalking behavior to what had happened in the car. "Yeah... it was. There were no roses. Usually, I can smell roses when he starts charming me, so I have some warning, and I can still talk to him and fight back. But this time, it was like he was using different powers altogether. He was touching me and I couldn't move or do anything."

"And when I caught him, he didn't use magic to fight me," Davyn said. "Since he fed on the Witch Doctor, his powers are exponentially greater than mine, so why didn't he blast me away? He could crush me if he wanted to."

"But he didn't," Reg said softly.

"Like he was a different person."

They looked at each other, trying to understand what it all meant. Or maybe Davyn already understood what it meant and Reg was the only one who was too slow to understand the importance of these words. They were both silent for a few minutes. Corvin continued to look at Davyn with animosity, but he didn't use his powers to break Davyn's hold on him. He remained trapped, held against the car by physical force.

"Can you come over here?" Davyn asked Reg. "Are you feeling well enough to stand up?"

"I'm okay." Reg got slowly to her feet, though, making sure that she was steady enough to approach him. She went to Davyn's side and looked at Corvin, trying to comprehend what it was she was seeing.

"It's not him," Davyn said. "Is it?"

Reg looked into Corvin's eyes and still saw the predator there. Not like the Corvin she knew, always warm and inviting and promising her that she would be compensated for her sacrifice. That dark temptation was gone, replaced by something that was wholly predatory. Something that wanted to consume and destroy her, not to give her pleasure in return for her valuable powers. Looking at him, she didn't even think he cared about the powers, just about destroying her. Corvin had never wanted that. He'd hungered for what she had, but he hadn't wanted to hurt her.

"No." Reg shook her head and swallowed. Her eyes were hot with tears, and she didn't even know why. "No... who is he?"

She knew it was Corvin, yet it was not Corvin. She had been talking to him just minutes earlier, and he had been wholly himself, talking to her naturally just like he always did. And then something else had sprung up and taken over.

"You don't know?" Davyn asked.

"No."

"You said that you connected with him in the coffee shop, and then he was acting like himself instead of intoxicated. Can you do that again?"

Reg wasn't sure it was a good idea. She didn't want to connect with this monster, whoever he was. She knew that the physical form was Corvin. That hadn't changed. He wasn't a doppelgänger, because he had been Corvin only minutes before. But she wasn't sure she could connect with the old Corvin if he were still there under the malevolent entity on the surface. She was afraid.

"You can do it. Try."

Reg looked into the wide, black pools of Corvin's pupils. Though afraid to hold his gaze, she did her best anyway. She reached out and touched his arm. Tentatively. Not his bare skin, but with a layer of clothing between them so that the electricity wouldn't overwhelm her. She felt the familiar buzz and tried to communicate with him psychically. She had been able to many times before. Once they were connected, they could exchange more than words. It was a kind of communication she hadn't experienced outside of the spirit world.

"Corvin." She said his name, trying to reach down under the surface of the pool and pull him back up. He was still in there somewhere. She just needed to make the connection. The being on the surface struggled, trying to fight back against her and break the hold. Just like she had tried to break away from him, but had been unable to use her powers. She tightened her grip on Corvin's arm. "Corvin, come back. Talk to me."

"No," the being growled. He writhed under her grip, trying to pull away from both her and Davyn. "You may not!" He struggled more, muscles writhing in their grips. "He is mine!"

"He's not yours," Davyn said firmly. "Release him."

"You cannot do this!"

Reg pushed harder mentally. She knew Corvin. She could find him despite what the being possessing him tried to do. Corvin was still in there, just suppressed.

Corvin's body howled, his head pulled out of Davyn's grip and thrashed back and forth as it tried to free itself. Then he suddenly relaxed. Reg didn't release her hold on him. It could just be a trick, a final attempt to get away from her.

Corvin blinked. He looked at her from the depths, then gradually rose to the surface.

"Reg…?"

"Hey. You're back."

He swallowed and looked around. He seemed disoriented by what he saw. Himself, pinned against the car by Davyn. Reg holding on to his arm, leaning toward him, inside his mind trying to figure out what had just happened.

"Where… was I?"

"I don't know. Something else took over."

Corvin blinked some more, like she was shining a bright light in his eyes. Reg tried to mediate her connection with him, soften it a bit, so it wasn't so overwhelming. It was not polite to invade someone's mind.

Corvin looked at Davyn. "Something else?"

"Have you been playing with sirens?" Davyn asked, humor coming into his voice for the first time. Reg hadn't seen Corvin and Davyn interact before. She had wondered what kind of a relationship they had outside the courtroom, but she had never seen it. There was clearly some history of brotherhood and teasing between them.

"Uh… one siren," Corvin admitted. He thought about that. "Is that what happened? She took over my mind?"

Davyn nodded slowly. "That would be my guess. When she left you there, asleep, she didn't leave you. She was just waiting for the right opportunity."

"That's why she didn't come back?" Reg relaxed her hold on Corvin's arm. Still keeping contact with him, but not so strong. "She didn't come back because she was… inside Corvin? Just waiting for me to come looking for him?"

"She knew about your connection," Davyn said. "She must have known something about your history with each other. That you would gravitate toward each other. She knew that he could charm you, so she used that to her advantage."

"But it wasn't the same. I didn't smell roses and I couldn't fight back the way I usually can because… it was her magic instead of Corvin's."

Davyn nodded his agreement. Corvin looked at the two of them, making the mental connections gradually. Reg could feel how tired and confused he was. Norma Jean had used his body and his mind, and he was depleted. She released her hold on his arm to make sure that she wasn't pulling strength from him.

"Reg."

Reg nodded.

"I'm sorry… I didn't…"

"I know. I get it. It wasn't you."

"I never intended to let her possess me. I didn't know that she was. I've never… experienced anything like that before."

"It's okay."

They were all quiet for a few moments, considering the chain of events.

"Where is she now?" Reg asked. "Is she still inside of Corvin? How could she possess him when she has her own body?"

Davyn raised his eyebrows and didn't propose an answer. Reg looked at Corvin. "Do you know?"

"I didn't know sirens had that power… I told you there are only a few around the world; they haven't been well-studied. She has mixed blood; maybe she is more than just human and siren. Or maybe she had help." He met Reg's eyes. "Someone like W."

"Yeah."

"Who is W?" Davyn asked, trying to follow the conversation.

"He's her lover... an immortal."

"How incredible... I've never heard of a siren taking a lover. I mean, clearly they procreate, but they almost always drown their prey."

"She couldn't drown an immortal."

"No. Of course not. It makes logical sense, but I've never heard of such a thing."

Reg persisted with her question, which still had not been answered.

"But is she still in there, or is she gone?"

"And if she is gone, can she return at will?" Davyn added his own question.

"I don't know," Corvin admitted. "I think... I think she's gone, but would I be able to tell...?"

Davyn withdrew gradually, releasing Corvin. They both watched him to see what his reaction would be.

"I'm not going to attack you," Corvin said after a minute.

Davyn shrugged. "Had to make sure." He looked at Reg. "You should be getting back home. I'd like to know that you are safely ensconced in your own domicile."

"Really?" Reg raised her brows. "Domicile?"

"You are safest if you are at home. And take my advice and do not let Corvin or your mother in if they come calling."

"Well, I wouldn't, of course. But I don't know if that will stop them. I can't stay in my house forever."

"No... of course not," Davyn agreed, "But at least while we're figuring this out. It's the best I can do."

"Are you going to take him home, then?" Reg nodded toward Corvin.

Davyn hesitated. He scratched his bearded chin, and Reg knew that he was not trying to decide, he was trying to figure out how best to tell her 'no.'

"Why not? What other solution is there? You want to leave him here in his car to sleep it off? That didn't work so well the first time. Who knows if he'll wake up on his own? Maybe he'll end up unconscious like Starlight, with no way to wake him up."

"But how would taking him home prevent that?" Davyn countered. "I admit I don't have a good solution to suggest, but what else are we going to do? I can't have anything to do with him. I shouldn't even be here talking to the two of you. But I also have a duty to the public, and I had to balance those two duties."

"You're still not going to talk to Corvin? How exactly do you plan to sort this out?"

Davyn looked at Corvin, then dropped his eyes. "I will have to investigate independently. I can't have direct contact and communication with him." He gave an apologetic shrug, aimed in Corvin's direction.

Corvin looked too tired even to care. He looked at his car. "I can probably drive home."

"No, you can't," Reg insisted. "There's no way. You'll end up crashing and killing yourself or someone else. You're exhausted."

"I can't ask you to drive me. And I can't ask Davyn to drive me. I'm pretty much up the creek if I can't drive myself."

"I can drive you. It's not far, right? I can't abandon you like this, even if he can." She glared at Davyn.

"What if *she* comes back out? Without Davyn there, what are you going to do?"

"Well, now I know how to fight her," Reg said, pretending confidence she didn't feel. "I know that I just need to connect with you. As long as we stay connected, she can't come."

"How are you going to stay connected?" Davyn challenged. "You'll be driving. You'll be focused on that."

"How much attention do I need for driving? It's pretty much all automatic. I can't keep eye contact with him, but I can touch him. If we're physically in contact, it's easier."

Davyn shook his head. "This is too dangerous. I can't allow it."

"Allow it? Since when are you in charge of me? I'm not in your coven."

Corvin smirked. Even as tired as he was, he could enjoy Reg's rebellion against Davyn's attempts to control her. Reg wasn't going to do what anyone told her. Especially not a warlock who refused to cooperate with her even when she asked nicely. Davyn made a calming motion with his hands, maybe realizing that he had pushed it too far.

"Reg. Surely you can see the folly in this. You need to go home where it is safe. You have wards there against malevolent forces. Out here, and in Corvin's car, you are at the mercy of evil forces. You can't protect yourself against them."

"Now that I know who it is and what to do about it, I can," Reg insisted. She motioned to the car. "Get in," she told Corvin. She started to walk around to the other side of the car to drive. "And unless you're going to help out, I'll be seeing you around," she told Davyn. She didn't expect him to jump in and change his mind. He was too stubborn, too much a rule enforcer. Reg, on the other hand, was not. "And you know what? I'm tired of seeing a shadow sneaking around following me here and there and everywhere. I don't know exactly how you do it, but stop. If you want to follow me, you stay visible. And I'd prefer that you not follow me. I don't like being stalked."

"I wasn't stalking you. I was trying to keep you safe." Davyn shifted his stance uncomfortably. "I am responsible for the members of my coven, even when they are under discipline. If Corvin were to hurt you again, then I would be held partially responsible. Knowing that he could be a danger to you, and yet you are still seeing him socially… I can't just ignore that. If I don't keep track of him or you… the only option is to bind him."

"Well, I've told you to take a hike, so you can report that. I don't want you following me. I can take care of myself."

Reg got into the driver's seat and pulled the door shut with a slam. She couldn't believe that Davyn would refuse to talk to Corvin, but still follow them around, monitoring whether he was keeping the rules of the community. She couldn't deal with him. If he wasn't willing to actually help her, then he was just one more person in her way.

"Okay, you'd better give me directions."

★ CHAPTER TWENTY-TWO ★

THEY WERE BOTH ANXIOUS in the car, neither knowing for sure what was going to happen. Even though Reg had told Davyn that she knew what to do if Norma Jean put in another appearance, she wasn't so sure. Corvin did his best. He kept a hand on her leg, keeping a physical connection to her as she had suggested. He gave her his address and then directed her, but his voice was sleepy, and he was drifting in an out. Reg was afraid of getting lost, or that the intruder would reassert herself when Corvin fell asleep, breaking his psychic connection with Reg. She nudged him.

"Stay awake. Come on. It's not much farther, right?"

"No." He yawned. "Nearly there."

"Do you think that Davyn will stay away? Now that I've told him to?"

Not that she cared what his answer was. She just wanted to keep him engaged so that he wouldn't fall back asleep. They needed to work together as a team if she were going to keep her mother's spirit away from them.

"I wouldn't count on it," Corvin admitted.

"Did you know that he could do that? Turn invisible?"

"No. We don't all share our powers with each other. Sometimes you know someone's biggest gift, especially if you've known each other for a long time because it can be hard to control them when you're a little kid. You go to school with someone, or you've known their family for a few generations, and you know what their gifts are or what gifts run in their family. But invisibility… no, I never knew that Davyn could do that. He's apparently pretty proficient at it, too."

"So he could be sneaking around, spying on the warlocks in his coven all the time."

"Why would he want to do that? Being part of a community like this doesn't mean policing everyone. That's not the purpose of a coven. He doesn't want to have to enforce discipline. What reason would there be for him to creep around and watch people invisibly?"

"I dunno. I'd take invisibility. I'd like to be able to see what other people were saying and doing when I wasn't around. See what they really think."

"You think that people are talking about you behind your back?"

"Of course they are. Don't you?"

Corvin squeezed her leg. He looked up the street and motioned with his unoccupied hand. "Just up there, at the end of the road."

Reg looked at the dark, forbidding houses. It was getting late, so she supposed it made sense that all of the non-magical practitioners were off to bed. But it made the neighborhood feel empty and lonely.

"Thank you," Corvin said. He shifted his hand, but didn't remove it from her leg. "I appreciate you doing this, especially knowing the danger."

"What should I do with your car?"

He rubbed at the corner of his eye. "I suppose… drive it to your house. Tomorrow, I'll either find someone to drive over with me and pick it up, or I'll take a bus and a walk to your house."

"Are you sure?"

"You can't leave it here. Then you wouldn't have a safe way to get home. I don't know if the buses are still running right now, and for sure they're not the safest place to be at night all by yourself. It would be one thing if you were out with a group of friends, but alone like this… I'd like to know that you are safe. I don't want to be worrying over whether you can make it home or not."

"Okay." Reg was happy to take his car. She didn't want to have to catch a bus or call a cab either. He could sort it out the next day when it was safe to do so. "Thanks. Um… I'll let you know when I get home. So you don't worry." She looked at the keys and unclipped the ring that held what appeared to be his house key. "You'll need that."

"Yes. Thank you." He lifted his hand slowly from her leg to take the key, and they both did their best to maintain the psychic connection between them. It was a strangely intimate dance, him slowly withdrawing and getting out of the car, both of them remaining connected so that the predator could not reassert herself. Corvin shut the car door and Reg immediately locked it. She let out a breath. They had made it safely. He couldn't reach her. She could go home and go to bed and not worry about being attacked.

Corvin walked up to his door, and she watched him in. He turned to wave just before shutting the door.

Once Reg got home, she would be safe and could go to sleep and forget the crazy magical world around her.

Reg breathed a sigh of relief when she reached home. She sat in Corvin's car in front of the big house for a few minutes, just breathing and looking around and feeling for any disturbing presence. She hadn't seen any shadow of Davyn, but that didn't mean he wasn't around. She wasn't going to discount the possibility. She could take care of herself, but if Davyn wanted to make sure she got home safely, why should that bother her?

She eventually got out of the car and walked to the cottage in the back. The blooms in the garden were giving off a heady scent, making her think of Corvin again. Reg couldn't help feeling a little bit sorry for him. She had lived with Norma Jean in her head for a long time. She knew what that was like. It probably wasn't the same for him. He couldn't hear her voice like Reg had been able to. But Reg hadn't had to deal with her body being taken over by Norma Jean, either. She'd only been a constant voice in Reg's head. It would have been a lot worse if she'd had to fight for control over her own body.

Reg pulled her phone out of her pocket and tapped a quick message to Corvin that she had reached home safely. The garden was quiet and peaceful, cool in the evening, and she breathed in the smell of the flowers and tried to relax her body.

If she could just know that Starlight was going to be okay, she would be happy and at peace. Until then, she was waiting for him to recover, always waiting and worrying.

Reg sighed and walked the rest of the way up to her door and let herself in. As she stepped over the threshold and pushed the door shut behind her, she heard and felt it thump against something. She turned to see what was blocking it from closing. A woman stood there in the breach, holding it open. Reg lunged, trying to slam the door shut. If she could shut it and close the deadbolt, she would be safe.

But Norma Jean wasn't about to let that happen. She put all of her weight into shoving it open so that she could enter the house.

"Reg? What's wrong, honey? I just came over for a visit."

"You can't come in!" Reg barked. "There are wards against you here. You can't come in!"

Even as she said it, Norma Jean floated into the room as if there were no barriers. Reg cursed under her breath. What was the point in having the wards there? They never seemed to protect her. It seemed like there was always some rule that she didn't know about. Some loophole that everyone else could exploit.

"What are you doing here? You shouldn't be here!"

Norma Jean just gave a puzzled smile, as if she couldn't figure out what Reg had to be upset about. "I came to see you," she said innocently. "Don't you want to see your own mother? We've lost so much time, Regina. Don't you think it's time to start recovering it? Why don't we have a little visit? We could stay up and watch scary movies. Make some popcorn. You're not tired, are you? It isn't the witching hour yet," she said in a teasing tone.

"I *am* tired," Reg said desperately, hoping that Norma Jean would listen to her. "I need to get to bed. It's been a long, tough day."

"Why don't you tell me about it, and I'll make you some tea. That will help you to get to sleep."

"No, really, I'm just going to fall into bed. We can talk about it later. Why don't you give me a call in the morning and we'll set something up?"

Norma Jean's smile was fixed and unwavering. "I can at least see my daughter off to bed. Do you know how long it's been since I was able to tuck my baby girl in?"

Her honeyed tone set Reg's skin creeping. She had looked at this same being in Corvin's eyes just an hour earlier. She'd seen the hate there. Now Norma Jean was behaving as if nothing had happened. She was using her sweetest manner to suck Reg in, to make her think that she was sincere in her wish to spend some time and mend fences with Reg. They were the same eyes, yet there was no hint of the malice that had lurked there earlier.

"I'll make some tea," Norma Jean repeated. She glided toward the kitchen. Reg stared at her. She sure as hell wasn't going to drink anything her mother made for her. She sat down on the couch and watched Norma Jean like a hawk, but didn't see her put anything into the drink. Reg was experienced with sleight of hand. She should have been able to see it, but Norma Jean moved slowly and smoothly, and her hands were in view all the time. Reg still couldn't see her put anything into the cup but the tea that Sarah had prepared for her and the boiling water.

"There. That will help you get to sleep much better," Norma Jean assured her. "It certainly is nice of that woman to take such good care of you. She isn't your mother, but she is so very nice to you."

"She's been a good friend," Reg said. "Just a friend. She's not trying to mother me and usurp your place." Reg didn't want Norma Jean going after Sarah next. Sarah was an experienced old witch and could, Reg was sure, protect herself, but it was better if she didn't have to, if Reg could head off Norma Jean before she even began an attack.

Norma Jean smiled. "That's nice, dear." She set everything out on the tea tray and carried it over to the living room, where she set it down on the coffee table. "There you go. Let's have a nice soothing cup of tea together."

Reg picked up one of the cups before Norma Jean could decide which one to give to her. She sat with it in her hands, staring down into the tea leaves. What was in her future? A quick but painful death from poison? A long and lingering one? Having to listen for hours to made-up stories of Norma Jean's past? Reg put the cup to her lips and pretended to drink.

"Where were you earlier?" she asked Norma Jean carefully. "I thought I'd see you downtown. Didn't you go there with Corvin?"

"Corvin?" Norma Jean's eyebrows went up. "Oh, such a nice man. But that was yesterday, sweetie—not today. I haven't seen him today. I was looking for you."

"Oh. Sorry I missed you."

Norma Jean beamed at her and sipped her tea. Reg couldn't tell if she was really drinking it or not, but she appeared to be. Maybe there was no poison. Maybe Norma Jean just planned to use a spell on her. Like she had on Corvin.

"Do you remember him from when I was little? He came to visit us once."

Norma Jean's brows drew down in a frown of concentration. "How could that be? No, I don't remember ever meeting him before."

"He had a cat with him. One like Starlight."

The small frown turned into a scowl. "I remember that cat," she spat. "Why did he come?"

"He came to help. The cat and Corvin were both there to help." Reg didn't mention her own presence there, as an adult as well as the child who belonged in the timeline. That would raise too many questions.

"I didn't need any help."

"You knew some dangerous people back then. People that could have hurt me. Or you."

Norma Jean took a thoughtful sip of her tea. "Do you remember much about that? You were just real little. I didn't think you could remember anything."

"I remember some stuff."

Norma Jean's thumb stroked the handle of the teacup. "I don't think it was that bad. I don't remember a lot of it, but I don't think social services should have taken you away. They're always doing that. You hear about it in the news. They take kids away for no reason at all, and then it takes the family forever to get them back, if ever."

"You were drinking, doping, and hooking."

"But that didn't hurt you. Addicts can still be good moms. Housewives get addicted to meth and their husbands and children never even know it. They shouldn't be able to take kids away just because of that."

Reg stared at her. Did Norma Jean truly not remember what kind of a mother she had been and what kind of life they had led? Was she telling herself stories and rewriting history, or was she just trying to fool Reg?

She didn't want to trigger the rage she had seen in Corvin's eyes earlier, but she also didn't want to let Norma Jean get away with the fiction. "You weren't a high-class mother with a pill addiction. You were mainlining." The image of her mother shooting up was burned into her brain, something she could never forget.

Norma Jean shrugged as if there were no difference. Reg kept her mouth closed. They sat and drank in silence. Or Norma Jean drank, and Reg pretended, hoping that wetting her lips would not be enough to poison her.

"I'm getting really tired," Reg said finally. "We'll have to put this on pause and get together again later."

Norma Jean faked a yawn and looked at her watch. "I suppose so. I thought a young person like you would want to stay up late."

"I have things to do in the morning, and it's been a long day." Reg stood up. Norma Jean stayed sitting there for a moment longer, then grudgingly got to her feet.

"I had to find a hotel. It's a nasty place, I would much rather have stayed with you."

"No, I don't have the space. I'm sure you'll be much happier there."

Reg shuddered to think of what might have happened if she had allowed Norma Jean to stay with her, forced to share the same bed or sleep on the floor. If Corvin was right about sirens needing a lot of territory and killing each other for it, Norma Jean probably would have killed her in her sleep.

She walked Norma Jean to the door and saw her out. Norma Jean eyed her before she stepped out the door, moving her body at an angle as if she intended to give Reg a hug goodbye. Reg shifted away to try to avoid any physical contact. Eventually, Norma Jean nodded and walked out of the cottage.

"We'll get together tomorrow," she suggested. "Maybe for lunch."

Reg nodded her agreement, though she didn't intend to go anywhere with Norma Jean. She would try to avoid any further contact.

★ CHAPTER TWENTY-THREE ★

REG HAD TYPED A text to Corvin almost before she finished shutting and locking the door. She sent it out with an accompanying swoosh sound and moved over to the window to see if Norma Jean were really leaving. She strained to see her mother walking down the path away from the cottage, but eventually was satisfied that she had left and wasn't lurking around just waiting for her first opportunity to return and attack Reg. She looked down at her phone, expecting an immediate reply from Corvin. But there wasn't one.

She tapped her foot and looked down at it, willing Corvin to message her back. She even closed her eyes and tried to reach out to him mentally to prod him along, but she was too exhausted after the day's events to raise the mental faculties. She went to the kitchen to check the fridge for something real to eat. And a trip to the cupboard to fetch a glass of Jack Daniels to replace the sleepy tea that Norma Jean had prepared. She looked at the tea, wondering if she could call Jessup and convince her to send it to the police lab for testing. Maybe they could find out what was in it. Maybe that would help her to save Starlight.

She would ask in the morning. Jessup would either be asleep or on duty, and neither one would bode well for Reg getting a favor if she interrupted her with a call. Reg looked down at the phone. Still no reply. She reached down to change the water in Starlight's bowl and had to stop herself. Starlight wasn't there.

She wanted to talk to someone about Norma Jean. Starlight was a good listener, even if he didn't contribute a lot of fresh content to a conversation.

Reg tossed her phone down on the counter, more roughly than she should have. It wouldn't help anything to break the phone. But she was frustrated and wanted to do something to show it.

There was some fried chicken in the fridge. Reg didn't remember when she had gotten it, but it still smelled good, so she put it in the microwave to heat.

No messages came in while she was waiting for the chicken to heat up.

When the microwave beeped, Reg pulled the too-hot dish out, and then left it on the counter, turning around to pick up her phone. She couldn't wait any longer. She dialed through to Corvin. If he wasn't going to answer her text, he'd have to answer a call.

It rang through to his voicemail. Reg hung up and tried again.

And a third time.

Finally, the call was answered. Corvin's slurry voice. "Reg? What is it?"

"She was here!"

"What?"

"Norma Jean was here. In my house!"

There was a silence while he considered that. "Well… why did you let her in?"

"I didn't! I tried to shut the door and she forced it open. And then she just walked in. I thought the wards were for my protection and were supposed to keep that from happening! Is there some loophole? Some exception for sirens or people who are related to me? I'm getting really frustrated with all of these exceptions!"

"If she walked in, then you must have invited her. Are you sure you didn't do anything that might have been construed as an invitation?"

"No. I didn't ask her in. I didn't open the door to her. I didn't give her a key. I tried to shut her out. I told her she wasn't welcome. And she still just walked in."

Corvin cleared his throat. Reg pictured him rubbing eyes sticky with sleep and trying to concentrate on what she was saying. It wasn't fair of her to put him on the spot like that. The poor man had been asleep, after the rather traumatic experience of having his brain and body ripped out of his power.

"The… has she been to your house before?"

"Yes, one time. But just because she's been here once before, that doesn't give her the permission to come back in again later, does it? Because that would be crazy."

"No. But she may have left something personal behind. Something that she would have to come back to retrieve later. In that case, she might have been able to break the wards."

Reg swore. She looked around the cottage, trying to see anything that was out of place. What had Norma Jean left behind?

"Are you okay?" Corvin asked.

"She gave me tea. I don't know if it was poisoned or not. I didn't drink it."

"Good girl."

"Do you think that's why she's here in Black Sands? To kill me?"

"It's a distinct possibility."

"Why? It doesn't make any sense. I haven't been hunting in the same waters. I'm halfway across the country from her. Why would she have to come here to kill me?"

"Sirens are very—"

"Competitive. Yeah, that's what you told me. Does she need half the world for herself? When she's not even a full-blooded siren?"

"I don't know. Sirens have not been studied very much. We know very little about how they live and socialize with each other and work out their territories and differences."

Reg sighed in exasperation.

"Go to bed," Corvin advised. "I need some sleep."

Both the drink and the chicken were still on the counter when Reg got up the next morning.

★ CHAPTER TWENTY-FOUR ★

'M SURE YOU MUST have fairies in your garden," Reg told Sarah the next morning. "I keep seeing things there every night—little lights and movement. I hear voices or bells or birds singing when they shouldn't be up. Maybe it's not fairies; maybe there is something else that I don't know about. But I was looking online, and those are things that it says you see if you have fairies."

Sarah smiled. "Google isn't the best tool for diagnosing illnesses or paranormal happenings in your garden."

Reg walked with her around the cottage to the back garden, and they looked around. Sarah had a big travel mug of tea and was wearing garden clogs. Reg had put on some flip-flops in order to join her in her survey of the garden, which was literally blooming under Forst's care.

"It's so beautiful," Reg said. "I can see why the fairies would want to come here."

But she was going by what she had found online, and those articles were talking about the little flying fairies. The fairies that Reg had met in real life liked plants and gardens and surrounded themselves with living things even inside their homes, but they were tall, pale, remote people, not little flying fairies like Tinkerbell. She couldn't imagine Lord Bernier or Calliopia's parents flitting through Sarah's garden to have a look at her plants. Even though Sarah's garden was spectacular, they would more than likely knock on the door and ask permission to have a look at it—excessively formal—than to flit in and make themselves at home. She didn't think they could turn themselves into the diminutive creatures that she'd seen on TV and the web.

"I don't know what you have been seeing, but I don't think we have been having visitations from fairies," Sarah told her.

Reg sighed. She'd liked the idea. She looked around for Forst. He was often camouflaged in the garden; she wouldn't even see him until he decided to speak to her. They waited for a few minutes before he showed up, pushing a wheelbarrow full of supplies. It was so laden down; Reg wasn't sure if she would have been able to push it herself.

Forst's face broke into a wreath of happy wrinkles when he saw her there. He put the wheelbarrow handles down and hurried over to her. "We are so pleased to have a visit from Reg Rawlins today!"

Reg's cheeks burned at his effusive greeting. Sarah might not be able to hear it, but she could certainly see the expression on his face and his eagerness to take her hands in his. Reg smiled, looking to the side in her embarrassment.

"Hi, Forst. It's so nice to see you again," she said aloud so that Sarah would be able to hear at least her half of the conversation.

Forst turned to Sarah with greater reserve. He bowed to her, doffing his red cap. He didn't say anything to her in his 'inside words,' knowing that, like most of the rest of the humans, she wasn't able to hear them. Sarah knew it was difficult for him to use his outside words, which was one reason she had stopped in at the cottage to see if Reg was available.

"Everything is looking so beautiful," she told him. "It is the most beautiful garden in the neighborhood. Everyone says so."

He smiled and nodded.

"I would like to add more wild herbs and magical plants," Sarah said. "I've always wanted a crafting garden, but I don't have the green thumb that you do. It's been the most I could do to keep a respectable-looking vegetable garden."

"What would the lady like in her crafting garden?"

Reg relayed the question to Sarah. Sarah had a notepad in her apron pocket, and she pulled it out to list off some of the plants she had thought of. When she had read it, Forst took it out of her hand. He looked at the list and looked around the garden, nodding and scratching his white-bearded chin. He pulled off his cap, rubbed his head, and put it back on again. He looked down at the list.

"I will get started on this," he agreed. "I will need to prepare the right location. Then I will find some good plants to start with. It might take a while to get it established. They are different plants; not all will like the same soil."

When Reg had repeated this to Sarah, she nodded. "You know much better than I do where they should be planted and whether they will compete with each other or be beneficial to each other. The list is only a starting point. You will need to decide how they will like it here and whether they will live together."

Forst smiled and nodded, happy that Sarah understood this.

Reg thought about Norma Jean and the idea that she thought Reg was competing with her, even though she lived so far away. When Norma Jean had visited, she hadn't expressed any animosity. And her behavior ensorcelling Corvin and then leaving him behind suggested that she might be acting instinctually without even knowing why. Maybe her negative feelings toward Reg, whatever they were, were unconscious as well.

"Do fairies like herbs?" she asked, not wanting to drop the previous topic. Now that Forst was there, maybe he could give her some clue as to what she had been seeing.

"Fairy folk? Certainly." Forst agreed. "Fairies like all natural plants."

"Maybe they'll come here to look at them. Or to ask for samples."

"Cuttings?" Forst suggested.

"Cuttings."

"Fairy folk do not come into the town," Forest said with a head shake. "Very rare. Only for important business. There are too many autos and houses, not enough living green."

"I thought maybe some of them have been in the yard and the garden. I thought I might have seen some."

"In Miss Sarah's garden?" Forst shook his head, chuckling, "They would not kommen here."

Reg tried to hide her disappointment. "I was sure... what do you think I saw, then?"

Still chuckling, Forst asked her what she had seen. Reg described it the best she could, and also tried to send him mental images of what she had seen and heard over the past few days. Forst's eyes lit up. "Not fairy folk," he told her. "Elves!"

"Elves?" Reg repeated aloud.

Sarah looked surprised. "Really? Elves in my garden?"

Forst nodded emphatically. "Elves. It is almost solstice. That is when they move house. Set up somewhere new."

"They're not setting up house in my garden, are they?" Sarah asked in alarm.

"No," Forst looked around, shaking his head. He walked through the garden, looking up into trees and down under bushes and around other plants that Reg was not familiar with. He shook his head again. "They come through here, mayhap. But not set up house here. You are on their way. They stop to refresh and frolic here."

Reg laughed, pleased. "What are they like? Are they little like on TV? Or are they big like the fairies? Can I see them, or can humans only see the lights? They're like little fireflies out here, swirling around."

"Elven folk take different forms. They may come through here as little people or lights. But they can also appear tall. Taller than me."

Not that Forst was particularly tall. But that meant they could be human height or tiny little lights. Reg was thrilled at the idea. And she was the one who had discovered them there. Of course, if Starlight had been around, he would have been the one watching them out the window. He would yowl at her to come see, and she would...

There was a soft touch on her arm. Reg focused on Forst's face. He was looking back at her with concern. "Reg Rawlins is not happy. What is wrong, fair maiden?"

Reg tried to shrug it off. She was sure he had probably already heard her woes. "It's just... my cat, that's all."

Forst turned and looked at the cottage, at the window where Starlight usually perched to watch him and the birds and whatever else appeared in his yard. Where he would have watched the elves frolicking. "Where is the cat? What has happened?"

"He's sick. Didn't anyone tell you?"

Forst shook his head. Reg looked at Sarah. Sarah might have at least mentioned it to Forst. But maybe she hadn't cared, hadn't thought that it was anything of importance.

Sarah shook her head. "I didn't think there was anything he could do, so why involve him?"

"No… no reason why you would." Reg gave a sad shake of her head. There wasn't anything anyone could do.

"Sick with what?" Forst prodded.

"He was poisoned… and magicked. He is unconscious." Reg didn't know whether Forst would know the word or what it meant. "Asleep. Near to death."

"Oh!" Forst took off his cap and wiped his brow. He wrung the hat with his hands, looking distressed. "Oh! You should have told me! How long? What physik has he had?" Forst shook his head. "These humans do not know good physik!"

"They've done everything they can. He's been at the doctor. I took him the plant, in case Starlight had eaten any of that. And there were all of the plants around for solstice. I didn't know that they could be poisonous to cats… But apparently… it looks like he was poisoned intentionally, he didn't just eat something without knowing it would hurt him."

"I must see him. Will you bring him here?"

"I don't think I can bring him here. Could you go with me? To the vet?"

"What is the vet?"

"A doctor for animals. Veterinarian. He is good at taking care of sick animals, but he doesn't know exactly what is wrong with Starlight, and he's not a practitioner. He doesn't know about the spell or how to counter it."

"Why would you take him to such a place?" Forst asked in alarm. "We must go to him. He cannot be left there, all alone, without an experienced physician."

Reg nodded. "Okay. Yes. If you want to come, and think you can do something for him, then please do. We can go over there…" she looked at the time on her phone screen. "They open in half an hour."

"We must go." Forst looked at Sarah. "The garden will have to wait for a few hours."

Reg translated for him and explained that Forst thought he might be able to do something for Starlight.

"Well, of course you must go see him," Sarah said. "The garden won't miss you."

Forst blinked at her, looking hurt.

"I mean, of course it will miss you," Sarah amended quickly. "But it will be fine until you get back."

"Yes," Forst agreed out loud, and gave a nod.

★ CHAPTER TWENTY-FIVE ★

R EG HURRIED BACK INTO the house to get her purse and grab a granola bar for breakfast, and then was out to the front to drive with Forst over to the vet's. Then she realized she'd left her keys in the cottage, and went back to get them, lock up properly, and unlock the car. Forst climbed into the passenger seat beside her, and Reg wondered if she should be using a booster seat to keep him safe. She didn't have one and it would probably be rude to ask, so she just kept her mouth shut about it. Forst watched out the window with great interest as they drove. Reg looked over at him.

"You don't drive much?"

"No. Gnomen don't drive."

"You probably could. It isn't very hard."

He looked at his short legs. "Must reach the brakes."

"Well, yes. But they can make extensions for the pedals. Or they can put in hand controls, so you don't need pedals."

He shook his head at the silliness of this idea. Reg shrugged. She didn't care whether he drove or not. It was only a suggestion.

"Do you think you will be able to help Starlight?"

"Cats are not the same as plants," he said slowly. "They are not as easy to make well. But I can try."

"Yeah. I sure hope there's something you can do. I don't know what I'll do without him if he doesn't make it."

"Do not think that way. We will see what is the matter and help him."

"Okay."

Reg looked in her rearview mirror for any tailing vehicles. She couldn't see Davyn anywhere. But then, he was difficult to see when she was looking for him. It was easier when she wasn't looking and just caught the movement out of the corner of her eye. She wondered what his other powers were. He was the leader of his coven, so he obviously had some ability to talk to people and get things done. He didn't seem to get bogged down in the bureaucracy; it came pretty naturally to him. He could turn invisible to follow her around. What else was he hiding? Corvin hadn't known about that power, but he must know about other gifts that Davyn had. He wouldn't be a leader of the warlock coven if he didn't have some power he could show his people, would he?

She looked back at the road and wished she could get to the vet without having to wait for all of the traffic lights. That would be a nice power to have. The ability to change traffic lights to what you wanted them to be.

It seemed like it took forever to get to the vet's office but, of course, it hadn't. She was just in such a hurry to see what Forst could do for her cat. He seemed quite confident in being able to do something for him.

Reg nodded at the receptionist. What did the woman think about her coming to the vet with someone different every day? That she was popular and had a lot of friends? Or that she was a flake and kept bringing all of these weirdos by because she couldn't bear to see her cat alone?

"Can we see him?" Reg asked, not sure what else to say.

"If you'll just have a seat, I'll have someone get him ready."

Reg breathed a sigh of relief. He wasn't dead, then. She wouldn't have said that to Reg if Starlight were dead.

She and Forst sat on the waiting room chairs. Forst's feet didn't reach the floor, and he watched his feet, swinging them back and forth. Eventually, the vet's assistant invited Reg to follow her. Forst jumped down behind her, and they walked in a line to the small examination room where they had brought Starlight. Forst stood up on one of the visitor chairs to be tall enough to look at Starlight. He ran his hands over the cat, shaking his head and making noises expressing his distress. Reg stood beside him, waiting for his verdict.

"Can you do something for him? Do you think you can help?"

"Poor beast," Forst said inside her head. "Poor, poor beast."

"Can you do something?"

The vet arrived. He looked at Forst with a slight frown, and Reg was afraid he was going to tell Forst not to climb on the furniture or that he wasn't allowed to touch Starlight, but he didn't. He just gave a bemused look and then focused on Reg.

"Still not much change," he said soberly. "But he hasn't declined, either, so that's good. I wish I could give you more hope, but..."

"Forst might be able to do something," Reg said, motioning to him.

The vet raised an eyebrow. He probably knew all of the vets in a hundred-mile radius and knew that Forst was not certified.

"The plant," Forst said aloud, in his curt way.

Reg looked at him. "What? I left the plant here so that they could test it," she said tentatively.

"We haven't been able to identify it, exactly," the vet offered. "I think we have the family narrowed down, but it is a very unusual—"

"Why did you not give it to him?" Forst asked Reg, using his inside words again.

"I thought you said it was poisonous. You said to make sure that he didn't eat it."

Forst shook his head impatiently. "No, he should not eat it. But if he has been poisoned, it is a remedy."

"The plant is a poison and a remedy?" Reg asked incredulously.

The vet looked at her, obviously thinking that she was off her head.

"Can you bring the plant here?" Reg asked him. "Forst thinks that we can use it to help Starlight."

"Alright... but I have to tell you... I can't in good conscience recommend you using a plant that we can't even identify, much less know the properties of."

"I don't care. Forst knows."

He nodded and left the examination room. He probably figured they couldn't make things any worse. Starlight would eventually die if they were not able to reverse the damage that had already been done.

★ CHAPTER TWENTY-SIX ★

T HE VET BROUGHT THE plant into the examination room. His assistant stood behind him, straining to see past him to what was going on. She wanted to see the show too, if there was going to be one. They probably didn't think that Forst could do anything about Starlight's condition, but Reg had hope. He was very confident, and she had seen some extraordinary things in the time she'd been in Black Sands. A gnome curing a cat would not be the weirdest thing.

Forst reached across the examining table to take the plant from the vet. He placed it before him very gently. He touched various leaves and bent down to examine them and to whisper to the plant. Even though Reg could hear his inside words, she couldn't make out what he was saying to the plant. The words were not meant for her. He pulled off a couple of brown leaves and examined the bent stems and the moisture of the soil. Reg felt a pang of guilt over neglecting the little plant. They had just thrown it into a box with all of the Yule decorations and then had left it at the vet's office without giving him any instructions on its care, thinking that it was the culprit in Starlight's poisoning. She hadn't cared how the plant was treated once she gave it to the vet. But plants were important to Forst. He could understand them and treated them like his children.

The vet watched this process without comment. He didn't roll his eyes, and he didn't sigh and leave, saying that he had better things to do.

Forst picked a couple of green leaves from the plant. He pinched them between his fingers and rolled them around, releasing a pungent smell into the air. He held it under Starlight's nose and, after a minute, he peeled back Starlight's lip and mushed the ball of crushed leaves into his cheek. He massaged Starlight's jowls and throat, and Reg imagined the healing juices from the leaves running down Starlight's throat a drop at a time.

Forst petted Starlight in long strokes, watching his face and waiting for a reaction. Reg shifted restlessly. Should they see a reaction right away? Would it take a day or two before they saw any change?

There was a low growling noise from Starlight.

Reg gasped and bent in closer. "Starlight?" She petted him, her eyes filling with tears. "Star, I'm right here."

Forst didn't try to stop her from touching Starlight. Reg scratched Starlight's ears tentatively, unsure whether he was waking up, or still deep beneath the surface.

"Is he okay?" she asked Forst. "Is he waking up? What should I do?"

"He is your beast," Forst said as if she should know what to do by virtue of that fact.

Reg wiped away a tear with the back of her wrist. The vet was edging closer.

"May I…?"

Reg nodded and withdrew to give him some space. Forst didn't move. He was still watching Starlight intently, one hand on his side. The vet did his best to work around Forst. He listened to Starlight's heart with his stethoscope, moving it from one place to another. He peeled back Starlight's eyelids to look at his eyes and Reg saw the big pupils shrink rapidly when exposed to the light of the room. She put her hand on Starlight, stopping the doctor.

"He should rest. I don't think we should be poking and prodding him."

The vet withdrew. "There is an improvement," he admitted. "I don't know what that plant is, but…"

"It is healing," Forst said. "But it will not cure all of his trouble. We need to take him home. Continue to work on him there."

"I wouldn't recommend it. Here, we can monitor his vital signs, keep giving him IV fluids, make sure that he's getting all of the care that he needs. If you take him away from here, he could go into shock, and be gone by the time you could get him back." He looked at Reg, making sure she understood these points.

Reg looked at Forst. He was the one who knew what to do and had finally given Starlight a treatment that was helping, not the vet. The vet could be as cautious as he liked, but that hadn't helped Starlight so far. He had kept Starlight alive, but that was all he had been able to do.

"If Forst says we need to take him home, then that's what we'll do," she said firmly. "There isn't anything else you can do for him, is there?"

"No. That's true."

Reg nodded at Forst. "We'll take him home."

The transfer was nerve-racking. Reg kept hearing the doctor's dire warnings and was worried that the minute they got away from the vet's office, Starlight would go into seizures and be dead by the time they could get either home or back to the vet. But unless that happened, taking him home was the right thing to do. Even if he died when they got there. He should be in his home, the surroundings that were familiar to him and the people he loved. Reg swallowed a lump in her throat and again checked on Starlight, making sure that he was comfortably wrapped in the towel the vet's assistant had swaddled him in and that he looked as comfortable as possible. Forst held Starlight cradled in his arms for the journey home, the little plant nestled in a jumbo cup holder so it wouldn't tip over. Forst checked both assiduously on the way home, and all arrived back at the house safely.

"He is doing well," Forst promised, when Reg leaned over again to see how Starlight was.

"Is he going to wake up?"

"He will. We will get him inside where he will be comfortable."

Reg wanted to take Starlight from Forst, but she refrained and let him carry her furry familiar to the cottage in the back, while she juggled her keys and purse and the potted plant. Sarah was watching for them and met them in the back yard, looking over Starlight and making sympathetic noises.

"Oh, the poor thing. You think you can do something for him, Forst?"

Forst nodded and followed Reg as she unlocked the door and entered. He looked around. "Does he have a bed?"

"He sleeps on mine." Reg motioned toward the bedroom. He took Starlight in and laid him down. He loosened the towel and spread it out and stroked Starlight's body and limbs gently.

"More of the plant, I think."

Reg had put it on the island in the kitchen as she walked by it. She trotted back out to get it and brought it to Forst's side. He again crushed a couple of leaves, whispering to the plant, and held them under Starlight's nose. The cat snorted and sneezed, but didn't wake up.

"What else can I do?" Reg asked. "Is there anything I can do?"

Forst scratched Starlight's ears, watching him. "You are his companion. Can you speak to him? Strengthen his soul?"

Reg knelt by the bed. She wasn't sure she could do exactly what Forst intended, but she would do like she had the previous couple of days. It had seemed to help a little bit. With the plant remedy in his system, maybe it would have a more significant effect. She stroked him gently, then held her hands over him and closed her eyes. When she reached out for his consciousness, it was closer. She hadn't been able to feel him in all of the time that he'd been at the vet's, but with Forst's treatment and in the comfort of his own home, she could now feel Starlight closer to the surface. Not yet awake and conscious, but sleeping beneath the surface. She tried to strengthen all of the defenses she had erected around him to protect him from the harmful magic, wishing that she were more experienced and understood better what she was doing.

"Come on, Star. I miss you so much. You need to get better."

She stayed with him for a long time but eventually had to withdraw and give herself some time to recover. Forst watched her with quick, intelligent eyes. He put his gnarled hand on her shoulder and squeezed it comfortingly. "This is a very strong curse. We have need of help."

She sighed. "I don't know who to ask. Corvin has tried. I've asked others for help, but..." Reg glanced at Sarah and trailed off. "No one seems to know anyone who can heal something like this. You are the first one who has been able to do anything."

"You need to rest and regenerate." Forst directed his gaze at Sarah. "Food and tea," he told her aloud.

"Oh. Yes, of course," Sarah agreed. "What would you like?" she asked as she headed toward the kitchen.

Forst bent over to listen to Starlight's breathing and to scratch him under the chin. He put the crushed leaves on the bed close to Starlight's nose and straightened up. "I must go back to the garden. I will return."

Reg watched him leave the room. Sarah returned, looking confused. "Is the food for you or him? Gnomes can be so difficult to understand!"

"Me, I guess," Reg murmured, petting Starlight again and resting her head on the bed.

"Okay. I'll get you something. You skipped your breakfast, didn't you?"

Reg thought about the granola bar she had intended to eat. She hadn't even had her morning coffee. It was no wonder she was feeling so tired. Sarah went back to the kitchen. Outside the bedroom window, Reg could hear Forst in the garden, his voice sonorous and slow as he sang to the plants.

★ CHAPTER TWENTY-SEVEN ★

R EG WASN'T EVEN AWARE of what Sarah made her to eat. She watched and listened to Starlight as he lay there, sometimes growling or purring, but mostly just quiet. She wondered if she should crush a couple more leaves and try to bring him out of his deep sleep, but decided she'd better leave that to Forst. He knew the properties of the plant and she did not. She had not even known that they had the remedy to help him on hand.

Partway through the afternoon, she lay down on the bed next to Starlight, her body curved in a protective crescent around his and, closing her eyes, had a nap, listening to the drone of Forst working outside in the garden. Sarah brought her more tea around suppertime, which Reg consumed, but she couldn't get any solid food down. As twilight fell outside, she heard Forst gather his tools, and then he returned to the bedroom in the little cottage. Reg moved to get up, and he motioned her back.

"No, no. Stay there beside him."

He bent over Starlight, laying his ear on the cat's side. He lifted his head back up and rubbed the white star on Starlight's forehead.

"Come on, little friend. It is time to wake up."

Reg's eyes welled up with tears. She'd hoped that Forst would be able to rouse Starlight from his deep sleep, but it would seem that he was running out of things to try. He was able to treat the poisoning, but the magic was too strong.

At the sound of bells, Reg lifted her head and looked toward the window. "There, do you hear that?"

Sarah, standing in the doorway, looked at her blankly, but Forst cocked his head, and a smile grew across his face. "Elven folk!" he exclaimed, delighted. He went over to the window and pressed his face against the screen, looking out. He called out to them in a language Reg did not understand. The bells stopped. Reg shook her head. He'd scared them away, like a dog running into a flock of birds to play. But after a moment, there were more bells in reply, up and down the scale. Forst banged on the screen and pried at it, attempting to get it out. Frustrated, he looked at Reg. "Invite them in!"

"What? You want me to ask them in? But Starlight...?" She looked toward the window. "I don't even know their language."

"Call them. Call them!"

Reg scrambled to get off of the bed and went over to the window. She could see the twinkling lights in the garden, but no human shapes. "Come in," she called, though she had no idea whether they would understand her, or what the proper protocol for inviting elves was. She might insult them with her bumbling words. "Please come inside!"

The lights twinkled out. Reg let out her breath in frustration. Why was she forever bungling everything? She heard Norma Jean's voice in her head. Not a spirit this time, but a memory.

You are such a stupid girl. You are so weak and stupid!

She tried to control the sob that came to her throat. She couldn't cry in front of Sarah and Forst, who would wonder why she was being so emotional over not being able to call the elves inside. She rubbed her eyes with her palms and turned away from the window to face them.

They were no longer alone.

★ CHAPTER TWENTY-EIGHT ★

REG FELT LIKE HER eyes were going to pop right out of her head as she looked around the crowded room. The elves had, apparently, responded to her invitation. They stood around the room, shadowy figures, men, women, and children. They had pointed ears and were dressed in muted greens and grays. Many had bundles on their backs. They examined her with the same curiosity as she felt in looking at them, something foreign that she had only ever dreamed existed. She had been watching them and listening to them for the previous few days, but she had never thought to find them standing around her bedroom looking back at her.

"Uh… hi!" she squeaked.

There was probably some long ceremony for properly greeting them. She was, after all, meeting real live elves for the first time. But she couldn't think of what to say, and Forst didn't provide her with the words. Sarah's eyes were just as wide as Reg's felt, and she was secretly glad that Sarah, who had lived for hundreds of years, was also seeing elves for the first time. It was possible she had seen them before, but it obviously wasn't very often, not if Reg were to judge by her expression of amazement.

"She is so strange!" one of the children exclaimed, his eyes shining. "Look at her ears! And her flaming hair!"

The other elves seemed to share this opinion. Reg blushed at being the object of their scrutiny. She fumbled for something to say to them.

"I've been hearing you the last few days. And seeing your lights in the garden. I didn't know… Forst was the one who said you were elves…" She indicated the gnome.

Several of the eyes turned to Forst, and they looked at each other and nodded. Forst smiled broadly at the elves.

Reg's eyes fell back to Starlight on the bed. She had, for a few seconds, forgotten his plight in her excitement about the elves. She went back to the bed and patted him and leaned in close to him. "I guess… maybe we shouldn't all be in here, where we might disturb Starlight."

One of the children, a girl who looked about six years old, stepped forward and spoke to Reg shyly. "Can I pet him?"

Reg hesitated. She didn't know if Starlight would like being petted by a stranger. Or would he even know the difference? She didn't like to turn the little girl down, remembering herself at four, so enthralled with Starlight, holding him close and loving him, like she hadn't loved anything else in her short, wretched existence.

"I… I suppose," she said. "Be very gentle; he is sick."

The little girl elf stepped closer and stroked Starlight's fur gently. Reg didn't think he would mind that. The elf petting him caused static electricity shocks, and the little girl laughed. Reg didn't think that the air was dry enough for static electricity, but she couldn't deny what she saw with her own eyes. One of the other elves came forward and touched Starlight tentatively and, before long, they were all crowding in close for a chance to touch him, and the tiny sparks transformed into something else, little elf-lights floating around the room and glowing through Starlight's fur. Reg watched in amazement. She looked over at Forst, and he gave a slight nod, saying nothing, but the smile on his face confirming that this was not unexpected and that it was not harmful to Starlight, but might be helpful.

"He has been very sick," the little girl told the other elves authoritatively. "He has a spell on him. Can you feel it? It's very bad. It was dreadful of the woman who put it on him."

The other elves murmured to her. Reg watched, hoping to see Starlight awaken, healed by the elven magic. Forst had said that they needed help. Was that what he had meant? Had he just been waiting all day for the dark, so that the elves would come and he could enlist their help?

★ CHAPTER TWENTY-NINE ★

"Y OU SHOULDN'T BE HERE!"

Reg jumped at the male voice that sounded from nearby.

"She's not answering her phone. I want to make sure she's okay."

That voice she knew. Corvin.

"If you weren't invited, you shouldn't be here. You're supposed to stay away from her."

"The coven can shun me, but they can't dictate who I am allowed to associate with. If I don't exist as far as the coven is concerned, then they have no interest in where I am or who I talk to."

"If you want to be reinstated, you need to leave Reg Rawlins alone." It had to be Davyn. She didn't know his voice as well as Corvin's, but he was the only one who would be putting conditions of reinstatement on Corvin.

Reg exchanged glances with Sarah. *Warlocks.*

The looked back toward the window, where the voices were coming in. It wasn't until then that she realized the elves were gone. She stood up straight and looked around, panicking. Where had they gone? She had been counting on them to counter the spell binding Starlight. At the sound of the two men arguing, they had disappeared.

"No, come back," she pleaded aloud, looking around. She hoped to see the little lights or some shadow that indicated they were still there. "Please, come back!"

Forst shook his head gravely.

Reg broke down. "No! No, no." Tears streamed down her cheeks. Were they ever going to run dry? She sobbed, sitting next to Starlight. She stroked his silky fur, searching for some sign that the elves had done their job and he was going to wake up. "Star… come on, buddy."

"Reg," Sarah said in a low voice.

"They didn't lift the curse," Reg wept. "Why can't anyone do it?"

"I think you'd better deal with those two before any harm is done."

Reg focused again on Corvin's and Davyn's voices. Why did she have to deal with the two battling warlocks? If they wanted to fight, why not let them have at it? But she could imagine the damage they might do to the garden if they got into a fight, either physical or magical, and that would hurt both Sarah and Forst. She sighed and pushed herself up off the bed. She leaned into the window. "Can't you guys knock it off? You're making things worse!"

They were both silent for a minute.

"Reg?" Corvin finally asked.

"Well, who do you think lives here? What are you even doing here?"

"Making sure you're alright."

"Well, I was until you showed up."

Corvin approached the window. "What's going on? What's wrong?"

"The elves were here and they were trying to reverse the spell on Starlight, and the two of you bozos scared them off. What do you think you're doing here?"

He didn't say again that he was just there to make sure she was okay. He probably figured she wasn't accepting that as an answer.

"Why are you lurking around back there? If you wanted to talk to me, why didn't you come to the door and ring the doorbell?"

"I already knew you weren't answering your phone; I figured I would have the same problem with you answering the door. I thought that if I just came around here, where your bedroom is, I could peek in and see whether you were asleep, or whether… you needed something."

Reg was silent. That was all she needed, Corvin sneaking around behind her house, peeking in the window to watch her sleep. That wasn't creepy at all. Especially when she still wasn't sure what all of his expanded powers were. She was still waiting for the day when he would just snap and decide that if he wanted in, he was going to go in, and that would be that.

"Your last message about your mother being here was disturbing," Corvin said. "I didn't know if she would be back here. I don't know if I could stop her from…"

"From ensorcelling you? Possessing you?"

He didn't answer, and it was getting too dark for her to see anything but his shadow out there. She couldn't see his body language and facial expression, and she needed to if she were going to judge whether he was telling the truth or not. He was a good liar, but not that good.

"Go around to the door like a normal person," she told him.

It was a moment before Corvin decided she wasn't just suggesting future behavior, but that she wanted him to go to the door now. He gave a nod and headed back around the house to the door.

Davyn took it upon himself to accompany Corvin to Reg's doorstep as well, which suited Reg just fine. Corvin would have to behave himself, or Davyn would have him before the council again and they would put a stricter consequence in place. Reg didn't want to think about that part. She didn't want him to be bound, but if that were the only way for her to keep her powers, she would have to deal with it.

She opened the door and let them in without a word. Davyn entered, but Corvin stayed on the doorstep.

"Are you inviting me in?" he asked.

Reg nodded and made an impatient motion for him to enter. Sarah had followed her out of the bedroom and objected.

"You're not going to allow him in your house! Reg, there could be consequences!"

"You're too late," Corvin told her, smirking. He stepped over the threshold.

"Do not let him leave anything here," Sarah warned Reg. "You watch him like a hawk."

"That's what I'm here for," Davyn put in. And he did look particularly hawk-like as he gazed at Corvin. Davyn didn't look at all happy with this development. Reg understood why, but as she had told Davyn before, her fate and Corvin's were bound together. Whatever Reg did to try to avoid him, she was always drawn back to him for one thing or another. Whatever she did, he was always right there.

"So," Corvin looked around at the assembled company, "Norma Jean is not here?"

"No. I was supposed to meet her today for lunch, but… I guess I slept through that. It's been a rough day." She sighed. "A rough week."

"How is Starlight?"

"Come and see." She set off toward the bedroom.

"He's here?" Corvin asked in surprise.

How else did he think the elves were going to heal the cat? Was that something that they could do remotely? Reg's spirits lifted a little. Maybe they could continue to work at the spell even though they had vanished from sight. If they were only invisible, or if they were still nearby, maybe they could still help.

Corvin, Davyn, and Sarah followed Reg back into the bedroom. She sat down on the bed beside Starlight and petted him again, wishing she could sense a change in his condition. His fur was still static-charged and gave off a crackle as she ran her hand over it. Corvin shuffled a little closer, with both Sarah and Davyn sticking close to his sides, making sure he didn't try anything.

Corvin looked at Forst and cocked an eyebrow in Reg's direction in question.

"He's been helping too," Reg explained. "He was able to counteract the poison. But the spell… That's another story."

"May I?" Corvin asked, motioning to him.

Reg nodded and moved to the side to let him reach Starlight. He raised his hands over the cat and held them there.

"Cat scan," he quipped to Reg.

She wasn't amused.

She could feel the heat start to come off of Corvin and knew that he was trying to give Starlight more energy to see if that would help. Maybe if he were strong enough, he'd be able to break the spell himself. Reg waited, but there was no detectable change in Starlight's condition.

"Come on, Starlight," she begged. "Come back to me."

After a few minutes, Corvin withdrew. "Sorry," he shook his head. "Not much I can do. I'm not sure what else to try. You've been working at it."

Reg nodded.

"I can tell. But we're not there yet. He's stronger, and having the poison cleared from his system is a big help. But I don't know what else to try."

Reg nodded.

Davyn spoke. "Have you tried a fire caster?"

Reg blinked at him. "A fire caster. I don't even know what that is."

Corvin shook his head. "I didn't think that would be of any help. Is this a spell a fire caster could help with?"

Davyn nodded slowly. "It may be. Do you know who cast the spell?"

Corvin and Reg exchanged glances. "We have some ideas, but no, we don't know for sure."

Davyn folded his arms so that the voluminous sleeves of his cloak hid them. "Do you want me to try?"

"Are you a fire caster?"

"Yes." Davyn looked sideways at Reg. "And from your activity at the tribunal, I suspect that you might have the gift as well, though it is undeveloped at this point."

"I wasn't the one who kept lighting things on fire."

"Lighting *me* on fire, you mean," Corvin corrected.

Reg tried to suppress a smile. As painful as the trial had been, that part had, at least, been satisfying. She let out a sigh. "I don't know anything about fire casting. If I did have anything to do with that… and I'm not saying that I did… then I don't know how to do it again, or how to manage it. I wouldn't want to… light Starlight on fire."

"No," Davyn agreed. "That would not be a good use of your power. How about you step back as far as you can. I wouldn't want you to light up in sympathy. Not when you can't control it."

Reg looked at him to see whether he was serious and decided he was. She backed up from Starlight until she was against the wall. She didn't want to be so far away from him but, as she had said, she didn't want to light Starlight on fire either. Davyn stepped closer to the bed. Corvin decided to step back as well and positioned himself just to Reg's left. Reg glanced at him to make sure he wasn't going to try anything, then watched Davyn.

Davyn unfolded his arms and rubbed his hands together briskly like he was cold and trying to warm himself up. Then he held his hands away from himself, positioned as if he were holding out an invisible basketball. Reg waited for something to happen and, at first, she couldn't see it. Then she managed to see the light that was starting to glow in the space between Davyn's hands.

It flickered and grew slowly, until it became a ball of flame, suspended in the air between his hands, not quite touching them. Reg took a step forward for a better look. Corvin put out his hand to stop her and motion her back. Reg was attracted to the fire and wanted a better look. Corvin put his hand on her shoulder and pushed her back to the wall.

"Don't get closer."

"But I want—"

"Your magic wants to join him. But it's not a good idea. Not when you don't know anything about how to handle it yet."

A tightness started to grow in Reg's chest. She breathed in and out slowly, trying to disperse it, but it continued to grow tighter and to get hotter and hotter.

"Just watch Davyn," Corvin tried to redirect her attention. He must have been able to see something in her expression. How much she wanted to light a fire. To see it getting bigger and bigger and burning out of control. She looked up to the ceiling, trying to suppress the hard knot of anxiety in her chest. She had known a few firebugs growing up in foster care. She had lit more than one fire herself, and she knew what it felt like, that feeling of power and that hunger to destroy.

She tried to do as Corvin said and focus on Davyn. The ball of fire cupped between his hands, he started to roll and manipulate it, looking like a baker working with a ball of dough. He bent closer to Starlight, held it over him. Pushed it down until it was almost touching Starlight.

Reg opened her mouth to warn him that it was too close, that he was going to burn Starlight. Then Davyn gave a sudden push like he was dribbling the imaginary basketball, and the ball of light disappeared.

Reg jumped forward, too fast this time for Corvin to stop her. She was at Davyn's side in an instant. "Where did it go? What did you do?"

She couldn't see the fire but, once again, Starlight seemed to be glowing with light. As if Davyn had taken up where the elves had left off. So maybe he was doing something helpful. He motioned Reg back but didn't touch her or answer her question. Reg stared at Starlight, hoping to see a change. His feet started to twitch.

"Is that it? Is it working?"

He jerked and danced like he was having a dream of chasing mice. Reg wanted to reach down and pat him, to calm him down and wake him up. But Davyn kept her back.

"Let it work," he whispered. "You mustn't touch him or interfere."

"Is it working?"

He nodded.

Reg's knees went weak with relief. Maybe there was hope. Maybe Davyn had been the answer all along.

"Can we do anything else? Can I help somehow? Does he need anything?"

Davyn raised his eyes from the cat and looked around. "Do you have any candles?"

"No… I… we had some, but when he got sick, I was thinking about things that could be dangerous to have with a cat around, and I thought candles would be too much of a hazard, so we took them all down again…"

"They are just at the big house," Sarah pointed out. "I'll go get them."

Reg didn't offer to go and help. She watched Starlight, hoping that at any minute he would open his eyes and see her there watching over him and know that everything was going to be okay. He would see that she had helped him and protected him, that she hadn't just sat around waiting for him to wake up.

★ CHAPTER THIRTY ★

SARAH RETURNED WITH THE candles and went out to the kitchen to find a box of matches in the drawer. Davyn gave Reg a mischievous smile and started to take candles out of the box, tapping the wick of each one to light it. He began to place them around the room. Reg was longing to light a fire herself after witnessing Davyn's power, and she tried to do the same as he had, tapping the wick to get a candle to light. She shook her head when they didn't immediately light up as Davyn's had. He shrugged.

"Keep trying."

Corvin watched Reg for a moment. "Why don't you just use your mind?" he suggested. "At the hearing, you didn't touch me; you just lit fires from across the room."

Reg looked down at the candle she held in her hand and focused on the wick, telling it that she wanted it to light. Nothing happened. She was getting more and more frustrated, but nothing seemed to be working. She looked down at the box of decorations, wondering if maybe there were something wrong with the candle she had taken out of the box. There was a 'whoomp' sound, and the entire box was suddenly engulfed in flames. Corvin and Forst jumped back. In the doorway, Sarah gave a little shriek. Davyn looked at the box and looked at Reg. Unhurried, he walked over to the box and gathered the fire together into a ball and scooped it up in his hands. Everyone watched in horror, but he wasn't burned, and he wasn't alarmed by the accidental inferno. He held the ball of light between his hands and approached Reg. He held it out toward her.

Reg stared at the small, controlled fire, and wasn't sure what to do.

"Just take it," Davyn said calmly. "Don't think about it."

Reg reached out both of her hands and swallowed. She put her hands beside his and inched them together until she could feel the warmth of the fire licking against them. But it didn't hurt. She slowly backed away from Davyn, holding it between her hands.

"This is weird."

He chuckled. "You need to learn control. Don't just send your fire out like that. Use your hands. Keep it small and controlled. When you have mastered that, you can move on to sending your fire out."

"What do I do now?"

He bent over the charred cardboard box and selected a candle. They were all somewhat melted after Reg ignited the box. He held out the single candle. "Hold the fire in one hand. Touch the wick with your index finger on the other."

Reg reached out her right index finger, cradling the fire in her left hand, and tentatively prodded the wick. It took a moment, but then it lit.

"I did it!" Reg said excitedly. "I really did it."

The fire in her left hand flared up. Davyn winced. "Stay calm. Fire is very emotional. If you get excited or angry, you will feed it, and if you are not careful, you will lose control again. Just stay calm and controlled."

"Okay." Reg took a few calming breaths, and the fire got smaller again. "Can I do another one?"

He handed them to her one at a time, passing them to Corvin once they were lit so that he could place them around the room. No one else wanted to get close to Reg while she was handling the fire. They all hung back.

In a few minutes, they had all of the candles lit, and every flat surface in Reg's bedroom flickered and glowed with the small flames. Reg looked down at the ball of fire still in her hand. "Now, what do I do with this?"

He took each of her hands in one of his and brought them close together until they were palm to palm, and the fire slowly flickered out. He opened her hands again and waited, watching to see if it would flare up again, then nodded and released her hands. "Your first lesson in fire casting."

"That was amazing."

"I'm glad you enjoyed it."

Reg looked back at Starlight on the bed. He was no longer twitching. She didn't know if that was good or bad. He was still glowing. "Is he okay?"

"We need to let him rest and let the fire work. It is a very strong curse… I don't know how long it will take, and if we'll need more help."

"It seems like everyone has already tried, and no one can counter it."

"It's very strong. What kind of a sorcerer cast such a spell?"

Reg looked over at Corvin.

★ CHAPTER THIRTY-ONE ★

"YOO-HOO, ANYONE HOME?" Reg looked toward the open bedroom door at the sound of the call. She had obviously left the front door unlocked after letting Corvin and Davyn in. Or Norma Jean had used her powers to unlock it. Reg still hadn't been able to determine how she was able to get past the wards in the house, but it was a little late to be worrying about it now.

Norma Jean walked through the cottage to the bedroom and looked in the doorway.

"Well, here everyone is." She looked around at all of the candles and visitors. "Exactly what kind of party is this? Are you having a seance?"

Reg tried to figure out what to say. She couldn't think of anything. Norma Jean shook her head.

"It's a pretty good scam, getting all of these people to believe in something that doesn't exist. You can't really talk to spirits."

Reg had been able to talk to Norma Jean when she had been dead, in the other timeline. She had spoken to plenty of spirits ever since she was a little girl. She studied Norma Jean's smiling face, trying to figure out whether she knew this and was hiding the fact, or whether she didn't believe that Reg could communicate with ghosts. Had she understood that was what Reg had been doing as a little girl when she talked to her imaginary friends?

Did Norma Jean understand that she herself had powers, or was it all accidental?

"And Corvin is here," Norma Jean purred, sidling toward him. "I wondered where you had gotten to, handsome."

"He was right where you left him," Reg snapped.

"What? Right where I left him where? What are you talking about?"

"You ensorcelled him and then left him on the street in a stupor."

Norma Jean's eyebrows went way up and she laughed. "I did what? Even if I could, sweetie, why would I do such a thing? That's ridiculous."

"You did. I don't know why. It doesn't make any sense. Maybe you wanted him to meet up with me and to take my powers. Is that what you were thinking?"

Norma Jean looked from person to person, her eyes narrow and calculating. She must know something. She might not know everything, but she knew what Reg was talking about and she was trying to figure out what everyone else in the room knew or guessed. She slid an arm around Corvin, and he made no move to stop her. The way he looked down at her was... it was very similar to the way that Weston had looked at her when Reg had gone back in time. He was clearly smitten with her, whether she was actively charming him or not. She snuggled up close to him and looked at Reg with fiery, watchful eyes.

Was that it, then? Was she jealous of Reg? She wanted Corvin and thought that he was Reg's boyfriend? She could have him if that were the case.

"Have at it," Reg said, making a motion toward Corvin. "Go ahead. I don't care."

Norma Jean frowned at this. Davyn gave Reg a warning look. Reg bit the inside of her cheek. She had forgotten that a siren's natural reaction was to drown the men she caught. She might have abandoned Corvin the last time, but the next time... she could drown him for real. And Reg had just told her to go for it.

"I didn't mean..." Reg shook her head. She didn't know whether that was Norma Jean's intention or whether she would be putting the thought in her head. That wouldn't be a good idea. She rubbed her head. It was starting to throb. She needed to be at the top of her game, but with how little sleep she'd had and the constant worry about Starlight, it was difficult to think things through clearly. She decided to switch tracks. Distraction was the best course of action. "I'm sorry I missed you for lunch today. Things got crazy. You know that my cat has been sick..."

Reg looked over at Starlight, hoping for some change in his condition. He did look a little different. Like he was sleeping instead of nearly dead. Reg couldn't think of what was different or how to quantify it, but he looked... fluffier. The glowing fire was dissipating, but he looked healthier. Maybe they were making progress. Maybe Davyn's fire had done the trick. And if Reg could learn how to cast fire, she would be able to do something herself the next time instead of being so helpless.

But there wasn't going to be a next time. She wasn't going to let it happen again. Once Starlight was better, she was going to protect him and make sure that nothing happened to him.

"Oh, you brought him home," Norma Jean observed. "How is he doing? He doesn't look too well."

"No thanks to you," Sarah snapped. "Are you the one who poisoned him?"

Reg's jaw dropped. She hadn't been expecting anything like that from Sarah. Sarah didn't even like cats and hadn't seemed very upset about Starlight's condition. She was usually sweet and Reg hadn't expected her to accuse Norma Jean straight out of being his attacker.

"Uh..." No words came out of Reg's mouth.

Norma Jean looked at Sarah, her mouth pinched into a sour, bitter expression. "What are you doing here? I thought your house was the big one over there," she gestured in the direction of the main house. "Why is it that I always find you over here? You're not Regina's family. You're just her landlord."

"I may be, but I look after her better than you ever did. What kind of mother are you?"

Norma Jean looked at the others in the room, not liking being accused in front of the strangers. "What I did or didn't do when I had Regina is none of your business. You're not her family. You're not a cop. And what happened was a long time ago. I've already paid the price for my mistakes."

"How have you paid?" Reg demanded, the words coming out of her mouth without planning. As far as she knew, Norma Jean had never suffered anything for what she had done to Reg. Reg had been the one to suffer from the abuse. She had been the one who had been hurt and neglected and who had been taken away from everything she knew and passed from one home to another as she tried to deal with her traumatic beginning. Maybe in this timeline, Norma Jean hadn't been tortured to death in front of Reg's four-year-old eyes, but in the timeline Reg remembered she had been, and that had been a terrible thing to live with.

Norma Jean's eyes reflected the flames around her, making her look like a demon. "Do you know what it's like to be addicted? To have your only child torn from your arms? You don't know what I went through. I was in recovery for years, and all the time, I was missing my daughter and knew that I didn't have any chance of getting her back. Can you even imagine what that's like?"

Reg shook her head in amazement. Norma Jean's self-pity was unbelievable. She acted as if she were a victim rather than the perpetrator of the abuse.

"What about me?" she demanded. "I'm the one you hurt! Do you even remember what you did to me?"

Norma Jean pressed her face into Corvin's shoulder, closing her eyes. "I know I did things I shouldn't have when I was under the influence. But that wasn't me. That was the drugs and booze. That isn't the kind of person that I am. I'm not a bad person."

"When you harm a child, an innocent child, that makes you a bad person. You can give all the excuses you like, but you did that, and I remember it."

"Until you have children of your own, you can't judge me. You don't know what it's like. An innocent child? You were never an innocent child. Right from the time you were a baby, you were manipulative. Had to have your own way. Get everything you wanted. You think I was the only one who hit? You hit and kicked me, bit and scratched. You imagine trying to take care of a little monster like that. You imagine what it's like to have to nurse a… a snake. You never wanted a mother. You just wanted someone who would fulfill your every demand."

The room was silent. Sarah, Davyn, and Forst looked from Norma Jean to Reg with wide eyes. Corvin was staring adoringly down at Norma Jean. Reg bit her lip and tried to control her rage. She didn't want everyone looking at her as if she were a monster. If they believed what Norma Jean was saying… Did they understand that Norma Jean was lying and just trying to throw the blame back on someone else? Surely they didn't believe that Reg had been a monster from birth, intentionally hurting her own mother and being manipulative and demanding.

Reg had seen her four-year-old self when she had gone back with Harrison. That child had not been mean or devilish. She had been sweet, scared, longing for attention and comfort. She'd had incredibly strong psychic powers that it had taken her mother and foster families and doctors years to beat down and stamp out.

Maybe that was how all sirens saw their offspring. They were competitors in a limited environment, rather than children to be nurtured. If they wanted to live, they had to run away or escape somehow, to survive on their own or in some other family where no one knew what they were.

The candles in the room flared. Davyn turned his head to catch Reg's eye. It probably wasn't the best idea to be in a room full of candles while she tried to control her fury at the woman who had given her such a difficult start to life. Reg tried to tamp it down, but could feel the fire building in her chest again.

Starlight stirred, turning his head to the side and curling together a little on his side—a natural movement for a sleeping cat. Reg's anger at Norma Jean was immediately forgotten. She dropped onto her knees on the floor, putting her face right up to the cat. She put her hand on his body, and he twitched and breathed. He felt normal like he was just sleeping. He still didn't wake up, though. Reg whispered to him as if she were the only one in the room with him, instead of all of the others being crowded into her bedroom.

"Starlight. Hey, Star, are you feeling better? How's it going? Are you going to wake up?" She rubbed his side and scratched his ears. He tucked his head in more tightly and flicked his ears, not waking up.

"What's wrong with him?" Norma Jean asked. All of the accusation and bitterness was gone from her voice; it was back to being honey sweet, as if she were concerned about her daughter and her pet. Reg felt like she was sitting on the swinging pendulum of Norma Jean's emotion, off balance and having to shift and adjust to each fresh swing.

"Don't you know?" Reg asked.

Norma Jean released her hold on Corvin. She brushed her fingers across his bearded chin, then stepped toward Reg, looking down at the cat.

"How would I know what was wrong with him? I'm not a vet."

"When you were here before, you did something to him." Reg turned her head to look into Norma Jean's guileless eyes. There was no knowledge in them of what had happened to Starlight, no hint of the jealousy or anger. Did she not remember what she had done from one minute to the next? Forgetting about charming Corvin and leaving him on the street. Forgetting that she had harmed Starlight. Forgetting how she had treated Reg as a child, pretending that she had been wronged by social services and everyone else who had dealt with her at the time.

Had the drugs damaged her brain and caused holes in her memory? Was it something to do with her siren nature warring with her human nature or whatever other species she was a part of? Or was it denial?

Or just lies.

"Why would I do something to your cat?"

"Because you don't like him. He makes you think of… something you don't like to remember. You think that he's done something to you. I don't know what. But something about him bothers you."

Norma Jean gazed at Starlight for a few long moments. Her nose wrinkled and her lip lifted in a sneer. "He's not so special. You'd be better off getting a different cat. Or a dog. Maybe you should get something else. Cats are useful for getting rid of mice and other vermin, but they aren't real companions. Having kitty litter in the house is so stinky and messy."

"Cats are very tidy," Reg insisted. "And I don't want a different cat or a dog. I want him. He is special. I need him back."

Norma Jean reached out her hand. Reg panicked, not knowing whether she should let her mother touch Starlight or not. Would she make it worse? Kill him? Or did she really not remember? If she had cast the spell that was keeping him unconscious, then she could remove it. But Reg didn't know what to expect. Did Norma Jean intend to help or harm him?

"What are you doing?" She touched Norma Jean's hand, stopping her before she could touch Starlight. It wasn't forceful or violent, just the barest touch, like a butterfly.

★ CHAPTER THIRTY-TWO ★

THERE WAS A BURST of light from Norma Jean's eyes. Reg found herself suddenly paralyzed. She was frozen in Norma Jean's gaze. Was that what Corvin had felt? Or had he felt the same type of warm, satisfying charm from Norma Jean as Reg felt from Corvin? Reg first tried to struggle physically, but there was no way she could move a muscle. Norma Jean pulled her arm away from Reg's touch, and proceeded to lay a single finger on Starlight's head, right on the star marking on his head.

Reg couldn't move physically, but that wasn't her only option. She tried immediately to block Norma Jean's magic and make a safe cushion of space around herself. She tried to extend it around Starlight to keep him safe from Norma Jean's spell.

She could feel the barriers she had built around Starlight on her previous visits to him at the vet's office. She could feel the strength that Corvin had given him and the heat of Davyn's fire casting. She could even feel the elves, the little pockets of energy, the tinkling bells.

Norma Jean was frowning. She looked at Reg in consternation. "What have you done?"

Still frozen, Reg tested out her voice and found that it still worked. "I've done everything I could to protect him and heal him. Please don't hurt him any more. Please."

Norma Jean stood there, touching Starlight, a scowl on her face. "You don't want this animal. You don't know what he is."

Reg was startled by this claim. She had wondered about Starlight's history. Who was his previous owner? What was his history before he had come into her life? Or in a past life, even before he had been born as Starlight.

"I might not know much about his life before," she said slowly, "but I know what he's like. What kind of a—" she caught herself before she said 'person he was.' But she couldn't bring herself just to call him a cat. She remembered how Harrison had cuddled with Starlight, called him an old friend. Harrison was the one person who knew what Starlight was and could counter whatever Norma Jean had to say about him. Harrison was an immortal, the one force that might be able to counter Norma Jean's spell over Starlight.

Harrison. Reg reached out to him in her mind. *Please come.*

She looked around the room, but he didn't appear with his usual aplomb. Reg was a little disconcerted. She had thought that he would always come when called.

Norma Jean was looking at Reg with cold, hard eyes. "What are you doing?"

"I was just… I just…" Reg looked around at the others, looking for help. With so many magical practitioners in the room, was there no one who could stand up to Norma Jean and counter her powers? Sarah looked like she didn't know what was going on and Forst like he wanted to run from the room. Corvin's eyes were still misty and lovelorn. Reg looked at Davyn. It was down to her and Davyn, but she hadn't worked with him before and knew nothing about his powers except that he could become invisible and was a fire caster.

"You can't call to one of them while I am in the room," Norma Jean said coldly. "You can't do anything here without my permission. You should say 'please, Mommy,' like when you were a child. Because that is all you are. You cannot usurp me."

"I'm not trying to usurp you. I just want my cat back. I want him to be healed. If you can make him better, then I don't need anyone else. You could do it for me."

"Why would I do that?"

"To show me how powerful you are. No one else has been able to heal him. You could show me that you're more powerful than any of them."

Norma Jean's eyes sparkled at this. The candles were dancing and throwing weird lights and shadows into her face. Reg could see that her suggestion had struck a chord. Norma Jean liked the idea of showing Reg how powerful she was. Even though she had already done that by cursing Starlight with a spell that no one else could overcome, by charming the charmer, and by being able to come and go as she pleased despite any wards against her.

Norma Jean tapped Starlight's white spot. He stirred and opened his eyes.

"Hey, Star." Reg found herself released and able to pet him. "Hey, buddy, how are you feeling?"

He stretched and yawned widely, then shook his head, his ears making the flapping sound that always made Reg laugh. She could feel his consciousness gradually growing as he blinked and looked around the room at all of the people and candles. He gave a snort and sneezed on Reg's arm. She didn't even care.

"Thank you. Oh, thank you so much," Reg breathed, looking at Norma Jean. "You don't know how much I missed him."

Standing tall, Norma Jean looked down at her. "Imagine how much I missed you."

Reg swallowed. She didn't believe it, but had to admit the possibility that Norma Jean might have felt something when Reg was taken away. Maybe she did have some motherly feelings toward Reg, deep, deep down.

Norma Jean turned and headed toward the bedroom door. She hooked a finger through one of Corvin's belt loops and pulled him with her. Corvin gave no resistance, following her lead.

"Wait, no! You can't take him," Reg protested.

Norma Jean arched an eyebrow. "You said that I could have him."

"I said that you could… you could charm him. I didn't say you could take him away."

Norma Jean rolled her eyes. "If I can control his mind, I can have him."

"No. You can't. It's… it's against the rules." Reg looked at Sarah and Davyn for their guidance. She wasn't actually sure what the rule was on the point. She had only ever seen one siren and talked to Corvin about what the rules were. She knew that Norma Jean was not allowed to take him down to the ocean. They were allowed to stop her if she tried. But with the strength of Norma Jean's powers, Reg was worried about what would happen if they tried to force the issue instead of reasoning with her. She had already disabled their most powerful member. Davyn watched her with wide, bright eyes and Reg suspected it wouldn't take much for her to draw him in as well.

"You cannot take him from here under your power," Sarah agreed. "He can only leave with you by his own choice."

Norma Jean gave Corvin another tug toward the door. "He is willing."

"You have him under your thrall. You must release him to make his own choice without your influence."

Reg remembered what it was like to be under Corvin's control. So foggy and deeply under his influence that she couldn't make a decision that would keep her safe. It was an intoxicating state to be in. Corvin would need more than just a brief release from her charms to return to his own mind and make a reasoned choice.

"Just leave him," she said. "You don't really want him anyway. You already got bored with him yesterday."

Norma Jean considered this, looking at Corvin. "He is a nice specimen."

Reg cleared her throat, trying not to laugh. "Yes… he is that."

"I think I will keep him."

She continued out of the bedroom with Corvin beside her. Reg swore and hurried after them. She didn't want it to come down to a knock-down, drag-out fight. Norma Jean was too powerful; she could paralyze Reg with a look. The only one that might be able to fight her—besides Corvin, who was already under her control, was—

Reg found Norma Jean in the living room, her finger still through Corvin's belt loop, standing frozen, looking at the man stretched out on the couch.

"Harrison!" Reg couldn't believe that he was there. She had called him, and he hadn't shown up. Or he had, but hadn't even bothered to go to the bedroom to help her out. He lounged on the couch, long legs stretched out in front of him, feet resting on the coffee table. He was dressed with his usual flamboyance, his outfit just missing looking human. The purple, long-sleeved shirt looked like something out of a Broadway musical rather than something a man would wear on a casual night out.

"Regina. So nice to see you and your mother again."

"Where were you? I wanted you and you weren't there!"

"Sometimes, humans don't know what they want. They think they want one thing when they are perfectly fine with another. You didn't really need me, did you?"

"Yes, I did!"

"Why?"

"To heal Starlight! You're the only one who is strong enough to reverse the spell—"

"That is clearly not true."

Harrison was looking past Reg, where Starlight was following her on rather wobbly legs. Reg stopped and picked him up.

"Well, Norma Jean could, obviously, because she's the one who cursed him in the first place."

"And she has reversed the curse. So there is no harm done."

"You need to tell her that she can't take Corvin away from here. She has him under her spell, and she could do him harm. She's part… she's part siren."

"Yes."

"You knew that?"

He gave a little shrug.

"Why didn't you tell me that part? Why do you always leave out the most important points?"

"I don't think that is true."

"What else do you know about her? What else is she? Human or immortal? Or something else? Where does she get these other powers?"

"She is a mixture of origins, like most humans. Like you yourself."

"Don't even get me started on myself, I'm still trying to figure out how *that* happened. Why can't you ever give me a straight answer?"

"I give you the best answer I can. I cannot help it if you are too human to understand the answers."

"What are you doing here?" Norma Jean asked, staring at Harrison. She gave no acknowledgment that they had been talking about her.

"Hello, Norma Jean."

"What are you doing here?" she repeated. She released her hold on Corvin and walked over to Harrison, towering over him like a mother who had just caught the child who had stolen the cookies intended for the church bazaar.

"It's nice to see you too," Harrison said politely.

"You aren't supposed to be here."

"Indeed."

He didn't look offended by her accusations. They didn't seem to faze him a bit.

"You were there." Norma Jean said, staring at him. She turned and pointed to Starlight in Reg's arms. "And he was there. And him," she indicated Corvin, still standing there like a lovestruck zombie. She looked at them all again. "Why were you all there?"

Reg wondered again why, if Norma Jean could remember them going back in time to visit her, that she didn't remember Reg as well. She seemed totally oblivious to the fact that she had been visited not just by the men, but by the adult version of her own daughter. Shouldn't she be more surprised that her grown daughter had been there too? Occupying the same time and space as her four-year-old child? All of the scientists and Star Trek writers had said that such a thing was impossible. It would cause a temporal paradox that would cause a rift in the universe. But apparently, it wasn't even worth remembering.

"We were there to help you," Harrison said. "To prevent further damage from being done."

"Damage? What are you talking about? Damage to what? To me? To my child?" She gestured to Reg. "Are you the ones who called Social Services and had her taken away from me? I always *thought* it was you."

"Called who?"

"You are the ones who called Social Services and reported me. You told them lies about me hurting Reg and had her taken away from me. Admit it!"

Harrison shook his head. "I would not contact more humans than absolutely necessary."

He was very good at avoiding a direct answer.

"And now you're here. Why? To send me back?"

Reg tried to wrap her mind around that. To send her back where? Back to Maine? Back to the point in time when Reg was four? Back to the siren's island, which should have been her real home?

Harrison's smile made Reg uneasy. "You don't need me to send you back," he told Norma Jean. "You can go back by yourself. Voluntarily. There is no need to involve anyone else, is there?"

Norma Jean's expression was fierce. She bared her teeth at Harrison like a snarling animal. "I didn't escape torture and death just to be forced back there by you! You have no authority over my life! I am a free creature!"

"Then what is your decision?" Harrison asked pleasantly.

She didn't move or answer. Harrison pulled his feet down from the coffee table and arose. Now Norma Jean had to look up at him. She held her ground and didn't back down. Harrison reached out and touched her arm.

"I am a free creature!" Norma Jean repeated, jerking her arm away from him.

"Then make your free decision. Choose to be free, not to be constrained by these humans and their rules. Go back where you belong and live a free life."

Norma Jean indicated Reg. "She is my daughter!" She didn't say it tenderly. It was more of an accusation.

"She is."

"She cannot be allowed to be here. We cannot both be here."

"Then what is your choice?"

She looked around the room. Her eyes stopped on Reg, holding Starlight in her arms. Reg tightened her grip, afraid that Norma Jean was going to strike Starlight with another curse. She had just gotten him back. She couldn't let him be hurt again.

Starlight's fur crackled with electricity. She could feel his strength, his growing consciousness. Starlight always helped her to focus her attention and her psychic powers. He magnified her gifts, or her control over her gifts. Reg took a deep breath and gathered as much of his focusing power as she could.

"Don't hurt him again. Don't hurt me again. I'm not doing anything to hurt you. I'm not competing with you, if that's what you think. I haven't done anything to disturb your… hunting grounds. And I won't. You go ahead and… do whatever it is you do. As long as it isn't hurting me or my friends." Reg reached out and grasped Corvin's arm, pulling him back toward her. "Just leave us alone, and quit these games about being a sweet mother and wanting to get to know me. Because you don't want to. We both know that."

Norma Jean scowled. She looked as if she were trying to decide whether to strike Reg down for being so impertinent. Was that the way for a daughter to talk to her mother? Reg had no idea how a siren daughter talked to her mother. Apparently, it was normally a battle to the death, but Reg preferred to talk things out. Her social workers, doctors, teachers, and foster parents had always taught her to use words to sort out problems. It was less messy. At least, there was less visible damage.

"This one is yours," Norma Jean said finally, indicating Corvin. "You claim him."

Reg nodded, hoping that wasn't going to spark a magical battle.

"You choose not to claim your heritage."

Reg nodded again. "I don't want to be a siren. That's not my thing."

"You claim these waters." Norma Jean motioned in the direction of the ocean. "This is your territory."

Reg hesitated. That seemed like a bad idea. She looked at Harrison, trying to get some clue from him as to what the right answer was. If she claimed a territorial right, would Norma Jean fight her on it? Or would Norma Jean accept Reg's claim and move out of her territory to establish her own? Harrison watched with interest but gave no clue as to the right answer. He was interested in human affairs, but they seemed to provide him entertainment rather than him being concerned with the impact on the humans involved.

She buried her nose in the short, soft fur at the top of Starlight's head, breathing in his clean cat smell and searching for inspiration.

"This is where I live," she said slowly. "I'm not going to be moving somewhere else, not in the near future."

Norma Jean's eyes were sharp. Her mouth was a thin line, drawing down at the corners. Reg's body was tense, prepared for attack. The memory of Norma Jean's anger were there, stored in her body, even if she didn't remember every separate episode. Her body knew to be ready.

"I'm not going to be hunting here," Reg said. "I just want to live in peace."

"You are what you are. It is in your nature. Sooner or later… you will."

Reg swallowed. "I'm not interested in that kind of life. I just want to live in this cottage in peace, with my cat, running my psychic consulting business. That's my nature. I don't have any interest in hunting."

"These southeastern waters shall be yours," Norma Jean declared. "If you venture north…"

"I won't. If I have to travel… do I have to call you ahead of time? Let you know that I am going on a trip?"

Norma Jean scowled. "Don't hunt in my territory. If you do, you will live to regret it." Her chin lifted slightly. "If you live."

Reg squeezed Starlight a little more tightly, making him squirm and start to kick his hind feet in protest. She relaxed her arms.

"Fine," she agreed. "It's a deal, then."

The wind suddenly picked up, blowing a cold blast of air through the open windows of the house, filling the room with the salty tang of the sea. Reg shivered, goosebumps popping up on her skin. Starlight rubbed his head against the bottom of her chin. Reg cuddled him and kissed the top of his head.

Norma Jean gave Harrison one more look of spite, and then without a word to her daughter, swept out the front door and was gone. Reg heard bells tinkling in the distance.

She gave a sigh and looked at Harrison. "Any more surprises?"

He cocked an eyebrow. "I am constantly surprised by humans."

"No, I mean are there any more surprises for me? Finding out that my father was an immortal and my mother part siren? Time traveling? What else?"

"There are always more surprises," he assured her with a beatific smile.

Reg shook her head. She shook Corvin's arm to try to wake him from his trance. He turned his eyes to her, foggy and shifting back and forth drunkenly.

"Regina? What are you doing here?"

"This is my house."

He looked around, puzzled. "Then what am I doing here?"

★ CHAPTER THIRTY-THREE ★

S TARLIGHT'S RECOVERY CALLED for celebration and, with winter solstice upon them, Reg decided on a loosely-organized Yuletide dinner with everyone who had been involved in his treatment.

Corvin was there, invited once more and in full possession of his faculties. Forst looked like a miniature Santa Claus with his white beard, round face, and red cap. Reg invited his twin Fir as well, thinking that it wasn't right for her to have one of them and not the other there for Yule. Jessup and Sarah had helped to pull everything together, helping Reg with the decorations—none of them toxic to cats—and the Yule feast.

Reg didn't know Davyn very well, but he had been a big part of Starlight's recovery, and he helped Reg to light candles and the Yule log, making sure that the surfaces Starlight might jump up on were clear of candles to prevent him from singeing his whiskers or starting a fire. Reg hadn't been sure whether Davyn or Sarah would come, knowing that Corvin was an invited guest, but they could apparently join in the celebrations as long as they didn't acknowledge Corvin's presence.

Reg caught Forst outside, standing on a ladder in order to reach the eaves, where he hung a couple of wind chimes that tinkled in the breeze.

"Mayhap the elven folk won't come by this way again," he said, face pink, "but the bells will tell them thank you."

"Oh, that's great. Thank you!"

"It is a great honor to be visited by elves."

"It was good of them to try to help, too."

Forst nodded his agreement.

Even the vet and his staff had been invited for the first part of the celebration, partaking in appetizers and drinks and enjoying the good feelings of the season. Everyone was delighted to see the guest of honor well again and treated Starlight like a king.

Reg sat with her feet under her and her hands wrapped around a warm mug of mulled cider. "It's hard to believe that it all really happened," she said to Corvin. "When I see Starlight and everything else back to normal, it feels like it was all just a dream. And a bizarre one, at that."

"For me, a lot of it was a dream."

Reg chuckled. "I guess so. Are you feeling stable again? Got your footing?"

He shrugged. "I'm not sure I will ever entirely recover. I still feel… longing for her. I can't believe that she abandoned me. Even though I realize that if she had followed through on her promises, I would be dead now."

"For what it's worth, I'm glad you're not."

"Thank you," Corvin said dryly, having a sip of the Yule wassail. "That's nice to hear."

Reg caught a movement out of the corner of her eye and turned her head to see what it was. She was half expecting it to disappear again. Instead, she smiled to see Harrison in full holiday regalia, dressed in red silk with white fur trimming from head to foot. Reg tried not to laugh at the ridiculous figure he cut. He seemed completely at ease with his costume.

"Seasonal greetings," he told Reg.

"Thank you. And you too, Uncle Harrison. I'm glad you could make it."

"Would I miss my god-daughter's seasonal Christmas Yuletide solstice celebration?"

"I guess not. You didn't have any other plans?"

"I always have other plans." He offered it as if it were a compliment, and Reg supposed that if he chose her party over whatever his other plans were, it was.

"Oh. Well, thank you for making the time."

"Making time," Harrison mused.

"It's just an expression."

"Indeed. What is your wish?"

"My wish?"

"Is there not…" he made a twirling motion with his finger to indicate all of the Yule trimmings and company, "…a wish made for this observance?"

"Well… I don't know if there usually is or not." No one else had mentioned making a wish to Reg. But she wasn't going to turn down the opportunity to let the universe know what she was hoping for. If there was one thing that living in Black Sands had taught her, it was that the unexpected could happen, no matter how unlikely. "I wish… for safety for Starlight. And wealth. I could use a little extra money, just to make sure I have something to fall back on."

Reg had not noticed Fir kneeling down to talk to Starlight. He rose to his feet and intoned a warning.

"Be careful of thy wishes. You never know which ones will be granted."

Did you enjoy this book? Reviews and recommendations
are vital to making a book successful.
Please leave a review at your favorite book store or review site
and share it with your friends.

Don't miss the following bonus material:
Sign up for mailing list to get a free ebook
Read a sneak preview chapter
Learn more about the author

Sign up for my mailing list at pdworkman.com and get Gluten-Free Murder for free!

JOIN MY MAILING LIST AND

Download a sweet mystery for free

Preview of

Gluten-Free Murder

Erin Price pulled up in front of the shop and shut off her loudly-knocking engine. She took a few deep breaths and stared at the street-side view. She hadn't seen it since her childhood, but it looked just the same as she remembered it. Maybe a little smaller and shabbier, like most of the things from her childhood that she re-encountered, but still the same shop.

Main Street of Bald Eagle Falls was lined with red brick buildings, pasted shoulder-to-shoulder to each other, in varying, incongruous styles. Each one had a roofed-in front sidewalk to protect shoppers and diners from the blazing Tennessee sun they would face in the coming summer. All different colors. Some of them lined with gingerbread edges or whimsical paint jobs. Or both. Some of the stores appeared to have residences on the second floor, white lacy curtains drawn in windows that looked down at the vehicles, mostly trucks, nose-in in the parking spaces. There was no residence above Clementine's shop. She had lived in a small house a few blocks away that Erin had no memory of. She had spent most of her time at the shop and did not remember sleeping over at her aunt's when her parents had brought her for a visit.

A US flag hung proudly on a flagpole in front of the stores, just fluttering slightly in the breeze. It was starting to get dark and she knew she'd have to find the house in the dark if she were going to stop and take the time to explore the shop.

With another calming breath, Erin unbuckled her seatbelt, unlocked the door, and levered herself out of the seat. She felt like she'd been pasted into the bucket seat of the Challenger for three days straight. She had been pasted into the bucket seat for three days straight, other than pit-stops and layovers. She wasn't tall, so she wasn't crammed into the small car, but she'd been in there long enough to want to get out and straighten her body and stretch her legs. And to go to bed, but bed was still a long way off.

Erin walked up to the shop and put her key into the lock. It ground a little, like it hadn't been used for a long time. Maybe it needed a little bit of lubrication to loosen it up.

The air inside the shop was too still and too warm. She remembered when the little shop had been filled with the smells of exotic teas and fresh-baked goods, but Clementine had retired and closed it years ago. It had been a long time since anything had been baked there. It just smelled like dust and stale air. Erin left the front door open to let some fresh air circulate while she took a look around. There wasn't much space to explore in front of the counter. She would need a couple little tables, with a limited number of chairs, for the few people who wanted to eat in. Most of her business would just be stopping in to pick up their orders. She walked behind the counter. Everything seemed to be in good shape. A good wipe-down and some fresh baked goods in the display case and she'd be ready to go. Maybe a fresh coat of paint on the wall and a chalk board listing the daily specials and prices.

She walked into the back. A kitchen with little storage and a microscopic office that might once have been a closet. The back stairs led to a larger storage area downstairs, she remembered. And what Clementine had always called the commode. There was a second set of stairs from the store front down to the commode for customers. Not exactly convenient, but it was a small, old building. The arrangement had worked okay for Clementine. As a girl, Erin had always been a little afraid of the basement. She would creep down the stairs to use the bathroom and then race back up again, always drawing a warning from Clementine to slow down or she would trip and catch her death on those stairs.

All the old appliances were still there in the kitchen. Even a decades-old industrial fridge stood unplugged and propped open. There was no microwave and Erin was going to need a fancier coffee machine, but everything else looked usable.

"What are you doing here?"

Erin turned around and saw a looming figure in the kitchen doorway at the same time as the clipped male voice interrupted her thoughts. She just about jumped out of her skin.

She put her hand on her thumping chest and breathed out a sigh of relief when she saw that it was a uniformed police officer. But he wasn't looking terribly welcoming, jaw tight and one hand on his sidearm. There was a German Shepherd at his side.

"Oh, you scared me. I'm Erin Price," she introduced herself, reaching out her hand and stepping toward him, "and I'm—"

"I asked you what you're doing here."

Erin stopped. He made no move to close the distance between them and shake her hand, but remained standing there in a closed, authoritative stance. His tone brooked no nonsense. Erin couldn't imagine that she looked anything like a burglar. A little rumpled from the car, maybe, but she hadn't been sleeping in it. Was a slim, white, young woman really the profile of a burglar in Bald Eagle Falls?

"I own this shop."

He raised an eyebrow in disbelief, but he did let his hand slide away from the weapon and adopted a more casual stance. Erin allowed herself just one instant to admire his fit physique and his face. He was roguish, with what was either heavy five o'clock shadow or three days' growth, but his face was also round, giving him an aura of boyishness and charm.

"You own the shop. And you are…?"

"Erin Price. Clementine's niece."

"If you're Clementine's niece, why haven't we ever seen you around here?"

"It's been years since I've seen her. My parents died and I lost all my family connections years ago, living in foster care. A private detective tracked me down."

He considered this and took a walk around the kitchen, looking things over. His eyes were dark and intense. "You'll be selling the place, then? Why didn't you just hire a real estate agent?"

"No, I'm not selling," Erin said firmly. "I'm reopening."

The eyebrows went up again. "This place has been sitting empty for ten years or more. You're reopening Clementine's Tea Room?"

"No, I'll be opening a specialty bakery, once I get everything whipped into shape." She folded her arms across her chest, looking at him challengingly. "I assume you don't have a problem with that?"

"No, ma'am."

But he didn't give any indication of leaving. Erin swept back a few tendrils of dark hair that had slipped from her braid, aware that she was probably looking travel-worn after several days in the car. She had put on mascara and dusty rose lipstick before getting on her way that morning, but she felt gritty and sweaty from travel and would have preferred a shower before having met anyone in her new hometown.

Erin strode toward the front of the store and the policeman moved out of the doorway and then back around the counter toward the front door.

"You shouldn't leave the door wide open."

"I wanted some air in here. I've only been here five minutes. Do the police always show up that fast in Bald Eagle Falls?"

"I just happened by. Thought it was strange to see Clementine's door hanging open. Didn't recognize the car."

"Well, thank you for looking into it." Erin waited until he stepped out onto the sidewalk and then followed, pulling the door shut behind her. He watched as she locked it again. "You see? I have the keys."

"Where did this detective find you?"

"Maine."

"Is that where you're from?"

"I'm from a lot of places. Now I'm looking at settling back down here."

Erin looked at the German Shepherd, doing the doggie equivalent of standing at attention.

"I've never heard of a small town like this having a K9 unit."

"Well," he looked down at the dog, chewing on his words, "this is the extent of our K9 contingent."

"He looks… very well-trained. What's his name?"

"K9."

Erin cracked a smile. "Seriously?"

He kept a serious face, nodding once.

"Okay. Well, again, thank you for checking in on my store, Officer…?"

"Terry Piper."

"Erin Price." Erin offered her hand and this time Piper took it, giving her hand a brief squeeze as if he were afraid of crushing it.

"Pleased to meet you, Miss Price. Or is it missus?"

"It's Miss."

"Keep safe. Give us a call if you need anything." He produced a business card with a blue and yellow crest on it. "We don't exactly have 9-1-1 service but there's always someone on call."

Erin nodded her thanks. "I'll keep it handy. A lot of crime in Bald Eagle Falls?"

"No. It's a sleepy little town. Not too much excitement. Rowdy teenagers. Some of the drug trade trickling down from the city. The occasional domestic."

"Not a lot of break-and-enters?" she teased.

He didn't look amused. "You can't be too careful. Where are you headed now? There's a motel down the way…"

"No. I got the house too. I'll be staying there."

"You can't sleep there tonight. Won't be any water or power."

"They've been turned on. Thanks for your concern."

He looked for something else to say, then apparently couldn't find anything, so he nodded and walked down the sidewalk with his faithful companion.

Erin kept one eye on the GPS and the other on her rearview mirror to see if Officer Piper had any ideas about hopping into his car and following her home to make sure that she was properly situated. But apparently, he couldn't think of any laws she had broken and he never appeared behind her. Clementine's house was only a few blocks away. Erin parked on the street in front of it and took it in. It was a pretty little house with white siding and green shutters, roof peaks, and accents. The living room had big windows to let in the light and a window up at the top peak hinted at an attic bedroom or study. Beside and behind the house, beyond the fence line, were shimmering green, dense woods.

Erin got out of the car and grabbed her suitcase before walking up to the heavy paneled door and inserting her key in the lock. This one didn't stick, but turned smoothly like it was welcoming her home. Erin lugged her suitcase into the front entryway and closed and locked the door behind her. No point in inviting more visitors. She really didn't want to have to deal with anyone else until morning.

The AC was on, so the house wasn't stifling like the shop had been. Erin hadn't been sure what to expect. Burgener, the lawyer, had informed her that the house was furnished, but she hadn't known what kind of state it would be in. But it was neat and tidy. Furnished, but not cluttered. There were a couple of magazines on the coffee table in the living room that were months old, but other than that, Clementine might have just left it a few days before. Or still be in the other room just awaiting Erin's arrival.

She wasn't a believer in ghosts or restless spirits, but Clementine's smell and flavor still clung to the place.

Erin left her suitcase at the door and explored the house slowly. Living room, small dining room, kitchen, Clementine's bedroom, a guest room, and what Erin thought she might call a sewing room. There was fabric, rolls of wrapping paper, partially finished crafts, and post-bound books of genealogy, painstakingly written in longhand.

There were pull-down steps to the attic. If there had only been a ladder, Erin probably wouldn't have explored any further, but the stairs were well-made and modern and raised her hopes that the attic had been properly developed and wasn't just a storage space full of boxes, bags, cobwebs, and dust.

She mounted the stairs. At the top, there was enough light from below to find a light switch. Erin switched it on and had a look around.

It was a beautiful, bright room. Erin knew she was going to be spending a lot of her free time up there. White paneling and built-in cabinetry, soft, natural-looking lighting; it consisted of a reading nook, a writing desk, a comfy-looking couch, and various other touches that would make it a paradisiacal oasis at the end of a tiring day of baking.

Or driving.

After exploring the attic, Erin shut off the light, descended, and pushed the stairs up until the counterbalance took over and raised them to snick softly into place in the ceiling.

Erin returned to the kitchen for a glass of water, not looking forward to the fact that she was going to have to go out and pick up groceries if she wanted anything to eat. She found a sticky note on the fridge on notepaper preprinted with the lawyer's logo and phone number.

Welcome home. You'll find some basic supplies in the fridge. JRB

Erin opened the fridge door and sighed. Milk, juice, eggs, bagels, jam, and some precut fruit and vegetable packs. That and the coffee maker on the counter would do just fine. If James Burgener had been there, she would have hugged him.

A quick snack and then she would be off to the guest room for some shut-eye. Ghosts or not, she wasn't going to be sleeping in the master bedroom until she had made it her own.

Never one to let moss grow, Erin set to work immediately the next morning. She found a sort of a general store which carried both the small appliances she needed and painting supplies. With the back seats folded down, she filled the cargo area of the Challenger with as much as it would hold. She went back to the shop, opened the windows, and prepped the walls to start painting. Best to get a fresh coat of paint on before installing anything new.

"Knock, knock?"

Erin was startled out of her thoughts. She yanked the earbuds out of her ears and turned to face the woman who was trying to get her attention.

"I'm sorry," the woman said, giving her a tentative smile. She had a pleasant face; a middle-aged woman with ash blond hair. Either she had the perfect figure, or her clothes were hand-tailored. "I didn't want to startle you, but you were pretty engrossed…"

Erin wiped her forehead with the back of her hand. "Yeah. A little caught up in my music and my work."

"My name is Mary Lou Cox. I heard a rumor that you were here. So, I just had to come over and extend a good old Bald Eagle Falls welcome."

"Erin Price. I, uh… Clementine was my aunt."

"Well, if you're kin to Clementine, you're kin to half the mountain. Welcome home."

Erin nodded awkwardly. "Thank you. That's very kind of you."

"So…" Mary Lou took a look around the kitchen. "A fresh coat of paint and then I hear you're opening up Clementine's Tea Room again? I'll tell you, this town has surely missed the tea room."

"Uh. No. I'm not reopening the tea room." Erin enjoyed a cup of tea at the end of the day as much as anyone, but she was much more interested in baking. The groove she got into while painting was nothing compared with the nirvana she would achieve while baking. "I'm opening a specialty bakery."

Mary Lou patted her hair. "We already have a bakery in Bald Eagle Falls."

Erin ran the roller down the wall, watching carefully for seams or drips. "I'm sure the town can support more than one bakery."

"But we already have The Bake Shoppe. We don't need another bakery."

Erin gave her a determined smile. "I'm opening a bakery."

"Angela Plaint owns The Bake Shoppe and does a really nice business, I'm not sure any of us would go to another bakery. It wouldn't be a very loyal thing to do."

"You could go to The Bake Shoppe for… whatever Angela Plaint is best at and then come to my bakery for gluten-free muffins."

"Gluten-free?" Mary Lou echoed.

"I assume you don't already have a gluten-free bakery."

"No, we do not. If you want that kind of baking, you have to drive into the city."

"Well, now you'll be able to get them in town."

"There aren't that many people that want that gluten-free stuff in Bald Eagle Falls. I don't see how you could make a living off it."

"We'll just have to see. I do other specialty baking as well. Dairy-free, allergy-free, vegan."

"We don't have a lot of those kind of people here. We like our meat. Whoever put meat in muffins anyway?"

Erin studied Mary Lou for a moment, trying to divine whether she was teasing or being sarcastic. "You might not put meat in a muffin, but you would probably put eggs and dairy."

"And you could make it without all those things? Who would eat such a thing? It would be like eating cardboard."

"Not when I make it."

"I guess we'll just have to see," Mary Lou said. "I sure don't cotton to the idea of you trying to take Angela's business."

"I guess we'll just have to see," Erin echoed.

Mary Lou was the first citizen of Bald Eagle Falls to express her opinion and welcome Erin to town, but she wasn't the last. Next came Melissa Lee, a woman with curly dark hair and a wide, even smile. And then Gema Reed, with her long, steel gray locks and a girlish complexion.

Erin did her best to explain to them that she wasn't there to horn in on Angela's business and take money out of her pocket, but to offer a new service that hadn't previously been available. But it was like talking to the wall. Or yelling at an avalanche. It didn't stop them from dumping advice all over her, while smiling and telling her she was welcome in town.

She didn't feel welcome.

At least Terry Piper did not show up with his K9 to give his input on the matter.

It was a long day and Erin never did meet Angela, her competition. The end of the day, the walls were freshly painted. Everything looked fresh and new. Exhausted though she was, Erin spent a few more minutes in the tiny office, going through the papers and plans in the folders she had brought with her from Maine.

Then she locked everything up tight and headed back home.

~ ~ ~

Gluten-free Murder, book #1 in the Auntie Clem's Bakery series is available now!

ABOUT THE AUTHOR

Award-winning and USA Today bestselling author P.D. (Pamela) Workman writes riveting mystery/suspense and young adult books dealing with mental illness, addiction, abuse, and other real-life issues. For as long as she can remember, the blank page has held an incredible allure and from a very young age she was trying to write her own books.

Workman wrote her first complete novel at the age of twelve and continued to write as a hobby for many years. She started publishing in 2015. She has won several literary awards from Library Services for Youth in Custody for her young adult fiction. She currently has over 50 published titles and can be found at pdworkman.com.

Born and raised in Alberta, Workman has been married for over 25 years and has one son.

~ ~ ~

Please visit P.D. Workman at pdworkman.com to see what else she is working on, to join her mailing list, and to link to her social networks.

~ ~ ~

If you enjoyed this book, please take the time to recommend it to other purchasers with a review or star rating and share it with your friends!

Lightning Source UK Ltd.
Milton Keynes UK
UKHW031458090820
367830UK00019B/1400

9 781989 415436